VAMPIRE'S TOY

Trembling, shaking his head, David dragged himself to his feet and limped back to his seat. He sat for a long time with his face in his hands. "Carter, no matter why you transformed me, you're like my father now; I need you to train me—"

"I know I promised I'd be Batman and you'd be Renfield the Boy Wonder," Carter began, "but, you see, that was just another lie. I have no intention of tutoring you or allowing you to stay here; in your inexperience you might draw attention to yourself and so endanger me. Besides, I made you a vampire to torture you, and your new existence will be more difficult and degrading if I cast you out. So, David, I think you'd better run along."

"I . . . I can't go out there again. Not alone, not tonight."

"You must, because I say so. You're my toy, David, and I'll break you if you become annoying."

"You don't understand—"

"No, *you* don't understand. You'll surely die if you don't go *now*, while you still have time to find a lair." Carter pointed at a window; the eastern sky was lightening to gray.

THE VAMPIRE'S APPRENTICE

RICHARD LEE BYERS

ZEBRA BOOKS
KENSINGTON PUBLISHING CORP.

For Dale

ZEBRA BOOKS

are published by

Kensington Publishing Corp.
475 Park Avenue South
New York, NY 10016

First printing: January, 1992

Printed in the United States of America

Chapter One

David Brent awoke to pain and darkness.

His whole body ached, with sharper pains in his abdomen and left nostril, down the sides of his neck, and, worst of all, in his mouth. Disoriented, he groped about, and discovered he was lying in a padded box.

Tiny cups adhered to his eyes. He scratched them off, but the world stayed black.

Nothing made sense. It wasn't supposed to hurt, and he wasn't supposed to wake up in a coffin.

He pushed the lid; it wouldn't budge.

He tried to call Carter's name and found that he couldn't speak.

With tongue and trembling hands he explored his mouth. Inside it, wads of cloth covered raw tissue. His canines had lengthened. Someone had sewn his lips together, and driven two long pins through the lower one and between his upper front teeth to make him smile.

Was it only a joke, or had he been embalmed?

The possibility revolted him. He imagined vomit trapped in his sealed mouth, choking him, and his nausea intensified. But he didn't throw up; maybe he couldn't anymore.

When the sickness abated, he drew out the pins, cringing as they scraped against his incisors and slid through his lip.

Then he worked his thumb and forefinger between his lips so he could pick at the thread with his nails. When it broke and he began pulling it out, he realized that the stitches ran all the way up into his nose. Once again the sensation of foreign matter dragging through his flesh made him flinch and twitch.

At last he could open his mouth. He pulled out the wadding, then cautiously fondled the sore spots. His undertaker had whittled him.

"Carter!" It hurt to shout, but he didn't care. "Carter, I'm awake; let me out!"

Nobody answered.

"Carter, it's not funny. Let me *out!*"

Still no reply.

It was a joke. Or a test, or an initiation. Unless something had gone wrong.

He was gasping, kneading the mattress; he struggled to calm down. Whatever was going on, he could free *himself* from the casket; he had powers now.

Carter was strong enough to muscle his way out of a coffin. But David didn't feel strong; he felt frail and afflicted.

Carter could also become intangible, a shadow who could slip through solid matter. Somehow that seemed like it might be easier, or at least more pleasant, than breaking his prison apart. If his body turned to mist, maybe it wouldn't hurt.

But he didn't know how to change; Carter was supposed to teach him.

It had to be mind over matter, didn't it? If he willed it to happen, expected it to happen, then it would. He settled himself as comfortably as he could, then concentrated.

My body is becoming thin as air. First my feet will disappear, then my calves, then my knees, then—

When it happened, it happened suddenly, startling him and breaking his concentration. An icy tingling stabbed his feet, then swept up his body, engulfing everything but his head and right arm. The pain in his abdomen vanished; he couldn't feel his legs at all.

He waited for the tingling to absorb the rest of him. Eventually he realized it wasn't going to.

Maybe nothing had really happened. Maybe he'd only

6

deluded himself, anesthetized himself with autohypnosis. He hesitantly raised his right hand and passed it through the empty space where his stomach should have been.

He was a severed head and arm. He tittered uncontrollably, had a mad desire to stick his hand up his open neck-hole and feel around inside.

He couldn't stay like this; he'd lose his mind. He fought to regain the meditative focus that had triggered the transformation, but dread and revulsion rendered it unattainable.

And now he somehow sensed he was in danger. His ghostly limbs and organs would disperse; already his left hand and right leg were breaking apart. He shrieked and pounded the coffin lid; his new fangs shredded his lip. *It isn't supposed to be like this! No, no, no, no, NO . . .*

His flesh congealed in a flash of agony. After a time the pain of reintegration contracted into a fierce new ache pulsing in his right thigh.

For a long while he just lay there shuddering. If this was a test, all right, he'd failed it. If it was a joke, he'd humiliated himself sufficiently to satisfy even the most sadistic prankster. So why didn't Carter let him *out?*

Because Carter really wasn't here. The coffin was probably in some funeral home; if he didn't get out, they'd bury him.

He didn't dare try becoming a phantom again. But since he had that capability, maybe he had superhuman strength too, even if he did feel like a terminal cancer patient.

He shoved the lid again, as hard as he could. Spasms racked his arms; it still didn't move.

Then he really was as weak as he felt. At last he found the courage to touch the sutured incisions in his neck, to slip his hand inside his shirt and finger the puckered hole. If he was in a funeral home, then of course he'd been embalmed, his blood pumped out and chemicals pumped in. That was why his powers didn't work right, why he was in so much pain; the mortician had crippled him.

Anguished, he howled and clutched at the padding above

7

his face; satin-covered foam rubber burst like a puffball.

He flexed his fingers, blinked in surprise. Even though he felt weak, he *was* strong, stronger than he'd ever been before. If pushing the lid didn't work, maybe beating on it would. He enlarged the hole he'd torn in the padding, then slammed his fist into the metal beneath.

It hurt worse than it would have before Carter bit him, because the impact jolted his entire stricken body. He kept punching anyway. The coffin rang like an anvil, thrusting spikes of noise into his ears.

After twenty blows his fist hurt as if he'd crushed it in a vise, so he switched to his other hand. When it was equally sore, he ran his fingertips over the lid. He'd cracked it.

He worked his fingers into the crack; its jagged edges pared flesh away. When he'd gotten as good a grip as he could manage, he pulled.

The metal screeched as it came apart. He expected light, or at least a darkness less absolute, but everything was as black as before.

He reached through the gap and touched stone.

He hadn't been able to push the coffin lid open because it was sealed in a concrete vault lying under six feet of earth; *they'd already buried him.*

He sobbed, and found that his eyes refused to tear. Everything hurt so badly, especially his hands. He couldn't smash and claw through another barrier; he just didn't have it in him.

But then again, he didn't have much of a choice.

Gravel showered into his face; dust sifted into his tattered mouth. Surely he'd flayed his hands; there couldn't be any meat left on them.

After an eternity the concrete turned to soil.

First he dug lying on his back, then sitting up, then finally standing, his body jammed into the suffocating shaft like a cork in a bottle, dirt cascading over his head and shoulders to land in the casket below.

Crazy fears came creeping into his mind. What if the coffin had been buried upside down; what if he was tunneling

8

the wrong way? Or what if it was daytime overhead; he'd be burnt to ash by the sun.

His hands broke free, pushed aside what must be a blanket of sod.

He scrabbled to enlarge the space above him. Then, clutching, kicking toeholds, he wormed his way upward, to emerge in a field of stones and flowers bleached by a skull-white moon.

Chapter Two

They'd buried him next to his grandfather.

He crawled over to the bronze veteran's marker to make sure of the inscription, then slumped down on the grass. Liz and his parents knew he'd died; he could never see them again.

Pain finally spurred him into motion, pain and the fear of discovery. He didn't want to be seen like this, a filthy *thing* with skinned, oozing hands and ragged lips.

Perhaps he could be healed. Only another Olympian could tell him, and Carter was the only one he knew. Carter must be dead or in trouble, but he might have left a journal or even some sovereign elixir in his house in Sulphur Springs. It was at least a possibility; it gave him somewhere to go and something to hope for.

He stood up, took a step, and nearly fell. He was knock-kneed; his right leg twisted inward, and extended an inch or two longer than his left. He was going to lurch and stagger as he walked.

Before he set out, he tried to fill the shaft he'd dug, but without a spade, it was hopeless. All he could do was re-arrange the squares of sod, knowing full well that some groundskeeper would discover the hole beneath them in a day or so. His mother's heart must be breaking already; she'd feel even worse when she heard his body had disappeared. He hadn't expected to grieve her, but still he felt ashamed.

Shadow drenched the field, though the sky above was

gray with city light. Angels and madonnas slipped out of the darkness to sneer as he stumbled by.

All too soon he ran out of graveyard. Beyond a low concrete wall lay one of Tampa's seedier districts, a tangle of narrow streets lined with shacks and decrepit cars. There wouldn't be many street lights or much through traffic, but he still couldn't walk all the way to Carter's house without somebody seeing him.

He turned up the collar of his grimy suit coat and brushed his hair down into his face, bowed his head and stuck his hands in his pockets. If people didn't look at him too closely, maybe they'd mistake him for a tramp.

Dirt pattered down from his hair and clothes; his right foot scraped along the pavement. Odors hung across his path like curtains: exhaust, skunk, acrid smoke from a trash fire. He turned down a side street to avoid a church; Carter had assured him that holy symbols and consecrated ground couldn't hurt him, but he wanted to keep his distance from the bingo players milling around outside.

After a while he began to get thirsty.

Dry mouth, clogged throat; it felt like any other thirst. Carter drank tea and wine, so maybe it was just an ordinary thirst. David didn't want to start craving blood, not now; he had problems and miseries enough without that.

Olympians didn't terrify or brutalize their victims; they seduced them, used them tenderly, then set them free with vague memories of an erotic dream. He'd fantasized about it a thousand times, never dreaming that he'd return maimed and repellent, with no one to teach him mesmerism or proper biting technique.

From twenty-four-year-old virgin to sexually retarded undead. It was almost funny.

He wished they'd buried him with his watch. It must be fairly late; he'd passed bars, a Circle K, and a barbecue joint that were open, but the other businesses he'd seen had already closed. If he couldn't reach Carter's before dawn, he'd have to find another place to hide.

His thirst grew gradually worse, waxing from a slight discomfort to a torment that rivaled, and at certain moments eclipsed, his other pains. Sometimes, when it was at its most unbearable, he blacked out; after his head cleared, he discovered that he'd stopped walking, or blundered off the berm and was zigzagging down the middle of the street.

"Satan rules!"

The shout burst out of nowhere, snapping him out of yet another daze. He lost his balance and sat down hard. The old red convertible, its scalloped tailfins reared like a dragon's wings, careened on down the block.

David shivered; they'd only missed him by inches. And now they were backing around; their headlights flicked from low to high beam, searing his eyes with glare. Maybe they were turning around because they'd seen his face.

He yearned to run, but somehow managed not to. Maybe they hadn't seen his face; maybe they were turning for some other reason. If so, he mustn't make himself suspicious. He got up and hobbled on down the street.

The convertible growled, then lunged forward. As it roared past, the kids inside, four long-haired metal heads in studded leather, hooted and threw a barrage of empty beer cans. One hit his shoulder; two others clattered at his feet.

His eyes squinched shut, burned with tears that wouldn't flow. All through school he'd been afraid of bullies; even after he grew up, tough-looking teenagers intimidated him just as much as ever. Now he was an Olympian, strong enough to rend rock and metal, and he was still petrified. It wasn't fair!

The convertible backed around again.

They hadn't seen his face, at least not clearly. If they knew he was a living corpse, they might flee or try to run him down, but they wouldn't taunt him or pelt him with garbage. They thought he was just a derelict, someone they could harass without fear of reprisal. Maybe he could make them lose interest before they found out any different.

In school, bullies generally got bored more quickly if he didn't resist or react. He lay down and curled up on the ground.

12

The convertible stopped a few feet away. Another hail of beer cans flew, clipping him on the hip and the back of the head.

"Hey, wino!"

"What's the matter, asshole?"

"Get up, gimp, and I'll give you a beer!"

"Yeah, get up, you fucking dirtbag!"

Don't let them get out of the car, he thought. Please, don't let them out of the car.

One of them threw a final can; then they laughed and drove away.

He waited for their taillights to disappear, then stood up. He told himself he should feel proud; he'd thought his way out of a dangerous situation.

But he didn't feel proud; his bowels churned with rage and humiliation. What good were powers and immortality if you were afraid all the time? If you had to let people piss on you?

He promised himself it wouldn't be that way for long; everything would change once he got to Carter's.

It was good he could pass for a mortal, but bad that he was encrusted with dirt. Other kids might accost him and so might a cop. He needed to wash and change his clothes.

He couldn't have entered a bar, store, or restaurant even if he'd had any money. But maybe he could find an outdoor faucet or laundry hanging on a clothesline.

Or maybe he could sneak into Johnson's Klean-Kwik 24 Hour Laundromat.

It was a long cinder-block building with no front wall, sitting at one end of an L-shaped shopping plaza. There were three cars in the parking lot, a couple of washers sloshing and driers groaning, but nobody visible inside. The customers must be waiting in the sandwich shop next door, or in their apartments across the street.

It wouldn't take long to drink and wash, then hunt for clothes that fit him. Someone might walk in on him, but he was willing to risk it. If he took a chance, maybe he wouldn't feel like such a coward.

13

Suddenly his thirst intensified; his vision blurred, he felt faint. If he blacked out now, he might stand in front of the laundromat like a statue, or even wander into the delicatessen. He broke into a cripple's run, collided with a wheeled metal cart and a Lance vending machine as he reeled toward the sink mounted on the back wall.

He frantically twisted the faucet handle, then bent over and guzzled. The water was cold, wet ecstasy.

He drank for at least a minute, the first pleasurable minute since he'd awakened. Just as he was straightening up, someone's finger stabbed him in the back.

"Are you doing laundry?" It was an old woman's voice, scratchy and querulous. "You shouldn't be in here unless . . . *What's the matter with your hands?*"

Where had she come from, had she been here all the—It didn't make any difference! All that mattered was keeping his back turned and getting out. Fortunately, there was a rear entrance just a few steps away.

"It's a skin condition," he babbled, "not contagious, not nearly as bad as it looks. Sorry I came in, I knew I shouldn't, I just—"

His stomach convulsed. He fell to his knees, clutched his middle, and retched; it seemed he could throw up after all.

"What are you doing?" the old woman yelped. "Go outside, go outside!"

He wished he could, but the pain wouldn't let him. The water came up mixed with waxy lumps of something the embalmer had pumped into him, a combination that resembled pus.

When at last he stopped heaving, he rose, trembling and ataxic, and dragged himself on toward the door. The old woman's footsteps came clicking after him.

"Just where do you think you're going?"

Why couldn't they leave him alone? "Please . . . I have to—"

"What you have to do is *clean that up!*" She grabbed his shoulder and spun him around.

She looked gaunt as a straw in her baggy flowered dress,

14

her receding hair like dandelion fluff. Her eyes bulged; she gasped in air for a scream.

Thirst blasted him. He knew what he was about to do and couldn't stop.

He lunged forward, slammed into her, carried her down beneath him. Her head cracked against the cement floor, but she didn't pass out. She was writhing, slapping, kicking, scratching, about to try to scream again. He grabbed her by the hair and collar and sank his teeth into the side of her neck.

She kept struggling and pulling away; blood splashed his face like spray from a trick boutonniere, ran uselessly down a drain. He bit again and again, until he'd savaged her throat into sponge. At last she stopped thrashing, though she still twitched and quivered, and he could lick and suck at her wounds.

Her blood tasted unspeakably vile.

Chapter Three

Her face.

Her white, contorted face.

He wrenched his eyes away, scrambled up, bolted. His foot slipped in a smear of blood and he crashed back onto the floor. The impact shrieked through his tortured nerves, shocked some of the panic out of him.

He couldn't run yet. He needed to wash and change his clothes worse than ever, now that he was spattered with gore. And someone would find the old woman within the hour if he didn't hide her.

When he bent to pick her up, he started shaking.

Come on, he told himself, damn it, come on! You sure didn't have any trouble touching her a minute ago. He thrust out his hands, then gasped and jerked them away.

She moved.

No, she didn't, it was just his imagination. She couldn't be alive, not with those gashes, not with her blood in his stomach.

Touching her was even harder the second time. He hauled her up and embraced her, then manhandled her across the floor. Her head flopped on his shoulder as if she meant to whisper in his ear.

He stuffed her into a drier, then pulled an Out of Order sign off one of the washers and stuck it on the window. If he had a quarter, he could send her tumbling around and around . . .

He ground his fists together until the pain cleared his head.

A mop and bucket were sitting by the sink. He flushed the blood and vomit down the floor drain, then stripped to the waist. His chest and arms looked gray and greasy, like hamburger beginning to go bad.

He didn't like facing the wall to wash. Driers were rumbling, and washers were whining through their Spin cycles; the faucet hissed. If she stirred, he might not hear her. Even if she climbed out and came creeping up behind him . . .

He moaned and whirled around. She was still where he'd left her.

He had to get away! He started raking through the driers, singeing his fingers in the process. In the second one he opened, he uncovered plaid polyester slacks, an aqua sport shirt, and a bright green golf cap.

Even dressed like an elderly snowbird, he'd be less conspicuous than before. At least the cap would help obscure his face.

He stepped behind a row of washers to change his pants; he might be a murderous monster, but nobody could say he was immodest.

After he'd dropped his old clothes in a garbage can, it was time to leave, but he felt compelled to take one last look at his victim. She hadn't changed.

But she might . . . after they buried her.

Carter had told him that an Olympian's bite wasn't contagious unless he wanted it to be. But David didn't know how his powers worked. What if he'd infected her without realizing it? If she came back from the dead, he wouldn't be a murderer after all.

But maybe she wouldn't want to come back. He couldn't carry her with him, so she'd be embalmed and return just as hideous, agonized, and alone as he was. She might go crazy. She'd certainly kill others, and certainly hate him. She might tell the police about him, or even try to hunt him down herself.

He couldn't let her come back.

17

He snapped the mop in two. The butt was left with a jagged point, so it wasn't too difficult to drive it in between her breasts.

Next he braced her shoulders under the drier door, then pulled her head out and twisted it. Her spine resisted for a moment, then cracked. Several rotations later her neck shredded apart.

Her temples were slick, awkward to support between his palms. He closed his eyes and squeezed until she crunched.

He couldn't incinerate her, but surely it wasn't necessary. Surely even an Olympian couldn't return with a punctured heart, a severed head, and a brain crushed to pulp.

And then she grinned at him.

He shrieked and hurled her into the drier, slammed the door and fled into the night.

Chapter Four

The river was an oily python oozing through the trees.

David sat on the sand beside it, weary, sore, and appalled at his own stupidity. He'd forgotten that he couldn't reach Sulphur Springs without somehow crossing the Hillsborough.

Actually, he was lucky he'd even traveled in the right direction. When he'd bolted from the laundromat, he'd been too terrified to remember where he was going. He'd simply run, pitching down one back street after another until suddenly plunging off a curb onto an eight-lane highway.

A block away, the light turned green; a wave of cars surged forward. His mismatched legs wouldn't carry him across in time. He stopped abruptly, almost fell, stumbled around in a half circle. Grabbing a street sign, he hauled himself back onto the curb moments before the first cars streamed by.

He hid his face behind the signpost and waited for a break in the traffic. Even at this hour, Hillsborough Avenue was busy; fortunately, it was the only main drag on his route.

Now that he'd stopped running, he felt less afraid. He'd better enjoy it while he had the chance; he'd probably panic again when the next horrible thing happened.

Had the old woman really grinned? She couldn't have; it had taken him days to awaken, so surely she hadn't done it in just a few minutes. He'd been hallucinating, yet another warning that he was on the verge of losing his mind.

Well, he didn't intend to lose it; everything would be all right if he could only get to Carter's.

Crossing the brightly lit street, he felt naked, agoraphobic; he scuttled like a cockroach for the shadows on the other side. Then he hobbled on north, a foul aftertaste still puckering his mouth. Apparently blood tasted nasty if you killed to get it; he promised himself he never would again.

An hour later he came to a dead end, limped around a guard rail and down the slope beyond. Water made gloating sounds as it ran over stones; the wind spat and whispered through the leaves. He stared numbly for a few seconds, then flopped down, closed his eyes, and tried to think.

Nebraska Avenue spanned the river, but there were too many bars on it; at night it was even busier than Hillsborough. Fortieth Street had a bridge, but it was more than twenty blocks to the east. If he walked that far out of his way, he might not make Sulphur Springs before dawn.

Maybe he didn't need a bridge. The river wasn't wide or deep; he knew how to swim. But the stories said Olympians couldn't abide running water, and Carter had never told him whether or not it was true.

It *probably* wasn't. After all, he'd washed in tap water without any ill effect. He'd even drunk it, and although he couldn't keep it down, it hadn't done him any permanent harm. Why should the same chemical compound, plain, ordinary H_2O, affect him differently just because it happened to be outdoors flowing down a natural channel? Kneeling at the river's edge, he poked a fingertip beneath the surface.

The water burned like acid; he snatched his finger back and stuck it in his mouth.

It wasn't right! Becoming an Olympian was supposed to set him free, but he'd never felt so trapped, caged by the river and his own gruesome body, by guilt, trepidation, and the imminence of sunlight. He couldn't cry, and there was nothing to smash, so he lurched to his feet and headed east.

Houses squatted at the top of the rise. Following the river, he was cutting through their back yards, but no one challenged him; the occupants were probably all asleep.

After a while the homes gave way to a park. Cigarettes glowed in one of the picnic shelters; someone else had sneaked in after hours. Farther ahead, a black arch straddled the river; white lights rolled along its crest.

He stopped for a moment, held his breath. If he moved or made a sound, the bridge might vanish.

He'd never lived in this part of Tampa, so he supposed it wasn't all that amazing that he'd found a bridge he hadn't known existed. Still, it felt like a miracle, or at least an omen. Maybe his luck had changed; maybe the whole world wasn't out to get him after all.

Once he slipped past the occupied shelter, he saw there were actually two bridges, one for trains and one for cars. If he crossed on the former, no one driving by would see him.

He climbed up the bank beside the graffiti-scarred pillars, peered up and down the track before he stepped between the rails. Then he dashed across, his crooked foot snagging on the ties.

When he reached the other side, he was in Sulphur Springs. Walking in the street was doubly nerve-racking after the loneliness of the riverbank, but he only had a few more blocks to go.

And then only half a block.

Carter's nondescript little house was as dark as he'd expected, but the one next door was blazing. Half a dozen people were lounging on the porch, drinking Busch and crowing over hitting the daily double at the fronton.

The porch light was too bright, the houses too close together. He hurried to the next street over, glanced around to make sure no one was watching, then darted up somebody's driveway. He'd approach his destination from the rear.

He paused beside an aluminum storage shed to get his bearings. Since only the bettors' house was lit, picking out Carter's place was easy. With his inhuman strength, breaking in should be easy too. He sighed to think that his troubles might be nearly over.

That was when it snarled.

The pit bull glided out from behind the shed, its teeth like

21

ivory daggers in the moonlight. David froze for an instant; after that he was still scared, but it didn't matter anymore. He couldn't let anything stop him now, not with his objective actually in sight.

There was a garden trowel lying on the grass. It would have made a good weapon, but the dog sprang before he could pick it up.

He flinched, staggered; the pit bull slammed against him and he fell. He threw up his arms to protect his face, realized too late that the animal was between his legs, fangs flashing, slashing at his *crotch*—

He was all set to scream, but he didn't have to. The pit bull abruptly scrambled back, head held low and tail between its legs. When he sat up, it retreated even farther, then crouched down to watch him.

It must have finally sensed there was something unnatural about him. Luckily for his balls, it was afraid to mix it up with the living dead.

He sidled on toward Carter's, keeping one eye on the dog. When he left its master's yard, it started barking.

Other dogs chimed in immediately, off to his right, to his left, then to his right again. Everyone on the block would look to see what the hell was going on.

Carter's drew him on, even though he knew he should run away instead. He couldn't force his way in without shattering a window or kicking in the door, not in the few seconds he had left. Even if the neighbors missed seeing him, they'd spot the damage.

The door swung open.

Carter was here! David burst into the kitchen, thumped against the far wall. He was gasping, his heart pounding with exertion and exhilaration. The lie that had kept him going was true: everything was going to be fine!

The ceiling light came on. "I didn't think you'd make it," said the dry familiar voice.

David meant to tell him it had been a piece of cake; then he saw the eyeless sockets in the brown, shriveled face.

Chapter Five

The night they met had begun like any other Friday evening.

Sunlight was streaming through the windows; crystals cast rainbows and the gaudy superhero posters glowed. The store usually looked a little dingy, but just before sunset, if the western sky was clear, Illuminations lived up to its name.

Wally Fulton sat behind the register, his ruddy moon face twisted, squinting into a hand mirror as he struggled to see his psychic aura. David, a mere employee, was actually working, plucking month-old issues from the rotating Marvel Comics rack. He was also trying not to peek out the window. Whenever he looked, glare caught him squarely in the eye, but every minute or two he did it anyway.

At last a battered silver Mazda wagon pulled up in the parking lot. He dropped a stack of *Captain America* and *Conan the Barbarian* and scurried out the door.

Liz Yarborough stood wryly regarding her car. Though the keys were in her hand, the engine was still coughing and sputtering; they waited half a minute for its shuddering death rattle.

The moment called for a quip, but he couldn't think of one. If Liz weren't quite so pretty, if her chestnut hair weren't so shiny or her brown eyes weren't so big, so bright and dark at the same time, maybe he wouldn't get so tongue-tied when he tried to talk to her.

"Open the back and I'll get the boxes," he finally said.

"You don't have to carry them all," she replied. "They aren't that heavy; I carried them to the car."

"You just hold the door."

She shook her head and unlocked the Mazda's rear compartment.

The first carton was heavy; he hoped she didn't hear him grunt. As he was stepping back from the tailgate, someone brushed him aside, nearly costing him his balance.

"I'll take some," said Steve Morales, and before David could tell him he didn't need any help, Steve picked up two cartons.

Steve worked at Cayman Jack's, the beach shop two doors down; with his swarthy tan, gleaming teeth, and Nautilus muscles, he probably sold a lot of sun screen and bikinis. He claimed he read science fiction, but David knew he didn't hang around Illuminations because he was interested in the merchandise.

When David returned to the car, he lifted out the last two boxes. They felt like they were full of concrete; they cut into his fingers and the top one blocked his view. He walked fast, so he wouldn't have to set them down before he got inside.

He was all right going through the door. His burden had grown heavier with every step, but it wasn't slipping out of his hands and he didn't think he was grimacing. Then he tripped over the pile of comics he'd left sitting on the floor.

He could see exactly what was about to happen. He and the cartons would fall against the Marvel rack, which would fall into the DC rack, which would fall into the first independents rack—

Strong hands gripped his shoulders. "I've got you," said Steve.

"Thank God," said Liz. "He always gets clumsy when he hurries."

David's face burned; he couldn't look at them. He mumbled a thank you, then knelt and started ripping at the boxes.

It took half an hour to check in the shipment. David and Liz worked side by side, unpacking the merchandise, counting it, and calling out their totals to Wally, who verified them against the distributor's invoice. Steve stood close to the girl, his thigh occasionally grazing her shoulder; if she turned her head, her face would be in his crotch. David wished she'd shift away, but she didn't.

The last carton was full of Tarot decks and metaphysical books. Steve grinned and pulled out a paperback; on its badly painted cover, a man who looked vaguely like Gandhi was meditating in the center of an iridescent pyramid. *"Empowering the Sahu;* what's a Sahu?"

"The High Self," said Wally. "It's a spirit guide, a teacher and protector, like a guardian angel except that it's actually a part of you."

"It sounds like something you yell when you're calling hogs."

Wally chuckled; Steve's incessant needling never bothered him. Liz sighed. "You should read that," David said. "Lord knows, you could stand a little spiritual development."

"I need development? Hey, *I'm* in college. *I'm* preparing for a career. *I* work out."

"And all that's important," said Liz. "Obviously I think so, or I wouldn't be doing it too. But there's a whole other side to life, a hidden side we discover through ritual and meditation. People who study it gain insight into why the world is the way it is. That gives us balance, and serenity."

"Is that all? I want to learn to bend spoons."

"You could," said David.

"Yeah, right, and leap over tall buildings at a single bound."

"Really," he said, standing up. He wanted to offer Liz his hand, but she rose before he could. "Psychic powers exist. It's proven; all you have to do is study the evidence." He didn't know if he believed what he was saying—some days he did and some he didn't—but he knew Liz believed it from the bottom of her heart.

"It's not proven, and it won't be until one of your New Age swamis performs under controlled laboratory conditions."

"Young souls can be so rigid," Wally said.

"Just because science hasn't validated metaphysical doctrine yet," said Liz, "that doesn't mean it isn't true."

"Maybe not, but then why should I take it seriously? Look, you mystical types claim the world is crawling with spooks and superbeings, but most educated people don't think so, and I've sure never seen any. If you want me to believe in miracles, show me one."

"All right," said a voice from the doorway.

They all jumped; the bell above the entrance hadn't chimed. The newcomer was tall and gaunt, with pale skin and white gold hair that shone like ectoplasm in the dusklight; he looked forty or perhaps a little older. His smile was as enticing as Steve's perpetual grin, but his eyes glittered cold and hard as amethyst.

" 'All right,' what?" asked Steve.

"All right, I'll show you a bona fide psychic-powered marvel, just as you asked."

Steve swallowed, cleared his throat; it was the first time David had ever seen him nervous. "Look . . . I don't know you. . . ."

"Oh, I'm just another crank. Don't you want a laugh at my expense?"

Liz laid a hand on Steve's forearm. "You don't have to do anything you don't want to do."

Of course he couldn't stand her thinking he was scared. "Hey, if he wants to do a trick, I don't mind watching, but I'll bet he's not as good as Kreskin."

Wally blinked, shook his head as if he was trying to clear it; maybe, like David, he had the feeling that everything was happening too fast. "Uh, friend, New Age is more or less my religion. If you're planning some silly stunt—"

"I'm not," said the stranger, stooping to peer into the display case. "I'd like a focus; please loan me that largest piece of quartz."

Wally fumbled for it, finally fished it out and handed it over. The pale man raised it to his eyes.

"I'm going to stare into this, but you shouldn't. I don't

want you thinking afterwards that I hypnotized you."

"What —" began Steve, and then they froze as motionless as statues.

After a while David hesitantly poked Steve's shoulder, then passed a hand in front of his face. Next, feeling gullible and frightened at the same time, he snapped his fingers under his nose. "Anybody got a match?" he asked at last.

"We're not buying it," quavered Liz, "so you might as well knock it off. Steve, I can't believe you made this poor man come here just to help you play this stupid joke."

"I don't think they're joking," Wally said softly. "I don't think there's anybody home."

They stood helplessly watching for another minute, and then the stranger smiled and lowered his hand. Steve gurgled and collapsed, thrashed about the floor with saliva foaming from his mouth. Wetness spread across his crotch.

"Damn," said the stranger. He snatched a piece of cloth off the counter, folded it several times and dropped to his knees, dragging David along with him. "It's like a grand mal seizure. Help me get this in the side of mouth, we don't want him biting his tongue."

David struggled to immobilize Steve until the stranger got the cloth between his teeth.

"What did you do to him?" shrilled Liz; her voice sounded a long way off.

The pale man ignored her. "Look," he said to David, who was placing a wadded up jacket under Steve's head, "you have a lot of positive energy flowing in your aura; I'm going to borrow some."

"I . . . okay."

"Close your eyes and concentrate on Steve's name. I need you to help me call him back."

The instruction seemed absurd, like a command given in a nightmare, but David did his best to obey it. And a few moments later, Steve stopped convulsing.

"He'll be all right now," said the pale man, standing up.

Steve's eyes flickered wildly back and forth. "Worms," he whispered.

Liz knelt beside him. "Where? What do you mean?"

"Everything was made of hungry little worms. Even my clothes—I had to claw them off. Even the ground—like quicksand—I kept sinking. Then my hands started to itch and wriggle apart and I realized that I—" He glanced up at the pale man, cringed. "Oh, God, *get me away!*"

"I think you should lie there and rest," Wally said. "I'll put up the Closed sign so nobody comes in and disturbs you. Or better still, maybe we should take you to—"

"Get me away!"

"Yes, baby, I'll take you home," Liz said soothingly. She helped him up and half carried him out, his brawny arm draped across her shoulders. She paused at the door to gaze at the pale man, partly in anger, partly in fascination.

"He really will be fine," the stranger said.

"What the hell happened?" Wally demanded.

"I astrally projected him. I know it sounds like a reckless thing to do to an unprepared ego, but I've used the same technique to enlighten many a skeptic, and nothing like this has ever happened before. Usually projection produces euphoria, but Steve panicked and I couldn't calm him down. Because he was frightened, he plummeted into a region of corrupt forms, and of course that only made it worse. By the time I retrieved him, he was so terrified that he couldn't get all the way back into his body, though for most people it's as easy as falling off a log. If David hadn't been here to lend me his strength, things might have gotten difficult. You should probably sit down, my friend; I really drained you."

"I'm fine," said David, and he was. When the stranger was supposedly leeching his psychic energy, he hadn't felt anything at all.

"Jesus," Wally said, "you're something. I don't know exactly what, but you're something."

"What I am is profoundly sorry. I humbly beg your pardon for bringing trouble into your establishment. If you forbid me to return, I'll understand."

"No, no," said Wally quickly. "I want to talk to you some

28

more. I have a lot of customers who'd like to talk to you too."

"I'll see you soon, then," the stranger said, and stepped into the night. David stood staring for a moment, then felt as if he'd suddenly awakened. He jerked open the door, almost expecting to see no one.

But the pale man was there, about to climb into a red Sentra. He turned and raised an eyebrow.

David realized he didn't know what to say. "I was just wondering who you are," he stammered.

"My name's Carter Cavanaugh," the stranger replied. "In a way, you could say that I'm your Sahu."

Chapter Six

David's parents had their usual trouble getting out the front door. First Molly discovered she'd forgotten her glasses. Then she decided it might be cold in the theater and went to fetch a sweater. On her way back across the living room she paused to straighten David's graduation picture, rearrange a pair of yellow roses in a spindly, milk white vase, and pluck a wisp of lint off the rug. Stan was grinning behind his luxuriant gray mustache; David was trying not to fidget.

"Well, I guess we can go," she said at last.

"Are you sure?" asked Stan. "Maybe we should pack a bag, or paint the house."

"Don't poke fun at me, or maybe we will. David, make sure your friends use the coasters."

"I will, Mom." He sighed; she'd reminded him three times already.

"And we don't want to come home to any bloodstains or cloven hoofprints," his father said.

"No problem; we'll hold the human sacrifice in the back yard. Look, if you guys don't take off, you'll miss the beginning of the movie."

"We get the hint," said Stan. Molly hugged David, kissed his cheek, and then they were finally gone.

David's shoulders slumped with relief, but a moment later he felt guilty.

He wasn't ashamed of his parents; he hoped they didn't

think he was. But if they'd still been hanging around when the New Age study group arrived, he wouldn't have felt like the host; with his mother fussing over everyone and everything, he wouldn't even have felt like a grown-up. And some of the group might take offense at his father's jokes.

He'd propose a family outing, just to show them he still loved them. Maybe his dad would want to take the boat out Sunday morn—

Someone tapped him on the back; he squawked and spun around.

Of course it was Carter, elegant as ever in a dove gray double-breasted suit and a dark blue shirt. "You should see your face," he said.

David told himself he wasn't angry. "Did you ring the doorbell? I didn't hear it."

"No, I walked in uninvited. I often do. It's a private joke, funny for several different reasons."

"I . . . guess I don't mind, but if my father had been here, he would have shit a brick."

Carter shrugged and sauntered over to inspect the trophies gleaming on the mantel. "Whose are these?"

"The ones for duplicate bridge are my mom's, and the ones for golf and bass fishing are my dad's."

"Where are yours? Don't you fish?"

"Some, but I'm not as good as he is."

"Stick with me and I'll make you a fisher of men."

"You keep saying these things . . ."

"And I never explain; it's all very Zen, don't you think? Show me your house; it will help me know you better."

The tour was disturbing. As he strolled, iridescent as an angel, from room to room, Carter was unfailingly complimentary. But whenever David followed his gaze, he saw something that made him wince. The bookcase stuffed with his mother's coverless Harlequins. A smudge on the dining-room wall. The Roach Motel under the kitchen sink and the garish painting of wild ducks his father bought from a roadside vendor. He'd always been proud of his home, but suddenly, somehow, it seemed almost shabby.

31

By the time they reached his bedroom, he didn't want Carter to see it. He tried to lead him past it, but the older man smiled, shook his head, and threw open the door.

The room looked full enough to burst, the dresser, desk, and bunk beds nearly lost among stacked cartons of comics. Dirty socks and T-shirts, paperback science fiction novels, and back issues of *Starlog* and *Fangoria* lay scattered everywhere. The X-Men, the Justice League International, and Indiana Jones were peeling themselves off the walls; spaceships and pterodactyls dangled from the ceiling.

David's face burned; Carter clapped him on the shoulder. "I think we should get out of here," he said.

"*What?* Look, I know it's not a mansion, but we met in Sarah's tiny little apartment—"

"You don't understand. I don't mind if the group meets here. Or it can meet in Antarctica, for all I care, as long as we don't have to attend."

"You're right; I don't understand."

"How many hours can you spend babbling about metaforms and the Huna before your brain turns to mush? Let's do something interesting for a change."

"But you're supposed to lead tonight's discussion."

"I will, but by remote control; come see." Returning to the front of the house, he lit the candles on the dining-room table, then extracted a handful of Tarot cards from his coat and laid them out in a triangle at the base of the candelabrum. "There: an exercise in occult cryptography. Something they can chew on without boring us. Actually, this is my way of imparting a great philosophical truth. If you seek enlightenment, you can find it; you don't need a guru to spoon-feed it to you."

"So you're really skipping group to teach a lesson?"

"No, but that's my alibi, and I'll stick to it."

"Well, if you don't want to stay, of course you don't have to, but it's my house."

"Leave Wally a note; he'll make sure that no one steals the silver."

"Yeah, but what will he think? What will the others think? Hell, I know what my parents will think!"

"We'll concoct an alibi for you too. David, I have things to tell you, things I can't say in a crowd."

"And . . . it has to be tonight?"

Carter shrugged. "It *is* tonight."

David found a pad and pencil by the phone.

Chapter Seven

The Sentra's interior reeked of pine. Carter turned the air conditioner to its highest setting, then floored the accelerator. Insects splatted against the windshield; in seconds the house was out of sight.

"Where are we going?" David asked.

"You'll see."

"I thought tonight you were going to give me straight answers."

Carter smiled. "I didn't say *that*, exactly."

"I bet you still won't do anything but drop hints and act mysterious, will you? Maybe there isn't anything to tell."

"Aren't we petulant. Does it really bother you so much to miss the séance? You can ravish Liz tomorrow night."

David's cheeks glowed warm again. "I don't know where you got that idea, but she and I have never even dated."

"Why not? She was impressed when I healed Steve, and I gave you part of the credit."

"Did you think she'd have sex with me just because you said I have a powerful aura?"

"Occultists have groupies, just like rock stars. After a while you can spot the type."

"You're wrong; she's not like that."

"Of course not, if you say so." The car veered left of

34

center to pass a bus, then raced on through a yellow light. David flinched at a sudden blare of horns.

"My God," he said shakily, "why do you always drive like this?"

"Driving fast makes me feel alive."

"Terrific; we'll crash and burn so you can get a rush. Look," he continued after a while, "I'm pretty sure you didn't really drain any energy from me, and there isn't really anything special about my aura, is there?"

The blond man chuckled. "There might be for all I know."

"You're supposed to know; you're supposed to be a New Age wizard."

"And does that credential impress you? Level with me: are you a New Age true believer?"

"Before I met you, I was keeping an open mind. I was interested, I thought it would be great if it was true, but I know a little about science, and, deep down, I guess I didn't believe very much of it."

"But when you showed up and astral-projected Steve, I started believing more. When you began hinting that maybe I could be some kind of disciple, I wanted to try it. Now . . ."

"Now it's been weeks, and I haven't initiated you or done any more tricks, and you wonder if that first trick was actually what it seemed."

"Well . . . yeah."

The Sentra turned onto Seventh Avenue, sped on into Ybor City. Wooden saints stared from a botanica; hooked black lamp posts arced over the narrow street.

"You're wise to be skeptical," said Carter, swerving into a parking space. "Most of New Age is nonsense. The paranormal does exist, but it doesn't work like Wally thinks it does." He switched off the ignition and opened his door. "Come on; our destination isn't far."

The block appeared abandoned; there were other parked cars, but nothing moving. The art galleries, cigar

35

shops, and Cuban restaurants were all closed, their grimy windows full of darkness.

"If New Age is garbage, then why do you hang around with New Age people?" asked David.

"Because I want to share what I have, and I'm more likely to find kindred spirits among students of the bogus occult than among people who aren't interested in the occult at all." They turned onto a smaller, crooked street. A few doors down squatted a tattoo parlor, its cinder-block walls painted with leopards, roses, and flaming skulls; beside it a bar rumbled with ghostly thunder. "There's the toughest heavy metal club in Tampa; it's kind of a headquarters for the skinheads."

David swallowed. "Is *that* where we're going?"

The blond man grinned. "No. Tonight I'm in the mood for a different scene."

They walked on without speaking for a while. David wanted to seem nonchalant, so he resolved he wouldn't be the one to break the silence, but soon he could contain himself no longer. "So what's the deal?" he demanded. "Am I a kindred spirit? Are you going to teach me what you know?"

"Probably," said Carter as they turned another corner. "Let's discuss it over a drink."

Just ahead and across the street stood a sprawling two-story wooden structure, an old house that had been converted into a night club. Candles flickered on the screened veranda, and Japanese lanterns bobbed in the branches of the surrounding trees. David blanched when he saw the neon parrot by the door.

"I've heard of this place; this is the Blue Cockatoo!"

"Right you are. You should see their drag show; it's hilarious."

"I don't want to go in *there*."

"You'll be all right as long as you don't bend over or use the men's room."

"Look, I really wouldn't be comfortable in there."

36

"Suit yourself, but I'm going in for a glass of wine." Carter strode on toward the entrance without another backward glance.

The thought of following made David queasy. Of course no one would rape him, no one could make him do anything he didn't want to do, but what if he had to watch them kissing? What if somebody touched him? And if Carter hoped to seduce him, he didn't want to spend another moment in his presence.

But Carter had never seemed sexually interested in him before, and if he wasn't, David didn't want to lose his friendship. Except for his parents, nobody else seemed to think he was special. Nobody else suggested he had some great untapped potential, or that his future held miraculous things in store. It was probably all bullshit, but he liked hearing it; lately there'd been a few days when he felt like it was all that kept him going.

Hell, it was just a bar, and the door would open from the inside too. He broke into a trot and caught up with Carter just before he went inside.

"There are lots of different rooms with different themes," the pale man said. "Leather, sports, country and western, piano—"

"Can we just sit on the porch?"

"Good plan; that way passersby can hear you scream for help."

They ordered drinks from the bartender stationed at the end of the veranda, then found a table for two beneath a hanging plant. David stared at the glass of beer in front of him so he wouldn't see the men holding hands, or the ones in dresses and cosmetics.

Carter sipped his Chablis. "It's always an event when someone new comes here, especially someone so young. Everybody's peeking at you, sizing you up."

"That isn't funny. I can't believe I'm sitting here. You took such an interest in me, right from the start. I didn't

37

understand, but I didn't think . . . I mean, why would you think—"

"Well, for one thing, you don't go out with girls."

"Look—"

"And there's the way you carry yourself, and that thing you do with your mouth when a boy your own age enters the room."

"Fuck you!" Eyes stinging, he thrust back his chair.

"Oh, for Heaven's sake, relax! You rattle so easily, there's hardly any sport in ragging you. Of course I know you're not gay and neither am I. I brought you here because I knew it would make you uncomfortable."

David slowly exhaled, then scowled and pulled his seat back up to the table. "Thanks a lot."

"I wanted one last assessment of your character. If you weren't even curious enough about what I have to offer to overcome your homophobia and follow me in here, then you wouldn't have been worthy to receive it. It's a pretty wimpy test actually; an old-fashioned master would have made you sit outside his cave in the snow for a few months. I might have myself, if we weren't in Florida and if I had a cave."

"Then you are finally going to let me be your student? Great, I guess, but I still don't understand: why me? Why only me, and not Liz or Wally?"

"Because of the kind of person you are. Your bedroom tells the story. You've devoted it entirely to fantasy, to imaginary marvels and adventures; it's the room of an introverted child."

David snorted. "Hey, this makes sense. You're going to trust me with your mystic secrets because I'm immature and maladjusted."

"Because you're miserable, and desperate for a life with magic in it. You haven't grown up because mundane existence doesn't sustain you; you're out of place in it. For our purposes, that's good, because if ordinary mortality

38

could make you happy, you'd never find the courage to forsake it."

"Forsake it . . . I definitely don't understand what we're talking about."

"Finish your beer and I'll show you."

Chapter Eight

The Blue Cockatoo's parking lot was a patch of sand-spurs and coarse grass lit by sickly yellow lights. Carter inspected the hood of a classic Mustang, dusted it with his handkerchief, and then sat down on it.

"Why didn't we park here?" asked David.

"Various reasons. I like to walk, and the car is safer where it is."

"Hm." He swiped at a mosquito whining by his left ear. "Well, is this it? Are you going to show me something now?"

"Soon."

"How did I know you were going to say that?" He brushed the mosquito away again. "Waiting for Jupiter to align with Mars?"

The older man chuckled. "You think I enjoy secrecy, don't you? Well, you're right, but even if I didn't, I wouldn't tell you what's about to happen. I doubt you'd believe me, and you might become alarmed. Aha!" He rose and took David's hand. "Let's walk."

David's skin crawled; he tried unsuccessfully to pull free. "Hey, you said—"

"Yes, I did. You're not, I'm not, and holding hands for a little while won't transform us. Humor me, David; I'll ask you to do stranger things than this before we're through."

"All right. If we have to. If it's really to teach me something, and not just more hazing."

40

Five minutes later they turned another corner, passed a pawnshop with steel-shuttered windows. The street ahead was deserted; somehow the illumination provided by half a dozen street lights only served to make the shadows blacker.

David frowned. "We're getting farther and farther from the car."

Carter's grip tightened. "I know."

Clouds crept across the moon. "Am I supposed to be seeing something, feeling something —"

"Not yet. Be patient."

Perhaps, behind them, something clicked. David glanced around but couldn't see anything alive.

Another minute passed. "I feel stupid." He stepped over the shards of a shattered bottle. "I feel like I'm failing an exam."

"You aren't, so relax and enjoy the stroll. No, this way." He drew him down an alley.

The narrow passage stank; cats were foraging among the overturned and overflowing trash cans. Many of the houses pressing close on either side were dark, with scabs of paint flaking from their gray corrupting walls. David almost expected to see ghosts staring from the windows.

Back beyond the mouth of the alley something crunched, perhaps a piece of glass cracking under a shoe. He stiffened, then told himself not to be paranoid.

"This isn't Tampa's prettiest neighborhood, but it's one of its most interesting," said Carter after a time. "Some of these houses are untenanted — that one and that one, for instance — and whores and drug dealers conduct their business in them. I read in the *Tribune* that the city wants to tear them down."

"I think you're trying to rattle me again."

"No, it's true; this is a high crime area. Don't worry, though, we're perfectly safe. Although I admit the average pedestrian wouldn't be."

Something moved off to the right, slipping across the

41

gap between two houses. David only saw it from the corner of his eye; by the time his head snapped around it had already disappeared.

"A number of the local toughs share your antipathy for homosexuals," his companion continued casually. "Of course the skinheads are notorious for it. Sometimes they mug people or vandalize cars in the Cockatoo's parking lot. Not too often anymore, though, because they know there are security guards."

David almost saw another flicker of motion, this one ahead and to the left; perhaps someone had just crouched down behind a rusting pickup. "Carter—"

"Now if some of them saw a gay couple walk off the Cockatoo grounds into their territory, they might follow and molest them. Particularly if the gays were obliging enough to proceed down a dark alley and if they flaunted their sexual preference with a public display of affection."

A soft jingling sounded at their backs. Suddenly two shadows were gliding down the alley, the one in the lead swinging a glittering length of chain.

David's mouth had gone dry. He tried to speak, swallowed, tried again. "I know this is just another joke."

Carter grinned. "Yes, but *they* don't know it." And David read in his face that it was so.

"Jesus, let go!" He tried to rip his hand free, but the blond man's fingers held him like a shackle. "We have to run! If these guys are muggers they could really hurt us!"

"No, I told you, we're safe."

"Oh my God, you're crazy!" He struggled madly to wrench himself loose, his fear intensifying with each futile pull. "You're crazy and we're going to fucking *die!*"

Then, abruptly, his hand was free; he stumbled back and nearly fell. No one stood before him; Carter might have melted like a wraith.

The shadows were trotting now, and only thirty feet away. David pivoted, darted for the gap between two houses.

He vaulted over a pile of trash; something soft burst beneath his shoe and sent him skidding. For an instant he was sure he'd fall, but then he was scrambling on past a splintered orange crate and a tricycle with its front wheel missing. Behind him drummed his pursuers' sprinting feet.

More junk littered the aisle between the houses. He kicked a can and it sprang away, clattering; something batted him across the shin.

The street beyond the gap was just as dark and empty as the alley. He spun to the right and raced on, past Condemned and For Sale signs, past closed doors and vacant windows.

He was already gasping, faltering; he glanced back. The one with the chain was no more than twenty feet behind him.

Then, just ahead, a porch light flashed on and a screen door started to swing open. With the last of his strength he plunged forward. Just as he drew even with the light he tripped, landing bruised and breathless on the grass.

An elderly black woman with a glossy jet wig was stepping out the doorway. She jumped and covered her mouth; her aluminum cane caught in the screen door when she tried to yank it shut.

"Please," David croaked. Someone grabbed his shoulder from behind.

"Please—the police . . ." The rest of the pack came loping up, their garments rustling. "Please . . ." The old woman shook her head; the inner door slammed and the porch light winked out a second later.

More hands seized him, hauled him to his feet. Gripping both his arms, they manhandled him around the corner of the house, back toward the alley.

David kept his head bowed and glanced at his captors surreptitiously; he was too afraid to look them in the eye. There were four of them, three men and a woman, all wearing work boots, jeans, and muscle shirts with heavy metal band logos stenciled on them; their naked arms were mottled with tattoos. Even the woman had her hair clipped boot camp close, revealing the swastika inked above her left ear. "Too bad you can't run as fast as your friend," she said.

"Listen, you can have my money! I don't want any trouble! I won't even report this!"

"You might as well save your breath," said the one with the chain. He was thin and long-legged, with a wide mouth and a broken nose. Now that he had David by the right forearm, his weapon dangled like a scarf around his neck. "You shouldn't have walked around down here. You shouldn't have made us chase you. Now they want to make you an example."

"Look . . . I know you don't like queers—"

"You don't know anything *yet*," crowed the man holding his left arm. He was pudgy and freckled, with little wire-rimmed glasses like Benjamin Franklin might have worn. "But you will!"

"—but I'm not a queer—I don't like them either—my friend didn't tell me where he was taking me—"

Swastika clucked like a chicken; the third man, a five-foot body builder who smelled of beer, spat and pulled David's wallet out of his back pocket.

David kept on babbling as they dragged him down the alley; he knew they weren't listening, but he couldn't stop. Then Chain said, "I guess this is far enough," and they shoved him back against a telephone pole.

Franklin started bouncing up and down. "Oh man, this is going to be so *cool!*"

"Well, we shouldn't take all night," Chain replied. "The other one got away, and that old nigger lady saw us too."

"I guess you're right," said Swastika. "Did you see that wig? Think I'd look good in one of those?" She rooted in her pocket, brought out a plastic spindle that suddenly spat a blade.

44

David thrashed and yammered, kicked and squirmed, but Chain and Franklin held him easily. The body builder drove stiffened fingers into his solar plexus and then he couldn't even struggle anymore.

"She's not going to hurt you *bad,*" said Chain. "You'll feel better if you take it like a man."

The knife point dented the skin at the corner of his left eye—

—and then they all looked up as if they'd heard someone overhead call their names, even though there hadn't been a sound. Carter hung twenty feet up the telephone pole. He wasn't gripping the metal rungs but adhering to the post like a huge white fly, his fingers simply pressed against the wood.

"Don't cut him or you'll make me a liar," he said. "If that happens I'll be angry."

The knife quivered, then jerked down to David's throat. "Stay away or I *will* cut him!"

Carter laughed, then kicked off the pole, launching himself into space. He seemed to fall too slowly, like a feather. When he finally landed, knees flexing to absorb the impact, his coat still hung properly and not a white-gold hair was out of place. "I've decided to damage you gentlemen in alphabetical order: first Bryan, then Ed, then Georgie."

For a moment no one moved. Then the body builder hissed and dropped into a martial arts crouch, his shoulders twisted and his fingers hooked. Franklin tittered and flicked open a switchblade of his own. Chain's weapon rattled as it slid from around his neck. "Look after this one," he said to Swastika.

"Don't do it!" she begged. "There's something *wrong* with him—we have a hostage. . . ."

"I don't think that matters," he replied.

The three men spread out to encircle their opponent. Franklin jabbed his knife out, waved it around in figure eights. The body builder's arms swayed like cobras; the

45

chain spun. Carter simply stood and smiled, allowing himself to be surrounded.

Swastika's lips were trembling; a tear oozed down the side of her nose.

Two of the skinheads attacked at once, Chain from the rear and the body builder from the side. The steel links flashed at Carter's ankles; the short man sprang in kicking at his groin.

Carter vanished from the middle of the circle.

The body builder's foot shot through empty air; the chain cracked against his knee and made him stagger. While he was still off balance Carter materialized beside him, whipped a fist against his temple and dropped him.

"That's Bryan," the blond man said.

Franklin blinked madly, then bolted. An instant later Carter appeared in front of him, his hand thrust forward as if he were a policeman stopping traffic. The flabby skinhead ran right into it. The collision didn't rock Carter at all, but Franklin rebounded with a lopsided jaw and broken teeth.

"And that's Ed."

Chain—Georgie—was charging, his weapon sweeping around in a murderous arc. This time Carter didn't disappear or even duck, and yet the chain never crunched against his skull. Instead it whizzed in a complete circle, lashing Georgie across the back and entangling his arms.

Before he could free himself Carter had him by the throat. He was forced to his knees; then Carter raised a fist.

"No!" Swastika shrieked. "Don't hurt him or I swear I'll kill your friend!"

"No, Val," Carter said. "Try if you like, but you'll find you can't." The punch snapped bone.

Val snarled, muscles jumped in her forearm . . . and then she shuddered, wailed, and dropped the knife.

"That's right. Now just stand there quietly for a moment."

46

She was twitching violently, her eyes ablaze with rage and terror. But within a few seconds her trembling abated; her face went slack, like a sleepwalker's.

Carter picked up the switchblade. "Would you like a souvenir?"

David flattened himself against the pole. *"What are you?"*

"I'll show you." He caressed Val's cheek, brushed his fingertips across her lips. He kissed her mouth, her ears, her eyes; his hands began to range across her body. Soon she was moaning and fondling him in return. David suddenly saw beyond the shaven scalp and tattoos, realizing just how beautiful she was.

His penis hardened — and then Carter bit her.

Chapter Nine

David soared on the night wind, his inhuman senses raking the darkness. Far below a car crashed into a tree. As he plummeted flames were already dancing beneath the crumpled hood; he jerked the driver's door off its hinges and carried her to safety an instant before the vehicle exploded. Quaking, sobbing, she pressed herself against him—

A wave slapped him in the face. Nighttime Tampa dissolved into daytime Key West; a beach ball bobbed just to his right and gulls screeched overhead.

He was glad to have his fantasy dispelled. He hadn't come to daydream but to bid farewell to sunshine. Turning slowly, he memorized blue sky and sparkling water.

When swimming began to bore him he retrieved his sandals and took a stroll down the beach. Soon he was smirking at the tourists. They looked grotesque with their wattled necks and bulging stomachs, their doughy thighs and reddening skin.

It was too bad they couldn't exchange their sunburns for an alabaster luster, their flab for perpetual leanness. What a pity that they had to age.

Of course, not everyone was homely. A luscious blonde lay dozing in the sun, her body gleaming. He remembered Val writhing in Carter's embrace and wondered if the sleeper lived in Tampa.

But at times that part of it still bothered him. If he

used mesmerism to make a woman love him, wasn't that a kind of rape?

No; Carter had taught him that it wasn't so. Rape was a mortal perversion. It was necessary and natural for Olympians to take human blood, just as it was for spiders to catch flies. Instead of agonizing over it, he should be glad he could manage it without hurting or terrifying his partners, and even offer rapture in return.

Besides, mortal seducers didn't play fair either; the successful ones practiced their own forms of beguilement. Guys with money, good looks, or a smooth line always scored; without hanging around with them you couldn't even get a date. Even if you were smart and nice, even if you really loved somebody and treated her like a goddess, she'd rather have a jerk like Steve Morales. Since love truly *was* blind, and women cared more about flash than what was in your heart and mind, then hypnotism was no sleazier than any other trick that got you laid.

Down the beach people had lined up before a yellow kiosk with a plastic ice cream cone on its roof. His mouth watered, but he hesitated; he planned to eat a huge steak and lobster dinner in just a couple hours. After a moment he decided to indulge himself. A milkshake surely wouldn't spoil his appetite, not when he was also saying goodbye to mortal food.

Actually, he was giving up thousands of small pleasures for an existence that would be difficult—or even painful—in many ways. He'd spend his life lying and glancing over his shoulder, at least until a day arrived when the majority of humans became imaginative and open-minded enough to believe that Olympians didn't pose a deadly threat. Carter had forbidden him to tell *anyone* about his incipient metamorphosis until he'd completed his century-long apprenticeship. He hated keeping the secret from his parents, but he also doubted they could ever understand.

Someday he'd watch them fade while he stayed young, and that would grieve him far worse than deceiving them. He felt treacherous, aspiring to immortality when they had to die.

But he could conceal his Olympian nature; in fact a part of him would relish the game. And every son, mortal or not, eventually had to mourn his mother and father.

Eternal youth was surely worth every sacrifice and sorrow it entailed. The certainty of decline cast a shadow on every man's life, but it wouldn't mar his. Mortals perished, having tasted only the tiniest portion of the joys the universe afforded, but he'd have time to savor nearly all.

He'd stride laughing down the ages, delighting in each new marvel. One day he'd explore the stars.

And he wouldn't be a nobody, either. Not with superhuman abilities, even if he did have to exercise them secretly. Not when a tiny investment today could mature into a fortune in a hundred years. Not when he could study until he acquired more skills and knowledge than any fifty humans could amass. He'd be a genius, a leader, perhaps the champion who led the Olympians into the light of recognition and acceptance.

Well, maybe that was a little grandiose. But he was sure that one day he'd possess erudition and charisma like Carter's. Then people would love and admire him; he wouldn't need magic to draw women into his arms.

It would all begin at dusk in his motel room, when Carter unzipped his thick black shroud and crawled out from underneath the bed.

Chapter Ten

The thing in the kitchen was dry and gaunt, like crumbling parchment stretched over a framework of sticks; from it seeped a scent of old decay. Its head, eyeless, noseless, and possessed of only one shriveled ear, was scarcely more than a fleshless skull. Several teeth were missing from its black and ocher grin, but not its long and needle-pointed canines.

It was wearing Carter's blue silk dressing gown.

David tried to scream. Before he finished inhaling the corpse leaped forward and ground its hand against his mouth.

The pressure set his tattered lips on fire. He lashed out, but the dead thing blocked his punch and threw him against the refrigerator. "Calm down! It's only me, for Heaven's sake!" Once again it spoke with his mentor's voice.

"C-Carter?"

"Of course. Sorry to maul you, but I couldn't let you shriek. My neighbors have never taken any interest in me and I intend to keep it that way."

David shuddered and averted his eyes. "Please don't do this to me. I've been through too much; I can't take it."

"Whatever do you mean?"

"You know what I mean! *Turn off the illusion and look like yourself!*"

51

"But I'm not casting an illusion. I couldn't; you're immune now."

"Then—oh no, not this—then I'm hallucinating again. It happened before, I saw something dead *smile* at me, and now you look ... look ... Carter, you've got to help me!"

"Come sit down and we'll discuss it." He turned and led David into the living room, his bare feet clicking on the floor.

The living room housed an eclectic library and a miscellany of masks. As usual, it smelled of air freshener, lemon tonight. The dead thing fished a matchbook from its pocket and lit a single candle. In the dimness the bookshelves loomed like basalt cliffs. The long-nosed leather face of Scaramouche leered above the front door, and a tusked ogre with yaktail hair snarled from the shadows in the corner.

Carter lowered himself into his favorite armchair, pressed together fingertips from which the last remaining scraps of flesh would soon have worn away. "Well now, let's hear all about your troubles."

"You ... you can see something's wrong with me." *Right, his eyes have rotted out but he sees, doesn't he?* "It's like I'm *dead!*"

"You are."

"Yeah, but—you know what I mean! They embalmed me, and I hurt and I see things and my powers don't work right! *I killed somebody!*"

Carter sighed and shook his withered head. "Sometimes you're a tad slow. Haven't you wondered why I gave your carcass to your parents instead of standing watch over it in Key West? Or why I didn't help you escape your grave?"

"Sure, but right now I don't even care. I just want to stop hurting and learn how to get blood without killing people. You can explain everything else later."

"How would you like to hear a story?"

"A *story!*"

"I promise you'll find it pertinent."

"I . . . I need. . . . All right." He slumped on the love seat, pulled off his cap and ran abraded fingers through his hair. "Anything, just as long as you help me."

"Splendid; you've made my night. I don't get a chance to tell this very often.

"Once upon a time there was a fortunate man, so fortunate he lived in Paradise.

"Paradise was a small town whose name you've never heard, and it would have seemed like Purgatory to you. The inhabitants had no jangling telephones or caterwauling radios to break the monotonous quiet, no comic books, televisions, or pornographic magazines to improve their minds. No one paved the fields to provide abundant parking for their wagons, or burned petroleum to perfume the wind. Without the prospect of nuclear war or ecological and social collapse, there was little to lend excitement to their days. But, no doubt because they didn't know what they were missing, the burghers who dwelt in this green and primitive place were well content.

"Our hero was even happier than most. He was the only son of a man who kept an inn, a hostel two hundred years old whose venerable reputation and situation on a major highway insured its prosperity, and so he wanted for nothing. Moreover, he was vigorous and well favored, with a tall, spare frame, golden hair, and brilliant blue eyes set in a fine-boned face; he looked like aristocrats should and seldom do."

David raised his eyes, hoping that the face he remembered, the face he'd just heard described, had replaced the cankered visage across the room. The corpse cocked its head; shadows squirmed like maggots in its sockets.

"Now when this chap was twenty-two, his father died of the grippe. The young man sorrowed, but it passed, and then he thoroughly enjoyed being the wealthy and respected master of the inn. With his money and natural graces, he could have had almost any bride he wanted, and within a year of his father's passing he married a radiant lass named Rebecca. She was a black-eyed dusky rose, even lovelier than your Liz, if you'll forgive my saying so, and with a disposition sweet as honey; she even got along with the young man's mother. She was the miller's daughter and came well dowered, but he might have wed her even if she hadn't had a farthing.

"For over two decades they were happy; their establishment continued to flourish, and she gave him a sturdy son and three fine daughters. Their boy Hugh had his father's face but not his temperament; he was a dreamer and doted on romances and volumes of natural philosophy. Margaret, the eldest daughter, loved dancing and flirtation; on Sunday mornings her swains would scramble and scuffle for a seat adjacent to the innkeeper's pew. Their second girl, Penny, was actually prettier, for she resembled her mother, but the lads didn't notice her because she was so quiet. Placid and dutiful, she was the child who never needed scolding. And Delores, the youngest, was a hoyden, a tree-climbing tornado with skinned knees.

"Well, one moonless December night when fresh snow lay on the ground—you've heard of snow, haven't you, my fine Floridian—a coach came racing through the town. A miserly old squire lay dying in a house just down the highway from the inn, and his niece was hastening to his bedside. It was a pleasant little house, and it takes time to settle an estate, so no one was surprised when she stayed on after his demise. Her name was Gretta Spelvin and as you will have guessed, she was a vampire."

"Vampire? You told me we call ourselves Olympians."

The dead thing chuckled. "I told me a lot of things."

"Carter, I . . . I always wanted to know about your past; I've asked you a hundred times. But I'm in a lot of pain. I hurt all over, every second. You still look the same, and I'm scared that if I stay crazy too long I won't ever snap out of it. Please, can't you do something for me now and finish this later?"

"All I have to offer you is knowledge."

"But . . ." David lifted his hands in supplication, then dropped them in his lap. "All right, I'm listening. I'm trying to follow."

"Good. One day the innkeeper sent Hugh on an errand to the brewer's. The boy had difficulty extracting his nose from the book he was reading, so he departed late and returned late. Night had fallen by the time he rode back into town, and as luck would have it, he met Gretta strolling on the common. She was a dainty creature with a mischievous smile and a turned-up nose; her cheeks were rosy with the cold, her heart-shaped face was framed in a fur-trimmed hood, and altogether she looked quite a fetching little elf. She spoke of sonnets and watercolors, eclipses and wildflowers, and of course Hugh wasted no time deciding that he loved her. Two months later he proposed and she accepted.

"His father was delighted. Hugh was such a romantic goose that he'd always expected him to fall in love with an eminently unsuitable girl. Instead he'd settled on a woman of means, indeed a member of the gentry, a wife who'd improve his family's position. The innkeeper did think it odd that they only saw her at night, but since he'd never seen any horror movies he didn't suspect that there might be something sinister behind it. She said she read, painted, and attended to her housework and business affairs during the day, and he saw no reason to disbelieve her.

"Needless to say, shortly after her arrival she'd begun preying on the humans in the area. No doubt this posed something of a challenge. In a great anthill like London she could have fed forever without anyone even realizing there was a serial killer at work; in a small community it was more difficult. Still, strangers passed through every day, many of them rootless vagabonds, and she managed."

"Why did she kill?" asked David. "Why was there anything to hide?"

"For now suffice it to say that she was evil. In April the innkeeper gave the lovers a betrothal party, and there Hugh presented her with a pair of silver earrings. She seemed quite taken with them, and promised that she'd wear them every day. That night Delores died in bed. The poor little hellion was only ten years old.

"The physician said she died of some mysterious 'heart failure.' The innkeeper didn't understand how such a boisterous child could have had a weak heart, but he didn't question the doctor's diagnosis. As far as he knew, he had no enemies, and in any case he would have had difficulty imagining a foe vile enough to strike at a father through his daughter, so it never occurred to him that someone might have smothered her.

"Well, they buried the child. The innkeeper grieved, oh how he grieved, but it was an age when parents were perforce resigned to the possibility of their children's deaths. He consoled himself with the thought of all he still had, of the grandchildren he soon would dandle on his knee. Then, a month later, the June wedding date fast approaching, Penny died. Diligent to a fault, she never overslept, and so her father, when he came to wake her, intended to tease her mercilessly, to accuse her of climbing out the window and staying out till sunrise with some beau. Imagine how his mirth turned to horror when he couldn't rouse her. When he embraced her cooling body, he found a silver earring in her bed.

"The innkeeper was no paranoid, but neither was he a dunce, and so when the town quack informed him that Penny too had succumbed to 'heart failure,' he began to suspect that Gretta was a murderess. Perhaps her uncle had left far less than people thought. Perhaps she was debt ridden and destitute; it was possible, impoverished

56

gentility wasn't rare. If so, she might be marrying Hugh for money, though the boy now had no wealth of his own, and wouldn't have until his parents died, when he and his sisters would divide the estate. And so, if Gretta needed *all* the family funds and properties, needed them before the year was out, she might expeditiously slaughter her fiancé's siblings, then his mother and father, and finally, in all probability, the lad himself.

"Ah, but all this was only conjecture, the tortuous spinning of a mind the innkeeper knew was at least half mad with grief. He didn't know that Gretta lacked for money or was sufficiently depraved to kill children in cold blood; to all appearances the exact opposite was true. The earring might have fallen onto the bed under innocent circumstances, although she hadn't visited the family on the night Penny died and it seemed unlikely that his daughter would have failed to discover the jewelry if it had been lost days earlier, or, having found it, would have simply left it tangled in her sheets.

"And so he didn't accuse her. If he was wrong, as of course he fervently wished to be, he'd have foully slandered a sweet young lady. She'd break off the engagement; how miserable Hugh would be, and how he'd despise his father! How people would laugh when the story came out! Why, Gretta might even sue, and win some ruinous judgment! And if he was right, the consequences might be much the same, because he didn't have a shred of proof.

"But of course he had to do *something;* he and everyone he loved might be in mortal peril. Perhaps if he searched her house he'd find evidence of her guilt or innocence, a diary obligingly filled with ghoulish confessions or, more happily, passbooks revealing she was truly rich as Croesus.

"No doubt he was foolhardy to enter what he suspected was a killer's lair alone, but remember, he was a fortunate man. Aside from the loss of his parents, which didn't occur until he was fully grown and was in any case a natural and expected part of life, nothing really bad had ever happened to him, and that kind of luck breeds recklessness. Besides, a tiny woman like Gretta might smother sleeping girls, but surely she couldn't overpower a strong, vigilant man with a pistol in his belt.

"He decided to break into her house in the hour before dawn. Though he never saw her by day and knew she kept late hours, he'd heard her speak of daytime activities and so didn't understand what a nocturnal creature she actually was.

"No matter how many employees one has and no matter what their skills, one can't run an inn without being something of a handyman. Once he'd climbed the fence and crept across the garden, he had no trouble jimmying the French windows.

"Inside the air smelled of lavender. There was no sound unless he made it, and the watery beam of his bull's-eye, sliding across a marble bust of Plato, a harpsichord, and a bowl of marigolds, was the only source of light. As I believe I mentioned, it was a small house, and the innkeeper, unacquainted with detective fiction and Gothic melodrama, didn't know he should examine the walls and furniture for secret chambers or that he should riffle through the pages of every book. Still, searching took more time than he expected; as the minutes dragged he strained to hear footsteps on the stairs, continually glanced over his shoulder, and winced whenever a drawer squeaked or a paper rustled. Even for a brave man, it was nerve-racking work.

"An eternity later he finished ransacking the ground floor. Having found nothing, now he could either descend to the basement or climb to the second story. He still expected to discover revelatory documents if he found anything at all, and he doubted that Gretta would keep them in the cellar. On the other hand, searching in even closer proximity to the bed on which she presum-

58

ably lay slumbering would be risky; examining the basement wouldn't take long, and he could be fairly certain he wouldn't wake her. So why not take a look? If she really was such a monster as he suspected, who knew what he might uncover?

"Well, from an investigatory point of view he made the right decision, for he found incontrovertible evidence of foul play. Suppose you're a killer ranging over the countryside disposing of transients. Once you've slaked your thirst, what do you do with the bodies? It's not very tidy to leave them where they lie, besides which you'd really prefer your neighbors didn't see them. You could bury them on the sites of their demises, but someone might notice the graves. If you have a home with a section that no one but you ever visits, why not conceal them there? Carrying them over hill and dale will be somewhat inconvenient but not too difficult or dangerous when you're prodigiously strong and can cloak yourself in illusion.

"Of course, after a few months they'll begin to pile up. Perhaps Gretta meant to truck them out by the wagonload, or to bury them in the earthen cellar floor, and had never yet gotten around to it. An indifferent housekeeper myself, I can understand her procrastination.

"At any rate, the innkeeper was halfway down the stairs when his lantern's beam, slipping back and forth across the floor below, fell upon what might have been a monstrous spider with some missing legs. He gasped, paused to make sure the thing wouldn't come scuttling up the steps at him, then realized he was actually looking at a hand. He swept his light beyond it, up the arm to which it was attached, and there, carelessly heaped atop one another, lay the corpses.

"Gretta had been a vampire for more than five years and so she no longer needed to feed every day. Thus she'd accumulated only about twenty bodies, but the innkeeper found that quantity impressive enough. They drew him like a flame lures a moth; he had to examine them more closely to convince himself he wasn't dreaming or insane. As he stepped off the staircase, rats squealed and waddled from the pile.

"In the first few moments, as he stood there with the stench searing his nostrils and the rats' claws ticking in the darkness, he didn't feel horrified, outraged, or even nauseated; he was too profoundly bewildered. Why would Gretta kill tramps? And how had she murdered so many without one of her intended victims managing to strike her down?

"What with the ravages of decomposition and the depredations of the vermin, it was surprisingly difficult to ascertain just how the poor unfortunates had died. After a few minutes, however, the innkeeper was reasonably sure that something had punctured each and every throat. Prosaic rationalist that he was, one can't help but wonder if, even then, he would have ever concluded Gretta was a vampire if he'd been left to his own devices. We'll never know, for as he crouched there puzzling over the carrion, the door at the top of the stairs clicked shut."

Chapter Eleven

"As he spun around," Carter continued, "she was already rushing down the stairs; he jerked the bull's-eye up and down, desperate to catch her in its light. When at last the beam struck her squarely, he shrieked and recoiled, tripped on an outflung limb and fell atop the mound of cadavers; the lantern rolled, rattling, across the floor.

"Perhaps she tried to look her usual pixie self but couldn't. In the last minutes before sunrise a vampire's powers attenuate and the illusions projected often fail, especially if the target has a strong will. Or perhaps she enjoyed terrifying mortals with her true appearance. At any rate, the countenance that threw the innkeeper reeling back in terror was little different than those of the corpses he'd been calmly examining mere seconds before. But this one was animate, its sunken eyes burning, its fanged black-lipped mouth snarling with rage; and, most horrible of all, it was still recognizably the face of Gretta Spelvin."

"She'd been embalmed too!" said David; at last the story was becoming relevant to his own situation! "She was like me!"

"That's right," said Carter. "She was just like you."

"Well, the lantern, miraculously still burning, came to rest against a cluster of old crates and barrels, its aperture pointing back at the center of the room. Gretta was lunging forward, a shadow in its gray and feeble glow.

"I said the innkeeper was brave and so he was; his panic lasted only an instant. He snatched his pistol out and fired.

"It's quite difficult to kill or cripple one of our kind, but it's relatively easy to cause us pain. The ball pierced her forehead and blew chunks from the back of her skull. Instead of pouncing on the innkeeper, she collapsed on him like an unstrung puppet, and he frantically rolled out from underneath her.

"But she was after him again instantly, her jagged nails snagging on his coat. He clubbed at her with the gun and she tore it away, then slammed him down on his back. Her head dipped; the long fangs slid into his neck.

"I'm sure you've heard that desperation can increase a man's strength, and it was unquestionably true that night. Gretta had brought him down within reach of the bull's-eye. It was sturdily made, and though it's awkward to bludgeon an assailant when supine, as he smashed it against her head it broke apart.

"Her teeth ripped out of his flesh; she tottered back screaming. Her gown and tresses soaked with oil, she was burning like a bonfire; he had to squint against the sudden glare.

"The oil had seared him too, but he didn't feel his burns or even his throat wounds, not yet. He was terrified, but at that moment, he didn't really feel that either. Before him stood an obscenity, a walking, talking tower of rot that had thrust its filth into his *body,* had killed his babies, and it seemed that now he had it at his mercy. Howling with rage, he began battering the poor blazing thing with kegs and boxes.

"It's my considered opinion that Gretta was too soft and stupid to survive. Even weak and lethargic with the approach of dawn, she had to be extraordinarily incompetent to let the innkeeper shoot her or set her on fire. And then, when she was in agony, she should have realized she could snuff the flames by becoming insubstantial; perhaps she'd never learned how or couldn't muster the necessary concentration. She should also have known that combustion probably wouldn't destroy her, but, if she didn't eliminate him, her adversary very well might. But she just stumbled around squawking and slapping at herself until the innkeeper wrested a long splinter from a shattered crate and rammed it into her heart.

"As soon as she fell dead, pain and weakness overwhelmed him. Dizzy, blood gushing from his neck, he staggered up the stairs and out into the lane, where he lost consciousness. Perhaps someone found him in time to summon the doctor, but if so, it didn't save him; our bite is virulent."

David shivered without quite knowing why. "You mean when we want it to be, don't you?"

"Why she used her transforming rather than her killing bite the innkeeper never knew. She didn't seem to have full control of her abilities and was in pain from her bullet wound, so perhaps she did it accidentally. At any rate, he awakened three nights later in his grave.

"I doubt you enjoyed waking up in your coffin, but at least you knew you were a vampire and could extricate yourself. This poor ass still didn't completely understand what kind of monster Gretta had been and so he didn't grasp what had happened to him; he thought he'd been buried alive.

"Surprisingly enough, he didn't go mad. He did what you may have done; he broke open his casket and dug his way out. Afterward he marveled that he'd had the strength, considering that his body hurt so badly.

"Fresh air didn't ease him as he'd hoped it might,

and he was growing hellishly thirsty, but he was jubilant as he stumbled down the highway toward the inn. Now that he'd thrown off his catalepsy, surely he could anticipate a complete recovery, and how ecstatic his family would be to have him back! A tankard of his best ale would extinguish the burning in his throat.

"He entered through the kitchen door; he wanted to greet his loved ones privately, before the tipplers in the common room swarmed over him. Margaret stood with her back turned, slicing cheese. Her shoulders sagged, and her hair was tangled, her accustomed gaiety altogether lost. Sunk deep in melancholy, she didn't realize anyone else was present until he enfolded her in his dirt-encrusted arms.

"When she saw the dead man's face, of course she screamed. He tried to soothe her with soft words and a smile, quite unaware that he was baring fangs. She screamed all the louder, and then Hugh burst into the room, several male customers behind him.

"The innkeeper was relieved. Severely startled, his girl had become hysterical, but his son and neighbors wouldn't. They'd help him calm her down, and then the celebration could commence.

"Hugh hadn't read all those fairy tales for nothing; when he'd examined the contents of Gretta's basement, he'd understood exactly what she was. Now he shouted it: *'Vampire!'*

"Did all the men massed behind him believe in the undead? Perhaps they never had before, but they were now seeing a walking corpse menace a pretty young girl, and so they surged forward to do battle. And as the innkeeper—revenant, rather, for he no longer owned an inn and never would again—stood frozen in disbelief, Margaret stabbed him in the stomach.

"When he felt that lancing pain, instinct took over and he began to fight. He didn't know how to dissolve, how to warp their perception and influence their thoughts, how to move like lightning despite the grinding agony, but his inhuman strength prevailed. His attackers fell back with gouged eyes, broken bones, and ruptured viscera, until not a mortal man remained on his feet. Then he picked up Margaret and carried her into the night.

"He meant to convince her that everyone was making a mistake, but he wound up tearing out her throat instead, and so finally understood that Hugh was right.

"Anguished, he contemplated suicide, but deep down he knew he'd cling to existence as even the most wretched and guilt-ridden often do. Perhaps if life hadn't been so sweet until that spring, he might have found the will to give it up. He did resolve that he'd never become a fiend like Gretta, and truly believed he could keep his promise. Why not? Except for the thirst, his thoughts and emotions were the same as they'd ever been. Whatever vampirism was, the devil's curse or some ghastly disease, it hadn't changed the man he was inside.

"I could tell you how he evaded Hugh and the other hunters, how he mastered his abilities, how he built a new fortune and sought out others of his kind, but I won't. It would take too long, and it might give you the impression that his new life was a glorious adventure. It wasn't; it was torment.

"For one thing, the pain never diminished. Curious, considering that his nerves were dead, but he suffered every waking moment. And bad as that was, his ongoing dissolution—his constant awareness that he was stinking, hideous, putrescent—was worse. He never found a way to procure blood without killing the vast majority of his victims. His mouth was poisonous, but serum obtained by other means than biting didn't nourish him, nor could he subsist on animal blood. How he

65

loathed himself, as he murdered again and again to prolong an existence that brought him nothing but misery!

"But the interesting thing is that in time he came to hate mortals just as much as he hated himself, an animus that emerged slowly over a number of years. For a long time, when he noticed how bitterly misanthropic his thoughts were becoming, he struggled to purge himself of spite and contempt, but still, I think inevitably, his capacity for benevolence eroded.

"Why did he despise them? Because they didn't hurt all the time. Because they enjoyed countless pleasures he'd never know again. Because they took their blessings for granted. Because they were so weak and dim witted—and if they weren't, he couldn't be a murderer. Because every single one of them would despise him in return if he showed them what he really was.

"Or perhaps he had to hate them because he desperately needed something to divert him, and cruelty is one of the few sports a vampire can actually enjoy.

"Finally, twenty years after his transformation, he stopped resisting his baser impulses, abandoned the scruples that were so ludicrous in a cannibal. To celebrate his liberation from hypocrisy he returned to the inn.

"That ancient hostel had been his pride and joy, and his own family stole it from him. He'd given his life to save theirs; in return they'd tried to destroy him. Actually, he knew such sentiments were unjust, insane, and yet he reveled in them. Even though he remembered loving Hugh and Rebecca, even though by any rational standard they hadn't wronged him at all, how splendid it would be to make them pay!

"He slipped into the inn at three in the morning, long after everyone had gone to sleep. Rebecca lay in the same room and bed they'd always shared. Her face had wrinkled, especially around the eyes, and most of her sable hair had turned white, but she was still a handsome woman. He gently shook her awake; for a moment she smiled at him, and then she remembered he was dead. He'd brought gags and rope, but found he didn't need them to control her; his mesmerism sufficed. He showed her how he really looked, then led her, silent and unresisting, down the hall.

"Hugh was in bed with the plump freckled wife he'd acquired sometime in the intervening years. The revenant barely glanced at her; his son's face fascinated him. The boy looked *exactly*, as *he* had just before his death; it seemed to him that a part of him had known it would be so, and that he'd returned primarily to retrieve his stolen image.

"The sleeping woman was of no importance; he killed her with a single blow. Hugh of course awoke. His will proved as strong as his father's, but his limbs weren't; a slap to the temple stunned him and before he could recover, he was bound and gagged.

"The revenant opened a clasp knife and cut off Hugh's face. The skin peeled away in strips, which he dropped in his coat pocket. It was an expensive garment and the stain ruined it; no doubt Rebecca, who'd always known the value of a guinea, deplored the waste.

"He was gratified that Hugh survived the flaying. He left them there, his wife still bereft of volition and his son still tied, and went downstairs. After splashing some naphtha around the kitchen and common room, he torched the inn and its outbuildings too. The old wooden structures burned as merrily as Gretta had. Only a couple of the guests got out, and it did them little good because he broke their necks. As the inn disintegrated, so did the last traces of his humanity, and from that night forward he was wholly and unrepentantly a demon.

"And that, I suppose, is really the end of the story."

David blinked. "It . . . it can't be the end. You haven't told me how you cured yourself of the embalming."

"How desperation clouds the intellect. I told you my story was set in a little country town a long time ago; the revenant never was embalmed."

"No. . . ."

"Yes, David; all vampires ache and rot and kill, not because of the undertaker's attentions, but simply because they're vampires. You're not hallucinating; you're finally seeing me as I really am."

David sprang off the love seat, fists clenched; if Carter persisted in his charade, he'd beat the truth out of him. *"Stop lying!"*

Carter pushed back his sleeve to pick at a flake of loose gray flesh. "I assure you I'm not; I thought you'd be able to infer the rest, but obviously my tale needs an epilogue. After the inn burned the revenant wandered on through the world, playing pranks on mortals. One of the funniest was to make other vampires; these fledglings suffered unspeakably themselves and inflicted grief on other people.

"Now, of course, he could transform a living man into an undead one without that person's permission, but after some experimentation he decided that that wasn't the best way to proceed. People who don't expect to rise as vampires often don't survive their first few weeks. A few commit suicide, and many others, altogether ignorant of their capacities and requirements, die by misadventure; some don't even make it out of their graves. And those who do survive sometimes create too many others like themselves, whereupon mortals recognize our presence and wage war. Occasionally they also seek revenge.

"And so the revenant determined that it would be preferable to change *willing* victims, fools who'd submit to his bite because he'd use his wiles and illusions to convince them that vampires were demigods. He'd choose the weak, timid, and unhappy—*losers,* in contemporary parlance—because they lacked the pluck to kill either themselves or the author of their misfortunes when they discovered the truth. Once he adopted this new tactic he soon found that seduction, because it posed a challenge, was a far more entertaining game than rape."

"It can't have been illusions. We spent too much time together—you'd have slipped—*I watched you fuck Val!*"

Carter flicked open his dressing gown to reveal the ragged, neutered place between his legs. David snarled and charged him.

The next instant something exploded inside his mind; it stunned him like an unexpected blow. His mismatched legs tangled and he fell; he tried to get up but couldn't move.

"I can't make you hallucinate anymore, but I can prevent your abusing my hospitality; I suspect I could make you dig your heart out of your chest if I really put my mind to it. So sit back down like a good boy."

Trembling, shaking his head, David dragged himself to his feet and limped back to his seat. He sat for a long time with his face in his hands, then said "Maybe you don't know why you did it; maybe it was because you're so lonely. No matter why it happened, you're like my father now; I need you, and I'll try not to hate you. Maybe science can help us. After you train me—"

"I know I promised I'd be Batman and you'd be Renfield the Boy Wonder, but you see, that was just another lie. I have no intention of tutoring you or allowing you to stay here; in your inexperience you might draw attention to yourself and so endanger me. Besides,

I made you a vampire to torture you, and your new existence will be more difficult and degrading if I cast you out. Knowing what I've already taught you, you have a fair chance of surviving for at least a little while. Call me occasionally, tell me how you're doing; and if I'm feeling generous I might share one or two tricks of the trade. But now I think you'd better run along."

"I . . . I can't go out there again. Not alone, not tonight."

"You must, because I say so. You're only my toy, David, and I'll break you if you become annoying."

"You don't understand—"

"No, *you* don't understand. You'll surely die if you don't go *now*, while you still have time to find a lair." He pointed at a window; the eastern sky was lightening to gray.

Chapter Twelve

David pulled his cap down, then peered out the kitchen door; there were no dogs lying in wait, and a second later Carter pushed him through. "Don't molest my neighbors," the dead thing whispered, "or you'll wish you *had* burned." The door swung shut.

Seeing the sky had shocked David out of his horrified daze, had submerged his anguish and anger in a brute determination to survive. He had, he judged, an hour at the most to find his refuge. Already he seemed to feel the somnolence Carter had described, but maybe it was just imagination.

He didn't know where to go, or how his crippled legs could carry him there in time even if — A car! Wherever he decided to go, he could get there if he stole a car, and if he didn't figure out a better place to hide, he could park it and climb into the trunk!

He crept around the house toward the street; next door the jai lai winners' party was still going strong. He could — No, no he couldn't; Carter would find him and kill him. Lurching along as quickly as he could, he turned and hobbled in the opposite direction.

A block away was surely far enough; it had to be, he mustn't delay any longer. Beside an azalea tree, in a driveway lined with Spanish bayonet bushes, sat a yellow Capri with a Carter-Mondale bumper sticker. The bungalow beyond was dark, and so were the homes on either side.

Crouching, he ran across the grass. As he rounded the corner into the back yard, he was suddenly sure there'd be another hostile animal, but there wasn't.

The screen door wasn't hooked but the inner door was locked; he looked for a key under the rubber mat and in a row of clay flowerpots. He didn't find one, so he gripped the doorknob and applied steadily increasing pressure. His fingers ached, all the muscles in his arm protested, and then the knob snapped off in his hand. The door still wouldn't open.

Useless tricks from books and movies danced through his memory. He could break a window quietly—with a glass cutter and tape. He could spring a latch—with a credit card. A competent vampire could melt right through a barrier, but even with his life on the line, he didn't dare try that again.

Great; he had superhuman powers, but he was going to die because he couldn't pull off a simple burglary. Chuckling, his mind tilting into craziness again, he kicked the door as hard as he could. It burst from its hinges and fell with a boom to the floor.

Stepping inside, he waited for the occupants to come running out of their bedrooms, and wondered what he'd do when they did. But amazingly, no lights flared on, no footsteps squeaked or clopped, and when he picked up the phone he got a dial tone.

Nobody home—the car here but nobody home. He'd be one lucky monster if only he could find the keys!

When men took their keys out of their pockets, they usually didn't stow them away; they left them sitting out where they could quickly pick them up again. Women usually kept them in their purses. As he examined counters and tabletops, the china cabinet and the home entertainment center, he noticed how well he could now see in the dark.

It shouldn't have surprised him, he decided. As

Carter had said, a vampire's nerves were dead; Hell, he saw without any eyes at all. Obviously then, their sight was psychic, magical, and thus might not require light. It was an interesting little marvel, relatively devoid of unpleasant significance, and contemplating it made him feel less afraid until he glanced out the window. The stars were fading fast; the easternmost clouds reflected a hint of pink.

Even if the Capri was locked, he could break a window to get in, but he didn't know how to hotwire an ignition. His father could fix anything mechanical, he'd know, hey, he could phone him. *Hi, Dad, I'm calling from beyond the grave to ask you how to steal a car.*

Where were the damn keys? He suddenly realized that if they were on the same ring with a house key, whoever lived here had probably taken them. But there might be a spare; he began yanking out and overturning drawers.

Clouds of paper and snapshots fluttered to the floor; a glass paperweight shattered. Soon he'd gutted all the furniture in the dining room, living room, and kitchen.

All right, he'd find the spare key in one of the bedrooms. Everyone kept one; there was no reason to get hysterical.

One bedroom was unfurnished; the door to the other was closed. He reached for the knob, then froze. Inside the room someone was panting; the air smelled, even tasted, of sweat.

Someone was home after all, someone cowering, hoping that the intruder would leave without discovering him. His keys were probably on his night stand.

Desperate as he was, David was still ashamed to show his face, nor did he want to fight or frighten anyone. Maybe he wouldn't have to.

Gretta's usual mask had been her living face. So was Carter's; maybe your own mortal appearance was the easiest illusion to assume. He closed his eyes and pictured his hands, visualized the raw flesh becoming smooth and pink again. After a few seconds he felt that *something* was happening, that he was straining a faculty he'd never possessed before.

He opened his eyes; his hands looked the same. But maybe that was okay; Carter had hinted that vampires didn't see illusions. Certainly his sensation of mental exertion hadn't vanished, and inside his head he still carried the image of his hands reformed, saw it just as clearly as the door.

All right, now his face; he mended his lips, shortened his canines, and put some color in his cheeks. After that he straightened his leg. As he extended the illusion, the strain intensified; he shivered and his forehead started throbbing.

Just changing the look of his body wasn't enough. If anyone saw him in his old man's clothes, he'd be taken for a burglar even if not for a revenant. Concentrating fiercely, his head pounding as if it were about to explode, he struggled to clothe his mental Doppelgänger in a policeman's uniform.

What did Tampa cops wear, anyway? It was all green—no, that was the county cops. The Hell with it; he had to finish this quickly, before he exhausted his psychic energy. Since it was the only uniform he could remember, he'd be a deputy sheriff; if the guy in the bedroom was half as scared as he was, he'd never notice the difference.

Had it actually worked? As he rapped on the door, he felt like the emperor in his new clothes. "Police officer." It came out as a whisper, so he took a deep breath and tried again. "Police officer! Are you okay?"

"Go away! I've got a gun!" It was a man's voice, shrill and quavering.

"I followed your burglar in, and I *think* I chased him

74

out; now I have to verify that the house is clear and you're all right. So come on, open up or else I'll have to kick the door down; you've got enough mess here already."

The floor groaned as the man approached. The lock clicked and then the door opened an inch; a pale blue eye gleamed behind the crack. David tensed and waited for the scream.

"Oh, geez," sighed the man in the bedroom, "am I glad to see you. I couldn't call—there's no phone in here and he was out there. . . ." He swung the door completely open. He was a scrawny, balding man who slept in an undershirt and jockey shorts; instead of a gun he was clutching a Louisville Slugger.

David slumped with relief; a second later the worst pain yet ripped through his skull. His knees buckling, he grabbed the doorjamb for support.

"Good lord, are *you* all right?"

"Sure," he gasped. "I mean, more or less. The burglar surprised me in your living room. He clipped me a good one, but I'll live."

The batter took his arm. "Come lie down on the couch. I'll call your station and an ambulance."

"No!" He shoved him backward into the room. "I'm okay, and I told you, I've got to check all around the house."

"You need to get off your feet; I think he gave you a concussion. Can't you see that everything's all right?"

It was a small room, furnished only with a bureau, the portable TV on top of it, a sagging single bed, and a painting of dogs playing baseball. On the chest of drawers there also sat a hairbrush, a copy of *Sports Illustrated,* and a glass jar half full of pennies, but no keys. "Look, I'm going to have to commandeer your car."

"Did he hurt your legs? You're limping something awful."

The illusion was falling apart! "Listen, I have to have your keys! Your burglar wasn't just a burglar, I was chasing him from before, he's a murderer and he killed an old lady in a laundromat! I know where he's going, and I can nail him if I only have a car!"

The batter stepped back, raised his weapon across his chest. "Please, please sit down. You can't chase anybody; you're delirious."

"I need your keys!" David turned and jerked open the top dresser drawer.

The pain surged again. He tried not to sob but couldn't help it; his visualization of Deputy Brent wavered and went out.

The other man gasped; his club clattered on the floor. By the time David looked around, he'd already vanished.

He'd lost his night vision; perhaps agony and exhaustion had shut it down, or maybe the approach of dawn had done it. Stooping, he peered into the drawer. The left side was stuffed with briefs and socks rolled into balls, but on the right were a wallet, a black plastic pocket comb, and a rabbit's-foot key chain.

He'd need money if he survived the day, he'd need a comb, for that matter, but he couldn't make himself take anything but the keys. Snatching them up, he ran for the front door.

It was open, and so was the screen door that led from the veranda to the yard. The batter was two houses down, beating on someone else's door and yelling at the top of his lungs.

David dashed for the Capri; the second key he tried unlocked it. He pressed the accelerator and turned the ignition; the car chugged forward and died.

A standard transmission; he hadn't driven one since

Driver's Ed. Pulling the stick into Neutral, he twisted the key again; the starter whined but now it wouldn't catch.

Above the batter the porch light flickered on. The door opened; the man pointed and yammered. Within seconds a huge woman in a red flannel robe and a wiry black-haired teenager in cut-off jeans were sprinting toward the car.

Finally the engine coughed to life. David revved it, then groped for Reverse.

He found Fourth instead; the Capri shuddered and nearly stalled. The teenager leaped over a rosebush into the batter's yard.

David tried again; the gears ground, but then at last he had it. The car jerked backward spewing exhaust, its untuned engine growling; the teenager tore open the driver's door.

He grabbed David's shirt and began to drag him out; David chopped at his forearm. Bone snapped and the boy screamed and stumbled back.

The Capri rolled out of the driveway. David fumbled for the pedals, then, the gears still rasping, threw it into First and wrenched the wheel.

The obese woman lumbered out into the middle of the road. Apparently she meant to block his path, like a pacifist protester standing in front of an army truck.

Well, fuck her! If she didn't have brains enough to dive out of his way, then she deserved to end up smeared all over the grille!

But he couldn't do it. He eased off the clutch and crept forward. Maybe she'd lose her nerve. If not, he'd swerve up onto the curb to get around her.

For a moment, as she stood bellowing and brandishing her meaty fist, it really seemed she wasn't going to move. Then her mouth fell open and urine splattered down between her feet. Robe flapping, she spun and fled down the center of the street.

He realized that his door was still hanging open and so the domelight was shining; no doubt she'd finally noticed his face. He didn't know whether to laugh or cry.

He passed the kneeling teenager cradling his fractured arm, then the batter still prudently watching from his neighbors' stoop. When the fat woman veered off the pavement, he stamped on the gas.

He still didn't know where he could hide. Since he'd been caught stealing, injured a kid, and even babbled idiotically about the woman he'd murdered, the police would look high and low for him, so he couldn't keep the car and sleep inside it. He couldn't even drive it all the way to whatever refuge he selected, because when they found it they'd surely search the immediate area.

In the same situation, Carter wouldn't have wound up with the same problem; he'd have blithely slaughtered all three witnesses. Maybe a vampire needed to be just that ruthless to survive; maybe he'd die because he wasn't.

His best chance would be to sneak into an abandoned building, but except for the tower near the dog track, he didn't know of any that were close enough, and kids climbed up inside that one all the time. When he'd decided to become a vampire he'd rented his own place, but his mom, who'd never been more energetic and efficient than when her father died, had almost certainly cleaned his stuff out of it by now; even if the apartment manager didn't notice that someone had broken in, he'd probably show it to prospective tenants during the day.

Say, there's a vampire hibernating in the closet.

Really? Well, don't worry, we'll spray before you move in.

The minutes slipped relentlessly away. He drove aimlessly, gripping the steering wheel tighter and tighter until the plastic creaked. He was going to burn if he didn't choose some building, get inside, and subdue whoever he found there; he couldn't survive the next thirty minutes without a roof over his head!

Or could he?

Just ahead sat four green plastic garbage cans, their lids askew, unseated by the shiny black bags bulging up inside. Jumping out of the car, he inverted the barrels and shook them until the overstuffed sacks slid out, then ripped open the knots and dumped the trash. A moment later, the malodorous bags on the seat beside him, he was racing for Nebraska Avenue.

Had the batter or his neighbors called the police yet? Of course, and he always saw cop cars on Nebraska. But every second counted; if he didn't take the quickest route back across the river, he'd never reach his destination before sunrise.

Turning, he ran a yellow light. The four-lane road was already busy, conveying travelers who started work early; some had switched off their headlights.

He hurtled south, his heart pounding; he almost rammed a bus because he couldn't keep his eyes off his rearview mirror, expecting any second it would pulse red and blue.

But he crossed the bridge without encountering a squad car. He turned down a side street as soon as he could, sped on to Park Circle and then Park Drive.

He abandoned the Capri on Twentieth, a little residential street than dead-ended after a few blocks; there it might sit undiscovered for at least a few hours. A hot breeze seared him as soon as he opened the door.

It couldn't be as hot as it felt, not at dawn. The air was like semisolid tar; he had to push his way through it. Heat sometimes made him drowsy, and despite his fear it was happening now. His head was full of cotton, his eyelids drooped, and his limbs were growing numb. If he sat down for a moment maybe he'd feel better.

No! If he rested he'd never stand up again. He staggered on through the clotting air, past trees full of twittering birds, down into the park and toward the railroad bridge he'd crossed before.

In the shadows just beneath it, where it separated from the slope, there grew a thick patch of brambles; with a lot of luck it might conceal him. He'd intended to gather leaves and branches to pile on top of himself, but the sky was blue and his skin was baking. He pulled two of the trash bags over his legs and burrowed into the bushes, then dragged the other two on over his head.

The river gurgled below him. As his awareness guttered out it seemed to speak, asking why he'd fought so hard to live.

Chapter Thirteen

When he awoke the world was black and airless. For one ghastly moment he thought he was back in his grave, but when he started thrashing about the bags tore and then he remembered what he'd done. All his old familiar aches were throbbing, and in addition a stinging itch was crawling across his flesh.

He sat up and pulled the bags off his head; his hands were swarming with red ants. They were all over him, maybe *inside* him by now, stripping away meat.

Thorns gashed him as he scrambled out of the bushes; he was almost to the water's edge before he realized what would happen if he immersed himself. His arms windmilling, his feet slipping, he stopped himself just before he toppled in.

He dropped to the ground and rolled, slapped himself, then pulled up tufts of grass and scoured his skin. When at last he'd rid himself of the insects he thought to look around. If anyone had seen him spring from the brambles he'd been smart enough to run away.

The sky was purple, dappled with rose in the west; a cool breeze was blowing out of the sunset. It was disorienting to flash instantly from dawn to dusk, and it made him queasy to think that *nothing*, not even the ants, could awaken him when the sun was up. He didn't think he'd even dreamed; by daylight he was truly one of the dead.

No point dwelling on it, not when his mouth already was so dry. Since he'd have to move among normal people tonight, he'd do better to take stock of his appearance. His flesh was, of course, even more hideous than last night and would have to be wrapped in hallucination. Unfortunately, the same was true of his clothes. Funny-looking and ill-fitting to begin with, they were now torn, dusty, and encrusted with coffee grounds, scraps of gristle, and various other bits of garbage that had stuck inside the trash bags when he'd emptied them. And he stank; it would be nice to believe that the stench had originated in the plastic sacks, but he doubted it. He wondered if olfactory illusions were more difficult than visual ones.

He conceived a mask for future use; he guessed he could conjure it up more quickly if he'd already imagined it once. He'd wear his black Levis and his blue Dreadstar T-shirt, and smell ever so faintly of Right Guard.

It was easier the second time around, no doubt partly because the night was young, but also, he hoped, because the ability was strengthening with practice. Maybe by the turn of the century he'd be able to disguise himself continually as Carter did; then he could live indoors like a human being.

He turned to climb the bank, and a wave of unreality swept over him. This wasn't happening. He couldn't venture into the streets to kill somebody for blood. He was no monster, no maniac; he was a *good* person.

But the thirst was searing his throat, mocking his pretensions to virtue. If he wanted to cheat it, his only chance was to plunge into the river before it became irresistible.

And he wouldn't; Carter had read his character exactly right. Even trapped in this nightmare, even though he knew right from wrong, he was just too chickenshit to commit suicide.

Well, if he was going to cling to life no matter what, it would be better to kill before the thirst drove him berserk. That way maybe he could do less harm, at least insure his victims suffered less. He didn't know if he had the courage to attack someone while he was in his right mind, but he'd find out before the night was over.

It was a long trudge back to Nebraska Avenue and then to Florida Avenue beyond. He thought of detouring down Twentieth, but it would be too risky to drive the Capri again even if it was still where he left it. Whenever cars, bicyclists, or pedestrians approached, he donned his mask, then dropped it as soon as they passed so he wouldn't exhaust his psychic reserves; it made him feel like a fan dancer.

By the time he reached the dog track the sky was altogether black. Passing the brightly lit Valet Parking Lot was unnerving enough; when he saw how Florida blazed with neon, how the traffic whizzed by in a never-ending stream, he nearly bolted. His cloak of air wouldn't shield him, not from that glare, not from so many living eyes; everyone would see that he was dead!

But if they destroyed him, he could return to his grave without murdering anyone else; if he died, then at least it would be over.

Ahead on the corner sat an Eckerd Drugs and, diagonally across from it, a Kash 'n Karry grocery and a Home Depot hardware outlet. He veiled himself, then, cap pulled low, head bowed, hands in his pockets, shuffled through the automatic door into the pharmacy.

Four customers were in line at the register, two others browsing at the magazine rack. If even one of them saw or smelled what he really was . . .

They didn't. He scuttled down an aisle toward the back of the store.

When he was nine years old he'd tried to shoplift once; the check-out girl who caught him slipping a bag of M & M's into his pocket locked him in the store manager's office and phoned his mother. She cried, his father spanked him for the first time ever, and he'd never done it again. Now he regretted that he'd never developed the skill, and that he didn't have a shopping bag or some voluminous garment with huge pockets. But maybe magic could compensate for his deficiencies.

He made sure no one was watching, then tried to replace his mental twin with absence, a vision of nothing at all.

It was harder to visualize nothing than something; the effort made his temples pound. Abruptly his mind blurred, lost its focus, and he didn't have any shield at all.

Panicked, he jerked his head around; he was still alone in the middle of the aisle.

Trembling, fingers twitching, he hastily evoked untainted flesh and clean clothes again. When that was done he added background to the picture, filled in the shelves of toothpaste, mouthwash, and dental floss that were actually behind him. Then he subtracted himself. This time it was easier, because even when his lying image faded away, he still had something tangible to imagine.

As before, his hands still looked the same; until someone reacted or failed to react to his presence, he couldn't know whether he was truly invisible or not.

His ears rang and the fluorescent light half dazzled him; if he was imperceptible, he couldn't stay that way for long. He stuffed a toothbrush, a floss dispenser, and a tube of Crest into his pocket, then scurried on to the next aisle for a bar of Lifebuoy, a traveler's plastic folding combination comb and hairbrush, deodorant, and a sample-size bottle of Suave dandruff shampoo for oily hair; he had a hunch that the grease and dandruff his scalp had produced while he was alive were nothing compared to what was developing now.

Now his pockets were bulging full; maybe he should leave. No, that was dumb, he was thinking like an ordinary thief. If he was a phantom he could carry things out in his hands; if he wasn't, he wasn't disguised at all, and the cashier was likely to react negatively to a walking corpse whether she could tell he was shoplifting or not. He grabbed a beach towel, an orange and white Rowdies T-shirt, a red baseball cap, socks and tennis shoes; there were Glad bags on the north wall, and a revolving rack by the photo-processing counter yielded a pair of UV 400 Blue Blocker sunglasses.

He took a deep breath, then hobbled out into the open area at the front of the store. The customers were gone; the cashier, a plump pretty black woman with a golden nail on her right index finger and reddish hair coiled on the back of her head, didn't look up from her *Seek-A-Word*.

It was miraculous; she really couldn't see him! For this one moment at least, vampirism was a little like he'd imagined it. If he weren't shaking so, if he

85

weren't so dizzy, he'd almost be tempted to play a trick on her. He could tweak her nose or tap her on the shoulder. Or if he wanted to be a real pig he could goose her or grope her tits. Or he could kiss her on the cheek, the ear, or the throat, kiss it, tear it, it had to be somebody, he was so thirsty and she—

He was already lunging when he caught himself. She flinched, dropped her pencil; unable to quite perceive him, she still somehow sensed she was in danger.

He made himself pivot, drove himself out into the night. He wouldn't; not her, not here, and not now. It was early yet and *he was in control.*

The alley behind the drugstore was deserted. Crouching in the shadows in back of a dumpster, he dissolved his illusory shroud. After a minute, when his pain eased and his head stopped spinning, he peeled off all his filthy clothes except his slacks. It wasn't easy; his shirt and socks stuck to his skin. Too bad Eckerd didn't sell pants, and too bad he couldn't wash before he changed. But he'd find a way later when it was really important, after his mouth was foul with the taste of blood.

Grimy as they were, peculiar as dress oxfords would look with the rest of his outfit, he was reluctant to drop his old shoes and socks in the trash bin. They were the last of his burial clothes and so the last things he now possessed that he'd also owned when he was alive. Eyes dry but burning, he pried his fingers open; the dumpster clanged like a gate slamming shut.

He put the rest of his booty in one of the Glad bags, then crossed the street to the grocery. As usual, they'd set the thermostat low enough to make him shiver. A scale sat near the entrance, and for a moment, morbidly curious, he wanted to weigh himself. He was probably pretty light already, and sure to become lighter every day. Maybe he should market the Vampire Weight Loss Plan. *Just follow my simple program: Die, rot, puke when you consume anything but blood, and let bugs chew away that ugly fat. Within thirty days you'll be skinnier than you dreamed possible.*

The plastic bag rustled when his fists clenched. Damn it all, why had this happened? Damn it all and damn Carter!

Alone beside the pretzels and tortilla chips, he switched from his life-mask to his ghost-mask. Then he scuttled from one register to the next, snatching the Jerry Lewis collection cans. He hovered, waiting until no one was looking, afraid that otherwise a shopper, cashier, or bag boy would see one float up into the air and disappear. The store was busy and he had to keep jumping out of people's way.

When at last he'd gathered all the cans, he rested outside again, then roamed through Home Depot. There he stole a hammer, a screwdriver, a glass cutter, and duct tape; he didn't know when he'd want to break into a house again, but next time he intended to be ready! The hammer and screwdriver could double as weapons, but he didn't want to think about that yet. Behind the check-out counters were brown paper shopping bags with handles; one of those would look less peculiar than his garbage bag and also be easier to carry. Not all the registers were open, so he didn't have to worry about brushing against anyone when he reached in and took it.

Back on Florida Avenue, he hid in the darkness between a used-book store and a Chinese restaurant until a southbound Hartline bus appeared. The night was kind; there were no other passengers. Sitting slumped in the back under a burnt-out light, his cap covering his face and his hands buried beneath the shopping bag, he tried to empty his mind as the long coach carried him to the killing ground.

Chapter Fourteen

Before David pulled open the door the night was quiet, but the brass handle shivered in his hand. When he stepped inside the music bashed him; he flinched and nearly let it blast him backward.

The bar was blue with acrid smoke; a lacquered collage encrusted the walls and ceiling. Hitler saluted Ozzy Osbourne while Ted Bundy and Aleister Crowley stood shoulder to shoulder with Metallica; demons clipped from Time-Life's *Enchanted World* books leered and capered among Uzis, mushroom clouds, and nudes from *Hustler's* "Beaver Hunt."

Three guitarists and a drummer were gyrating behind a chain-link fence; a thrashing, stomping mob packed the dance floor in front of it. Some of the audience were skinheads and some had shoulder-length hair like the band; some dressed nondescriptly, while others were living fetishes of chrome and leather. They all looked like they'd enjoy breaking a wimpy little bookstore clerk in half.

David turned around. The bar was too crowded, and the people who made up the crowd were too intimidating; if he was nervous when he tried to kill he'd botch it. Better to start with some poor fruit from the Blue Cockatoo and return to "the toughest heavy metal club in Tampa" when he felt a lot more confident.

Damn it, no. Gays gave him the creeps, but that

didn't mean they deserved to die. Maybe thugs who molested innocent people did; he had friends who thought so. If he took the blood he needed from a fellow predator, then *maybe* he could live with himself afterward.

For appearances' sake he bought a draft Busch at the bar, then found a table in the corner. The band howled a final number and filed offstage; the room thrummed for half a minute after. A few seconds later "Night Prowler" started playing on the jukebox, but fortunately it wasn't nearly as loud. Now people would talk and he could eavesdrop.

He meant to find a victim as vicious as the foursome who'd assaulted him, but it wasn't easy. The bearded duo at the table on his right looked like Vikings plotting a raid on a monastery, but as they argued the merits of the new Ronnie James Dio album they sounded more like Siskel and Ebert. The pimply adolescents on his left prattled on endlessly about how they'd been "sure it was all over" when the bartender asked to see their fake ID's.

But no doubt the skinheads were gloating over past atrocities or devising new ones. He sharpened the false self-portrait in his mind, then drifted toward the five clustered around the pool table.

He twisted and sidestepped but still people jostled him; once he elbowed someone's head and quickly apologized. He almost felt like screaming; so many enemies pressing close on every side. If his mask slipped, they'd tear him apart.

Frustratingly, when he finally got close to the pool players they weren't saying anything significant. The one with the high tops and the screaming eagle tattoo was kidding the shortest one about dating a beanpole of a girl; the Neanderthal was trying to convince a hatchet-faced guy with piercing green eyes, and a moose with blue suspenders, that the Post Office really did intend to put the Three Stooges on a stamp.

Come on, David urged silently, reminisce about the last time you sliced somebody's face up or gang-raped a girl or sold drugs to little kids. At least say you're Nazis and hate Jews and blacks. Give me an excuse!

But they stubbornly went on talking like ordinary people.

His head was pounding in time with "Burn in Hell." The smoke, the noise, and his anxiety were partly to blame, but it was also a reminder that he couldn't stay disguised forever. If he didn't choose a victim soon, he'd have to leave without one, and the bloodlust might become uncontrollable before he could return.

They wouldn't have to say anything incriminating if he could read their minds.

It would be dangerous; what if his shroud dissolved when he diverted his concentration? Why not simply choose one at random? Surely they were all cruel, bigoted, and violent; why else would anyone become a skinhead?

But that wasn't good enough. Before he killed he wanted to *know* that his quarry made a habit of victimizing innocent people; the slightest doubt might eventually drive him crazy.

He stared at the Stoogeaphile, told himself that in a moment his mind would ring with the apeman's thoughts.

But it didn't. After a while he relaxed, then tried again, this time laboring to still all his own thoughts. When being empty-headed didn't help, he imagined an iridescent shimmer streaming out of the Stoogeaphile's forehead and into his. That didn't work either.

He wasn't surprised he'd failed; his untrained, untested abilities never functioned easily at first. But when he'd initially tried to dissolve into a shadow and veil himself in hallucination, *something* had happened. This time there'd been nothing; if he hadn't seen Carter pluck the names of his attackers out of the air, he would have concluded that vampires couldn't read minds.

The Stoogeaphile sank the three in the side, then looked up at him. "You want in?"

David started; beer slopped over the rim of his glass. Oh no, he'd done something after all, his target could feel it, feel him fumbling at his mind! And now that he was rattled, his life-mask began to blur; he squinched his eyes shut, plunged his fangs into what remained of his lower lip, and forced the image back into focus.

"You want in?" the Neanderthal repeated. "You been watching for a while. Put a quarter up and you can play the winner."

"What? Oh. Thanks, maybe in a little while." He stumbled to a chair beside the cue rack, where he eventually stopped shaking.

Well, what now? Maybe the skinheads were criminals, even fiends, but he couldn't prove it by probing their thoughts and apparently they weren't going to discuss their ties to the Manson Family or how they helped assassinate JFK. His throat burned; before long he might start blacking out. He despised himself for ever considering it, but perhaps, after all, he'd have to kill one without proving him a psychopath; better to murder someone who was probably scum than delay, run amok, and slaughter whoever was in reach.

Then the skinheads waved and hooted. By the time he turned toward the door, Benjamin Franklin was weaving his way across the room.

David nearly laughed out loud; something had answered his prayers. He could bite *Ed* and feel like Dirty Harry!

92

His prospective victim was still chubby, although naturally he'd dropped some weight in the weeks since Carter broke his jaw; his teeth were gapped and jagged in the front. He almost scurried, his shoulders hunched and his eyes darting from side to side behind his glasses. There was a goat's head and pentagram design stenciled on his T-shirt, and a medallion hung from the thong around his neck.

David jerked down his cap and pushed up his sunglasses; it had suddenly occurred to him that this encounter wouldn't be all that lucky if Ed recognized him. He couldn't alter his mask, not with other people watching; maybe a vampire adept like Carter could project an illusion into one viewer's mind while generating a second, different phantasm into other people's, but he certainly couldn't. He'd just have to hope his quarry wouldn't place him.

"Merlin! How you doing?" boomed the Stoogeaphile. "You haven't been around much."

Ed fidgeted. "Things to do."

"Hey, I'll bet," said Green Eyes. "Curses. Rituals. Serious supernatural shit. So what do you hear from the Antichrist?" High Tops and Shorty laughed.

"You better be nice," the Stoogeaphile said. "You make fun of his powers and he might turn you into a turd."

"Yeah, and I'm sure he can," said Green Eyes, " 'cause I can see he already tried it on himself."

"Fuck you!" Ed spat. He snatched the bridge off the rail, trembled, and then slammed it down again.

"Hey man, be cool," said the Stoogeaphile. "Nobody means any harm."

"I will," said Green Eyes, "if he touches that cue rest again."

"We don't mean anything, it's just that it's hard for us to take it seriously when a guy we've known since third grade sets himself up as a witch doctor all of a sudden."

"You never made fun of Frank's ceremonies."

"Frank can do things you can't."

"Like read," said Green Eyes. "Get laid."

"And find his ass with both hands and a flashlight," High Tops added.

"How can you laugh when Val is dead? I'm only going to warn you one more time: everything they sing about on all these fucking records is *real!* I'm going to study it, worship it—and you should too, because there are *things* out in the dark that want to hurt us!"

For a moment they stared, then Green Eyes snickered, and a few seconds later they were roaring. Blinking, cheeks flushed and lips compressed, Ed retreated to a seat at the bar.

Cheer up, thought David, I'll help you convince them that the boogeyman was really out to get you. Gazing intently, he tried to implant a suggestion. *You want to leave; they ridiculed you, and if you stay they'll do it again. This dump is dead tonight anyway; you'll have more fun someplace else.*

His temples throbbed; once again he felt he was opening a part of his mind that hadn't even existed a week before. Ed shifted restlessly on his stool. *You want to leave; the seats aren't even comfortable.* The skinhead wriggled again, looked at the door for a few seconds, then pulled out his wallet and beckoned to the bartender.

Maybe he had a strong will, or perhaps David needed a lot of practice before he could actually influence anyone. Whatever the reason, his magic wasn't working. If he wanted Ed to walk out into the night, he'd have to talk to him.

When he sat down beside him Ed turned and glared. For a moment he was afraid Ed knew him, but then he decided that his chosen victim would have bestowed the same sneer on almost anyone with hair. He belonged to a clique, and even though some of its members had just humiliated him, it was still outsiders he disdained.

"I'm glad to see you up and around," said David. "It's a shame about Val, but soon she'll be avenged."

"Who the Hell are you?"

"A friend. You and I practice the same religion."

"Yeah, great. Now get lost. Did my friends put you up to this? I take a razzing from them, but that doesn't mean I'll take it from you."

David pretended to sip his beer. "Now you're displaying the proper attitude. 'To know, to dare, to will, and to keep silent.' "

"I just read that! That's supposed to be the magician's creed!"

"Right, and keeping silent helps you in many ways; it keeps fools from making fun of you, for one thing. But there comes a time when the wise confer, to pool information and resources."

"Huh . . . Well, maybe. You know I'm sort of new at this. I've been into the music for a long time, but mainly just because I liked the sound. So if you're for real, I guess I could use some pointers. But if you're blowing smoke I'll make you sorry."

"That sounds fair; I think I can convince you I'm sincere. My name is David Waite, but inside my coven I'm called Hastur. I belong to a Satanic brotherhood that colonized the New World in 1609, a full eleven years before the *Mayflower*. In 1972 the Dark Ones instructed us to monitor you stoners. Our job is to ferret out the special few who truly understand the messages in the music and recruit them. We also clean up after morons who aren't fit to meddle in the occult but do it anyway. Sometimes one of them liberates something he can't control, and then we're obliged to hunt it down. And that's why I'm talking to you now."

"You calling me a *moron?*"

"Not at all; you have a tremendous aptitude for sorcery. I suspect you were a great Ipsissimus in several of your past lives. Eventually one of us would have invited you to join us, but I've come in haste because you and I have other business now; you've crossed paths with the product of some incompetent's bungled conjuration."

"I . . . I did meet *something.*"

"Don't be afraid to call it by its proper name; it drank Val's blood and so you know it was a vampire. And you're in trouble, because demons of that sort eventually seek out any mortal unfortunate enough to behold them; it'll kill you if we don't destroy it first."

Ed shook his head. "I don't know. I saw what I saw, but that doesn't mean I should believe every fairy tale anybody tells me. If you're a warlock, then you should be able to prove it."

"I'm sure you don't expect me to do it in front of the whole bar."

Ed shrugged.

"Come on outside."

The night had turned cool and windy; moths battered the small white light above the door.

"Okay," said Ed, "let's see it."

"This is still a little public, don't you think?"

"I'm not walking all the way to Transylvania."

"Of course not, but let's at least step around to the side of the building."

The skinhead preceded him into the shadows.

Chapter Fifteen

David knew he should attack while his quarry's back was turned; one hammer stroke would stretch him in the dirt. He reached into the shopping bag and gripped his weapon, then found he couldn't pull it out.

Ed turned to face him. "This is as good as it gets."

"Fine." Soon he'd pounce, drink, and revenge himself, but he'd realized he couldn't do it here. He'd have to con his victim a little longer, and that meant he'd have to show him some magic.

The easiest stunt by far would be to dissolve his shroud, but even now he cringed at the thought of standing naked. He could try becoming invisible, but he had a hunch he wasn't powerful enough to completely deflect the regard of someone who was already staring at him. "Look at my right hand. As I'm sure you know, a mage can change his shape."

Closing his eyes, he shifted memory into fantasy. Hairs lengthened, coarsened, sprouted on his fingers and his palm. His hand grew broad and heavy, like a grizzly's paw; his nails hooked into blades of yellow horn.

As usual, the new illusion wasn't easy; for a moment the image flickered, the fur and talons nearly fading out to expose the raw gray reality beneath. But he was slowly learning how to transcend pain, and he redefined the semblance without staggering or crying out.

"Holy shit!" whispered Ed.

"Of course if I chose to, I could transform my whole body, but I don't want to waste the energy. I suspect we're going to need it later."

"Holy shit! You're real, you're real! Are you going to teach me that?"

"If you like," he said as he returned his disguise to normal. "We can hunt the Everglades together; you haven't lived till you've run down a hog, or ripped out a gator's belly. But first we have to concentrate on keeping you alive."

Ed's grin twisted to a frown. "Yeah ... the vampire. You're for real, so it's true it's really after me."

"Yes, it is. And now I want you to show me where you fought it. Have you ever heard of a genius loci?"

"Huh-uh."

David sighed. "Well, I suppose you couldn't be expected to learn everything you need to know about the subworlds just by listening to Motley Crue. Some spirits are tied to a particular area, a home base to which they return at frequent intervals. Your vampire is like that, and if we're in luck it attacked you near its lair."

"I guess I understand, but do you think we should go there *tonight?* Why don't you teach me some magic first, so I can help you zap it?"

"It grows stronger every time it drinks, and unfortunately its power would increase more rapidly than yours. In other words, the longer we wait, the worse our odds. But don't worry; at this stage in its development I'm sure I can handle it. And you will be able to help; I'll teach you an exorcism as we walk."

"Look, I don't know. I mean, we just met —"

"Do you want to live? Do you want to learn sorcery? You won't unless you're brave enough to trust your teacher. I always did, and that's what made me what I am today."

"Well . . . okay. What the Hell. It might not even be there."

"Don't be a pessimist; I'm fairly certain it will."

They rehearsed prayers to demons as they crept down the dingy streets: "Ashtaroth, defend me; Belial, guide my sword!" Occasionally David patted the skinhead's shoulder.

After a while Ed said, "I don't know whether I should be jumping for joy or pissing in my pants. Maybe I should just be expecting to wake up. How can this be happening to *me?*"

"Believe it or not, you've earned it."

"Fuck if I know how. I mean, let's face it, I'm nobody. I always wanted to be important, but I know I'm just your basic high-school dropout."

"You should keep practicing that incantation."

"I think I'd rather die young trying to kill a monster than live a hundred years just flipping burgers. At least for a few minutes you'd know you were a goddamn warrior, not just another rat in the fucking maze. My dad's worked in the same office—"

"Shut up! Look, I—I want to hear all about you, but later. If everything goes as expected, we'll be fighting in just a little while. Let's concentrate on preparing ourselves, and not let anything distract us."

"Yeah, okay. Lucifer, Son of the Morning . . ."

As they approached the mouth of the alley David froze, then pressed his fingertips against his temples. "I sense it! We're close, aren't we?"

"Yeah! Damn, how'd you know?"

"The same way I knew who you were. Let me lead the way from here."

The alley was as black and close as he remembered.

A cat screeched from the shadows. Maybe it had lapped Val's leftover blood; maybe it had even chewed her throat.

They stopped beneath the pole where Carter perched. "You saw it clinging right up there."

"Right again," Ed replied, looking around nervously. "Fuck if I know what you needed me for."

David peered up and down the alley; there was no one else in sight. He'd been sure that here, on the very spot where the skinheads tried to mutilate him, he could become enraged, but he just felt hollow and queasy. He remembered the knife point looming at his eye, Ed giggling and bouncing with glee, and *still* he couldn't find the hate he needed.

"I think I feel it," Ed whispered. "Damn, I really think I do! Is it here?"

"Well, yes and no," said David. He pulled off his cap and set it and his shopping bag on a trash can, then removed his sunglasses, folded the stems in, and laid them down on his cap.

"What do you mean?" asked Ed.

It must be too dark; he stepped closer. "Look at me, and then you'll understand."

Ed shrugged helplessly. "Uh, sorry, I don't. Remember, I'm just a beginner."

And then at last the anger started flowing, a trickle that quickly swelled into a torrent. "You piece of shit. How many people have you tortured, that you can't even remember all their faces anymore?"

Ed's hand leaped into his pocket. David grabbed him below the elbow and squeezed; his hands ached horribly but he laughed when the arm bones crunched.

"Oh God oh God," Ed moaned.

"You're forgetting your lessons; a little turd like you ought to pray to Satan like I taught you." He hooked

100

his good leg behind one of Ed's and dumped him on the ground. "I think I'm getting the hang of this," he said as he knelt beside him. "Last night I had trouble killing a little old lady, and now here I am beating up on a big bad skinhead."

"Look, man, I don't know . . . *you were the one from that night!*"

"Better late than never. Well, maybe not in this case."

"Don't hurt me anymore, man, I swear I'm really sorry!"

"Sure you are. Exactly what were you going to do to me?"

"I . . . I don't—"

"You weren't the one holding the knife, so if you tell the truth I'll let you off easy, but if you don't I'll tear you apart."

"She was going to carve 'fag' on your face."

"Thank you; that's just what I needed to hear." It was finally time, and he might as well enjoy it; he'd kill mercifully every other night. The more frightened Ed was, the more fun it'd be, and so at last he let his mask disperse.

Ed freaked out. For a few moments, as they writhed and grappled, David was afraid he might actually break free, but even in a frenzy the skinhead couldn't match his strength, and before long David had fractured his other arm and his left hip.

He covered his quarry's mouth. "No more screaming or I'll pop your eyes." When he lifted his hand it left a patch of slime.

"Oh God," Ed whimpered.

"How do you like my new look, Ed? I bet you'll remember my face from now on. Especially since yours will look just like it."

"Oh God no—please!"

"Relax, you'll probably like being a vampire; you already get your kicks by hurting people."

Ed was panting; tears oozed down his cheeks. He kept shuddering convulsively, each tremor jiggling his broken arms, and David fancied that Ed might be in even more pain than he was.

"But if you really don't want to die and be like me," he continued thoughtfully, "maybe we can work out an alternative. You are kind of cute, and nosferatu don't live by blood alone. Instead of me sucking you, how would you like to suck me? Answer when I ask you something, Ed."

"I . . . I . . ."

"I know you don't like queers even when they're alive. And I admit my cock is a lot like my hands, all skinned and oozing, and my come's so nasty I'm embarrassed to describe it. But hey, revenants need love too. Give me a blow job, and I'll let you live."

Ed retched; for a moment David was afraid he might strangle. Then, after another shudder, he opened his mouth.

David closed it with a backhand slap. "Sorry, but even that won't save you. I may be undead, but I'm an undead heterosexual. Carter—the vampire who killed Val—just made you think we were gay to bait his trap."

"*Carter?*" Ed was so astonished that for a second he seemed to forget his pain and terror. "That *thing* that hit me—that was Carter Cavanaugh?"

"Yeah," said David. He knew he should bite Ed immediately before his anger drained away, but a part of him demanded that he listen. "I guess you know him."

"I—I do, but *that* wasn't him. He's only a year or two older than me!"

102

"We can look however we want, remember? Your Carter's a skinhead too, isn't he? He got you started harassing the guys who go to the Blue Cockatoo."

"Yeah!" Ed said eagerly. "You've got to believe me it was *his* idea! I mean, we never *liked* queers—some of the guys had punched out one or two and we sure would have kicked the shit out of any that bothered us—but it was Carter who convinced us that we ought to try to shut that damn club down so we wouldn't have to look at them anymore. At first most of us thought it sounded like more trouble than it was worth, but he has a way of talking you into things."

"Yeah," said David, "he does, doesn't he?"

"After they hired the security guards we slacked off, but the night before Val died Carter was bugging us to start up again; somehow he kind of charged us up with hate. Bryan, George, Val, and I decided we'd watch the parking lot the next night and see if we could give some homo a bad time. I don't know who thought of the face-cutting; I swear to God we never did it before."

"I imagine it was *his* idea, just like everything else. You know, he told me himself that he likes sadistic manipulation. I should have realized you wouldn't have shown up and attacked me right when he was supposed to demonstrate his powers if he hadn't influenced you to do it."

David's head was swimming; everything looked far away and he wondered if vampires ever fainted. It couldn't be true that he'd tortured a human being. He had the strangest feeling that, like Carter before him, he'd been on the brink of destroying his mirror image.

What a jerk he was! In the comics Spider-Man and Green Arrow went patrolling night after night and always found subhuman devils to attack, but skinheads weren't like that and neither was anyone else. Real people always had dreams and feelings, and at least a little goodness in them somewhere; and now that he realized it, he could never justify preying on even the worst of them again.

He shook his head, raked his fingers through his hair. Guilt and despair would have to wait until later; Ed was still scared and suffering. He concentrated and recreated his life-mask; pain surged through his head, and he was glad.

"Everything's going to be all right," he said. "I promise I won't hurt you again. Look, this is the real me; it was the dead thing that was only an illusion."

Ed's eyes were glazing, his face white as paper; maybe he was going into shock. "Please please don't *play* with me anymore!"

"I swear I'm not; I'm going to take you to a doctor." He projected another suggestion: *The torment's over; you can trust me now.* Maybe this time it would work, since that was something Ed must desperately want to believe.

"I don't understand . . . anything."

"My coven had to be sure of your courage. It's a cruel, difficult test — and I apologize — but Satan only recruits warriors."

Ed nodded, apparently too dazed to realize that what David had just told him didn't gibe with what he'd said about Carter a moment before. "And I was just a rat after all."

"No! You were scared but you fought back; you were going to bite my cock off if I gave you a chance. That's the kind of bad-ass attitude we need." *You proved you're brave, and now you need some rest.*

Ed smiled drowsily. "Everything's so weird . . . was there really a vampire?"

104

"I killed it before I came to see you."

The skinhead's eyelids drooped shut. "I think I'm dreaming after all . . . nothing really makes sense and my head's all funny . . . did you bring me something for the pain?"

"Yes," said David, and with a sob, he whipped the hammer down at his victim's forehead. Ed didn't deserve to die, but he needed blood.

Chapter Sixteen

When he finished he stared at Ed's chest, then pressed his wrist and the untorn side of his neck; Ed wasn't breathing and didn't have a pulse.

But he did have a wallet. David fumbled it out of a back pocket and riffled through the bills. Twenty-eight dollars, not bad, it —

He wailed and threw the wallet down the alley, then crumpled and dug his fingers into his face.

He'd committed *premeditated murder.* It was horrible enough that he'd killed the old lady, but at least then he'd been out of control and didn't completely understand what he was doing; this time there was no excuse at all. The thirst hadn't overwhelmed him, not quite yet. He could have let Ed live, but he knew someone had to die and he just . . . didn't.

Eventually he dragged himself to his feet. It would be pretty wasteful to take someone else's life to preserve his own, then turn right around and let the cops catch him crouching over the corpse.

Hiding the body seemed like too much trouble; so did trying to wipe off some of the blood. Funny how just a couple hours ago he'd been so concerned about scouring the foulness out of his mouth; now it didn't really seem to matter.

He vaguely remembered that he'd planned to spend the rest of the night looking for some refuge safer than a thicket; he supposed he might as well follow through.

MONSTER! First you tortured him and then you KILLED him—

He trudged back onto the street; a station wagon sped toward him, its single headlight glaring. Uh-oh, at some point, either when he was guzzling gore or castigating himself afterward, he'd allowed his shroud to disappear. He could conjure it up again, but it seemed kind of stupid to make his head hurt.

The driver zoomed by, apparently without noticing anything unusual.

Like Carter said, the area had more than its share of vacant houses. Some were tumbling down, but so far he hadn't spotted the particular ruin he felt he deserved. His house should be huge, old, and rococo, a crumbling monstrosity full of bugs and rats. If he was going to haunt one, it might as well be a decaying mansion in the grand tradition.

He wondered what would have happened if Ed had managed to pull his knife out. Was there any chance he could have saved himself? What if Ed had popped his eyes? Could a fledgling see without them the way Carter did? It would make sort of an interesting experiment.

And what if he'd been stabbed in the chest? Legends said you trashed a vampire by driving a wooden stake into his heart, but a steel blade might kill him just as dead. That would make a neat experiment too.

He limped around another corner, and there before him, across from a day-care center, of all things, squatted just the house of horrors he'd been seeking, one of its turrets thrust into the moon. It was a green three-story castle with shutters hanging askew and chipped gingerbread; wasps' nests swelled like tumors under the eaves and bare branches gouged at the staring windows. David grinned and scuttled toward the porch.

What if Ed had nailed him with a really heavy-duty weapon, like an axe or a machete? What if he'd missed his heart but hacked the hell out of the rest of him?

Well, he knew one thing: vampire wounds usually didn't repair themselves. If they did the holes the undertaker had punched in him would have begun to mend and Carter would have grown his pecker back. That being the case, if Ed had lopped off an arm or a leg, it probably would have permanently crippled him; if his head had been cut off, he almost certainly would have died.

But then again, everything about being undead was magical and illogical, so maybe not. Possibly a vampire's severed limb would regrow or bond itself back onto his torso; perhaps his head would live on by itself if no one destroyed his decapitated body. If the devil invented vampirism, maybe he'd rigged things so his creatures had to bear the discomfort of minor wounds for all eternity but recovered from crippling injuries so they could continue to do harm.

As David's chemistry teacher used to say, it was an empirical question. He could settle it by lying on a train track.

Someone had boarded the front door shut, but the mesh of scrap lumber pulled away easily in his hands. Apparently another intruder had worked the nails loose. When he wanted in he could tug the barrier free in one piece; when he left he just stuck it back in position and the door looked undisturbed.

Since someone was already using this house, maybe it would be smart to find another. But the place was gigantic; surely the other squatters wouldn't begrudge him one measly little bedroom.

The door swung open silently. Too bad; he'd been hoping for an "Inner Sanctum" creak. What he could see of the first floor was unfurnished. Footprints in the dust revealed that visitors usually went upstairs, and he supposed he might as well do the same.

The third riser snapped when he put his weight on it; his foot plunged through and the jagged hole bit a ring around his calf.

He chuckled as he pulled the splinters out. What a shame he was so clumsy; he'd make a lousy first impression on any other ghosts who were already in residence.

At the top of the stairs shimmered another barricade; a banana spider with legs as long as his index finger had sealed off the second floor. Its huge web sagged, weighted down with a bumper crop of roaches, flies, and termites. He scowled and raised his fist, then wondered why for an instant he'd hated it so.

He considered trying to become a shadow so he wouldn't break its handiwork, but in the end he settled for wiping away the right-hand moorings; maybe it wouldn't have too much trouble reconnecting them. After he sidled through the gap he found himself festooned with insect husks and wisps of gossamer; they tickled but it seemed like too much bother to pick them off.

Someone had hauled some stained yellow mattresses up to the bedrooms; graffiti slashed the walls, and candle stubs, condoms, cans, and cigarette butts littered the floor. Despite the lack of running water people had pissed and shit in the toilet and the bathtub too.

Running water . . . Damn, that stuff stung! Strange

how for vampires, no less than humans, some deaths were so much easier than others. A clean sudden stake through the heart and you'd never know what hit you; dying of thirst would be a long slow Hell. But eventually you'd go insane, and after that it might not be so bad. It was hard to guess how much the sun would hurt. It might incinerate you in a split second; on the other hand you could burn for half an hour.

The third floor wasn't nearly so full of trash, perhaps because no one had carried up anything to sit or have sex on. In the middle of the master bedroom's ceiling, at least ten feet above the floor, gaped a square black hole.

He hoped he could get up there and sleep with the other bats; maybe he could learn to hang from the rafters by his toes.

Down on the first floor someone laughed.

He could avoid them by becoming invisible, but it would take a lot of effort and somehow it even seemed like cheating. He sat down on a window sill that commanded a view of the stairs.

They probably wouldn't climb to the third floor anyway. If they stayed below he'd sit quietly and leave them alone.

Excited whispers buzzed up the stairwell; risers groaned. He hoped the banana spider hadn't started rebuilding yet.

Last night he might have cursed the rotten luck that drew other people into the house after him, but by now he'd learned to take such things in stride. He'd never have any peace; mortals would hound him every waking moment of his unending life. It was the natural order of things, all part of the rollicking fun of being a vampire.

A pop top clicked and the opened beverage hissed.

Stairs creaked again, louder and louder.

They were going to find him; it was obviously predestined. Nevertheless, it wouldn't hurt to give them one last chance at a pleasant evening. He tiptoed around the corner, where they wouldn't see him as soon as they reached the top.

A flashlight beam stabbed the space he'd just vacated. "Next time *you* carry the fucking cooler," said a voice that started out bass and squeaked in the middle.

"It didn't kill you, so take a chill pill," another boy replied. "The best window's over this way." To David's surprise, they went into a room on the opposite side of the hall.

He sank down in a corner, his knees drawn up and his face pressed against them. He wondered if vampires could fall asleep before sunrise. It was worth a try.

The cooler sloshed and thudded to the floor; feet scuffled and metal tapped metal.

"Let me take the lens cover off—there. Look over that tree; that's Jupiter."

The cooler lid thumped shut; another drink can clacked and sighed. "Fuck Jupiter; show me the *girls*."

"You are such a pervert it's pathetic, but okay. Somebody ought to be going to sleep by now. . . ."

I wish it was me, thought David, but as he'd expected, it wasn't. How could you doze off when your whole body hurt? He'd be awake till dawn snuffed out his mind.

"So where are they?"

"Not there yet."

"You are so full of shit—"

"Look, Joe, I can't *make* them go to bed, so give me a break, okay? We can look at the planets till they do."

"I knew I should've gone to the movies. . . ."

111

David wondered if drugs could make him sleep; according to Carter he was settling in a neighborhood where they were readily available. But if his system rejected ordinary water, how could it process narcotics? Hm, it would be interesting to find out. If he took them orally he'd just vomit, but if he injected them . . .

Lost in dreams of poison, he didn't hear someone prowling restlessly through the house until Joe had already stepped into the room.

Remaining motionless, David eyed him through the crack between his thighs. Joe was about fifteen, a chunky Hispanic boy with a gold stud in his left earlobe and a can of Mountain Dew clutched in his hand. "Vinnie! Vinnie! Come look at this!"

"I've seen this whole house a million times," said Vinnie from the other room.

"I'll bet you twenty bucks you didn't see this!"

"Oh, Jesus Christ," his friend said irritably. "All right, hang on."

Vinnie was Hispanic too, a tall scrawny kid with jug-handle ears and a few black hairs sprouting on his upper lip. "Shit!" he whispered. "Is he passed out?"

"He's dead, you dork; look at his hands!"

"Did you check him out?"

"What do you think, I want to get maggots?"

"Then you don't know he's dead; you can't hardly see him all curled up like that. Hey mister! *Mister!*" He bent down and reached for David's shoulder.

David decided he didn't want a shaking, so he uncoiled and grabbed Vinnie's wrist. "Your friend's right," he said. "About me being dead, I mean. I don't think I have maggots yet."

Vinnie froze and wet his pants; Joe squawked and stumbled back against the wall. "Am I squeezing too

112

hard?" asked David; he loosened his grip a little. "Sorry my hand's so grubby; be glad you don't have on a long-sleeved shirt."

"Let him go," Joe pleaded as he inched toward the door.

"If I do you'll *both* run away, and then I won't have anyone to talk to. Can you guys help me get some drugs? I want something that'll really zonk me out."

"No, really, no! Please don't kill him; he didn't do anything to you!"

"I won't, don't worry. I've already eaten."

Joe bolted for the stairs.

"Well, now it's just you and me," said David when the front door banged. "You really can't help me with the drugs?"

Still paralyzed, Vinnie only stared.

"Shit. I guess that means you're a good kid. Which is too bad for me, because it means you'll want to kill me."

The boy made a tiny whining sound.

"Hey, relax, it's okay. I'm a vampire, a dead damned murdering monster. You're *supposed* to want to kill me. You could do it too, if you caught me during the day."

Vinnie frantically shook his head.

"No, really." David stood up and dragged him into the hall. "I sleep during the day; I can't wake up no matter what. If you found me—and *that* wouldn't be hard—you could stake me right out and I'd be history."

Vinnie was starting to cry and still shaking his head.

David grimaced; was this kid stupid or what? "It would be *okay;* you'd be a hero. If you were too squeamish to do it yourself, you could call the cops and they'd do it. Now do you understand?" Incredibly,

113

Vinnie shook his head again. "Look, damn it!" David released him and ripped a newel out of the banister, then started picking and scratching at one end to make a better point. "You take a fucking wooden stake—"

Vinnie screamed and lunged forward, slammed David aside and bounded down the steps.

"Come back . . . I only wanted to *teach* you something—you're forgetting your telescope!" The front door banged again. David pivoted and hurled his makeshift spear into the wall, then sat down on the landing. His dry eyes pulsed and burned.

He couldn't go on, not like this. Even now, despite everything, he didn't really want to die, but he'd be better off dead than crazy with remorse.

He forced open a second-story window that some fool had painted shut and crawled out on the roof overhanging the front porch. He'd bet himself that before sunrise he could think of a way to survive without hurting anyone. If he won, he won the right to go back inside.

It might be a problem with no solution. An undead couldn't live unless he bit humans and his bite either killed them or turned them into vampires too. The rules seemed brutally straightforward; no wonder Carter never found a loophole.

Could he somehow neutralize his poison? Smiling crookedly, he imagined himself gargling with iodine or some other disinfecting agent just before attacking. No, he couldn't believe it would work; no matter what chemicals he rinsed it with, his mouth would still be a dead decaying vampire orifice sucking an open wound.

He could change every victim into a revenant, but that was no solution either, since it was just as cruel as killing them. Besides, he'd be responsible for all the harm they did.

The eastern sky was bleaching. Shit, this was ridiculous! No doubt vampires had been wrestling with this dilemma since the dawn of time; of course, he couldn't expect to solve it in just a few hours. Who could blame him if he stayed alive and tackled it again tomorrow night?

The person he'd kill tomorrow night, that's who. He dug his fingers into the shingles as if to anchor himself.

He wished Carter weren't so damn clever; it was hard to believe there could be an answer if he'd never found it. David could picture him pondering the problem by candlelight, dressed in his peruke and ruffles or whatever, in those long-ago days before he embraced depravity.

Already the air felt hot and heavy. He started getting sleepy. . . .

Long-ago days!

Carter had tried to solve the puzzle in a vastly different age. Maybe he hadn't found the answer because it didn't exist *then,* but it might today. Maybe if David thought about the billion ways the world had changed he could uncover it.

The sky was pink and violet when he climbed back inside. Lethargy dragging at his limbs, he limped back up to the third floor. Even with his twisted leg it wasn't difficult to leap up and grab the open hatch.

There were no bats, just cobwebs, rat droppings, and a lot of old trunks and boxes. Cocooned in new garbage bags, he smiled and waited for oblivion.

Chapter Seventeen

The hissing spray and foaming lather couldn't alleviate his pain, but at least they sluiced off the itchy grime. He hated seeing his dead naked body and watching bits of himself swirl down the drain, but he enjoyed the shower anyway.

But pleasurable as it was, he'd better hurry; he'd feel pretty awkward if someone surprised him while he was undressed.

He toweled off and sprayed on Right Guard, an exercise in futility if there ever was one, then pulled on the green pajamalike shirt and pants he'd taken from a closet. He stuck his shopping bag in the cabinet under the sink; he'd look peculiar carrying it and it was easier to stash it than to hide it in illusion.

As he stepped out into the corridor a tinny amplified voice announced that visiting hours were over and would resume at one o'clock tomorrow afternoon; a moment later it repeated the same thing in Spanish. People began emerging from the long line of bedroom doors and shuffled toward the elevators.

Outside the nurses' station stood an empty IV rack; it looked like a robot sentry or a high-tech gallows. He made certain he was masked, then stepped inside.

A swarthy brunette with a mole on her wrist was

writing in a green plastic hospital chart, and a stout gray-haired nurse was putting pills in little paper cups. "May I help you?" the older woman asked.

"I'm supposed to review records," he replied. "I can start with any you're not using."

The ward clerk smiled and shoved some across the table, but the nurse squinted at his chest and asked, "Who are you?"

Belatedly he noticed they both had plastic photo ID's clipped to their clothes; no doubt everybody was supposed to. "I'm David Yarborough, the new medical student. I work under Dr. Santisteban." The physician's name was inscribed on several charts.

The nurse—Carmen Alvarez, according to her badge—plucked a microphone from its desktop stand. "Dr. Santisteban, please call the station on Three. Dr. Santisteban, please call the station on Three."

"I think he's already gone home," the dark woman said.

"Then I'll page Dr. Truman."

"He's gone too," said David. "Look, what's the problem?" *Everything's all right,* he told her silently. *I'm a nice young man; don't give me a hard time.*

"The problem is that I don't know you." She seemed utterly unaffected. "These records are strictly confidential."

"I'm sure it's okay," said the brunette.

"Somebody was sure at Tampa Metropolitan last year. It wound up in a twenty-million-dollar law suit and dirty laundry all over the St. Pete *Times.*"

David did his best to look mystified, then startled as he glanced down at his chest. "Oh, my badge! Now I understand. No problem; I've got it right here." He'd slip his hand in his hip pocket and bring it out holding an illusory ID. Unfortunately, when he ran his

117

hand down his thigh he discovered he didn't have any pockets.

Carmen scowled.

"Uh, of course, it's in my *street* pants."

"If you are a student, why didn't you start your rotation when the others did? I think you'd better—"

"All right!" David roared. "Keep your damn charts! Why not? Tomorrow on rounds Santisteban will ask me one stupid question after another and I won't be prepared, but it's no skin off your nose, right? What do you care if I don't make it in this hospital either?" He spun around and slapped the window that looked out on the corridor, not hard enough to break it but with enough force to make it bang and rattle. *This isn't worth the aggravation, Carmen. I'm a complete pain in the ass when I don't get my way.*

After a long embarrassed silence the brunette said "Maybe he could show us his badge the next time he comes up here."

"Oh good grief, " Carmen growled. "But he'd better conduct himself in a professional manner from now on, or I'll have a little talk with Dr. Santisteban. There are *sick* people here, and they don't need any disturbances!" She slammed a can of Hawaiian Punch down on her tray of medication cups and stalked out onto the ward.

"Is she always this bitchy?" he asked.

"She lost her last job because she bent the rules," the brunette—Julie Hillyard—replied. "What's *your* excuse? No, don't tell me, just get busy and get out before she comes back."

David thought the sixth record was the one he wanted, but he was too ignorant of medical jargon and abbreviations to be sure. He stuck it in front of Julie and pointed at a notation. "DNR—what's that mean?"

"Do Not Resuscitate; don't you know anything?"

"Just making sure I've got it right. So when this old guy starts to die, they're just going to let him? I don't know if I agree with that."

"You don't? Well, this changes everything; let's get the attending physician on the phone. Look, Dave, Mr. Bronson's had Alzheimer's for the past twenty-five years; he doesn't even recognize his family anymore. Now he's riddled with inoperable cancer; he'd be in horrible pain if he wasn't doped up. So what would *you* do? This is a good hospital. We don't just—"

"I get the point," he said as he pushed back his chair. "I'm going to grab a Coke; be back in a minute."

He passed Carmen in the hall; he smiled and she didn't.

Mr. Bronson had a roommate, a black man with one leg in traction and a bandaged head. Fortunately, he was snoring softly. David shut the door and tiptoed past him, then pulled the curtain that halved the room completely closed.

Mr. Bronson reminded him of Carter; he didn't look rotten exactly but he was just about as withered. Entangled in tubes and restraints like a bug in a web, he twitched and slobbered in his sleep.

David wondered if any vampire had ever tried to survive this way before; of course, until recently the option hadn't existed. In centuries past, when people got too sick to function even marginally, they died. Today, however, the miracle of modern medicine had produced a sizable population of incurable invalids who lingered and suffered on and on and on; many of them didn't even have minds anymore. He wouldn't enjoy killing them, but he dared to hope that he wouldn't despise himself afterward either.

119

Brushing aside the yellow hose that had slithered up the old man's nose, he lowered his head and bit. He tried to penetrate cleanly on the first try, so he'd make neat inconspicuous little holes.

Chapter Eighteen

And another sunset; pain, thirst, and loneliness as usual. Drizzle pattered above him; rats or mice scurried somewhere below. When he was alive he'd loved to roll over and snooze for another few minutes, especially on school and work days, but of course it wasn't possible anymore. Sitting up, he pulled the trash bags off, then checked himself thoroughly for insects.

No little scavengers tonight; maybe it was a good omen. Perhaps he could drink and wash without a lot of hassle and then, since he still had clean clothes and money, spend most of the night trying to enjoy himself. He put on his Walkman and dropped down to the third floor to watch the stars come out.

Vinnie's telescope and cooler still sat beside the window; you'd think after six weeks he would have found the courage to retrieve them. Not that David wanted him to; he enjoyed looking at the moon and planets. But he had plenty to feel guilty over without having this particular "theft" on his conscience too.

The thirst seared his mouth and made him shiver. The dusklight was nearly gone; he supposed he could be on his way.

But he wouldn't; that wasn't the routine. The sky wasn't *all* black, Sting wasn't *quite* done singing "King of Pain," and as usual he'd stay until both things came about. The thirst wasn't in control, *he* was.

121

He absently tapped the post embedded in the wall as he started down the stairs; by the time he reached the bottom he was invisible. He peered out a window, then climbed through; he avoided using the door so he wouldn't dislodge the scrap wood barrier.

Actually, it was a silly thing to worry about. Adventurous kids, street people, prostitutes and their customers, and other assorted riffraff wandered through the house all the time; Joe and Vinnie had even *seen* him here. If he really wanted to be safe, he'd move, but a part of him needed a certain level of risk. He was still a murderer even if his current victims were wretched unreasoning shells. Sleeping in the attic made it easy for the universe to destroy him; when he woke and found that it hadn't, he felt like he'd been given permission to exist for another few hours.

He limped through the knee-high grass and past the For Sale sign; a few houses down the street he put on his life-mask.

Just a block away was a Seven-Eleven that usually had a few unsold copies of the *Tampa Tribune*. He bought one to read while he waited for his bus; the cashier didn't speak and neither did he.

He still hadn't made the papers. He'd hoped that by being careful and cleaning up after himself he could avoid detection for a little while, but it was amazing that no one had discovered his depredations by now. Apparently when a charity patient who was expected to die in the immediate future did, nobody really bothered to check on what killed him; it was enough to destroy a person's faith in doctors.

He'd revisit Royal Palms Manor tonight, a cheerless establishment that was close by and warehoused a number of ancient husks who couldn't even get out of bed or recognize their own names anymore. And since their physician was a befuddled alcoholic who probably wouldn't notice if David dismembered his patients with a hacksaw, all in all it was an ideal hunting ground.

Riding the bus wasted too much time and boxed him in with strangers; he hoped one day he could buy a car. But even though he shoplifted much of what he wanted, it was difficult to accumulate much money when he only robbed Jerry Lewis. A cashier wouldn't lose his job or get arrested if a little merchandise vanished from the shelves or a collection can turned up missing, but he might if his register total came up short.

A wraith once more, he hobbled into the sooty gray brick rest home and on past the nursing station. He suspected he was aggravating his headache for nothing; the burly sister of mercy behind the desk probably wouldn't have pulled her nose out of her Barbara Cartland novel if he'd marched through blasting fanfares on a tuba, and the silent scarecrows slumped in front of the switched-off TV in the lobby seemed nearly as oblivious.

He'd planned to kill Mrs. Wu, but her bed was already empty. No problem; Mrs. Tyler next door was every bit as sick.

After he finished he examined the wounds: not bad. They weren't humongous, and he hadn't splashed too much blood around. He washed her neck, then sat her in a chair, changed her sheets and her nightgown, and tucked her in again. Once he showered, brushed his teeth, and put on fresh clothes he was ready to leave; he'd carry her gore-spattered shift and bedding away with him and toss them in some other building's dumpster.

According to the clock on the olive wall behind the Coke machine it was 9:15. He had plenty of time for recreation, if only he could think of something he wanted to do.

He could read his new comics or catch the new Chuck Norris flick, but now that his own existence was full of danger and violence, escapist fiction wasn't as thrilling as it used to be. He'd heard all his tapes too many times and didn't feel like stealing any new ones; Saturn's rings would look the same as always.

He didn't want to spend another night alone.

When he wanted company he sometimes went to a bar and talked to the other patrons, but it often made him uncomfortable; he kept thinking how repulsed his companions would be if he lost his veil. It was frequently more pleasant just to spy on people, usually the people who'd crept into his house.

They'd certainly given him an education; he'd never seen anyone smoke crack or divvy up the loot from a robbery before. He liked to watch the hookers most of all.

And suddenly he wanted to gag as he pictured the leering voyeur corpse with its dead shriveled cock dangling between its thighs savoring the greatest pleasure it had managed to extract from its immortal existence.

A freckled woman with tousled hair threw open the lobby door. She was as red as catsup, with coppery curls, flushed cheeks, a scarlet blouse, purse, and shoes, and a rose bouquet in her crimson-nailed hand.

"I had to stay late at work," she said as she bustled up to the reception desk. "I hope he isn't asleep already."

"Oh dear, I'm afraid he is," the nurse said sweetly. David was sure she hadn't left her seat since he'd arrived.

"Shit," said the redhead. "Well, let's look; maybe he woke up."

"Certainly," sighed the nurse; she closed her paperback on a tasseled unicorn bookmark. Still invisible, David followed them down the male patients' wing without quite knowing why.

The old man's room was as shabby and dimly lit as the rest of the building; all that red shone like a fireworks display. "Sonny?"

"Please, let's not disturb him," whispered the nurse.

The visitor looked at the night stand by the bed. "Where are his things?"

"Safely put away in that bureau."

"Why?"

"Please check them if you like; I'm sure they're fine."

"I'm sure they are, but how's he supposed to *use* them?"

"Ms White, I hate having to say this, but he wouldn't use them in any case; he's completely withdrawn and disoriented."

David had skimmed Sonny Ford's chart. According to the doctor, admittedly not an unimpeachable source, the old man still had lucid intervals. If the Cartland fan was right, he'd found another meal, but for the redhead's sake he hoped she wasn't.

"He talked for me last week. Do you people *try* to draw him out; does he get therapy?"

"Of course, but he doesn't respond."

"Damn it, he's not that bad!" She gently shook his shoulder. "Sonny, it's *Karen*. Come on, sugar pie, wake up!"

"Please don't do that."

"Come on, rise and shine! I brought you some flowers and a present."

Sonny looked just as feeble and desiccated as Mr. Bronson and Mrs. Tyler had. His toothless face was

125

seamed like cracked dried mud; arthritis had twisted his hands into paralytic claws and his flesh exuded a musty, sour smell. After a little more prompting his eyes jerked open. He glared at Karen, then twitched away from her hand.

"You see?" said the nurse.

"Look at me, Sonny, it's Karen." When he kept his face averted she strode to the green metal bureau and, after a moment's rummaging, removed a boom box from the second drawer. "I've got some new tapes."

"I'm sorry, but that's not allowed past eight."

"Damn you! Why are you all like this? I wish to Hell I could take him out of here!"

"I'm afraid that's a decision the *family* would have to make."

Karen jabbed the Play button; Dixieland jazz came strutting out of the speakers.

Sonny just kept staring at the wall; after a minute Karen fumbled some Kleenex out of her purse and the Cartland fan smiled and patted her on the back.

God damn it, Sonny, open your ears and listen! Your favorite music's on, just pay attention!

David silently shouted the commands till his head felt ready to split; then the old man slowly rolled over like Lazarus reviving in his tomb. "Jelly Roll," he murmured with a grin.

"That's right!" said Karen. "The Red Hot Peppers, 1928! I brought 'Fatha' Hines and John Coltrane too!" She hurled herself across the room to hug him.

For a moment David was as happy as she was. Then something twisted in his chest.

Everybody had somebody to love them, even senile invalids shut away in squalid nursing homes. Everybody but him. As he watched Sonny and Karen chatter, laugh, embrace, he couldn't help realizing just how

126

empty, how *lonely,* his new existence really was.

He didn't know how he was going to manage it, but somehow he was going to get his friends and family back.

Chapter Nineteen

The New Age study group had cleared a space in the middle of Wally's living room and had set white candles on the carpet to define a five-pointed star. Now they stood in a circle at its center, eight chimeras gazing intently at the implements laid out on a three-legged table.

Gaunt as a praying mantis, Carter stood out from the others even with the grimacing Iroquois demon mask concealing his hideous head. Liz was on his left, strands of her chestnut hair protruding from behind two smiling basketwork faces stacked one on top of the other. And Wally stood on his right, readily identifiable thanks to the white short-sleeved dress shirt stretched over his paunch. His head was bowed as if his horned, lacquered noh mask was too heavy.

David crouched on the terrace just a few feet away, spying through a gap in the curtains in front of the sliding glass door, terribly afraid that Carter would spot him but too fascinated to leave.

A moment after he'd resolved to contact his family and friends, he'd realized how much the prospect terrified him. How would he feel when he witnessed his parents' grief? What if someone he loved discovered what he'd become?

Eventually he'd decided to begin by looking in on Wally, precisely because his former boss didn't mean as much to him as Liz or his mother and father did. Still, by the time he stepped off the bus in front of Wally's apartment complex he felt too jittery to actually talk to him; perhaps tonight it would be enough just to see his face.

Wally's second-story terrace was no higher than the attic hatch, so he jumped up and swarmed over the wrought-iron railing. When he peeked into the apartment, he discovered that the study group was meeting.

Once he actually saw his friends, he *did* want to greet them, desperately yearned to hear the sounds of their voices. But he didn't dare approach them, because Carter was present too, and the elder vampire had promised to kill him if he annoyed him.

For some reason he'd assumed, now that Carter had seduced him into becoming one of the undead, he would have no reason to remain in the group. And yet, here he was, still hanging around. But why? What kind of diversion did participation afford him now?

The answer became apparent as the ritual progressed.

Carter was presiding. When everyone had presumably meditated into the proper state of mind, he rang a bell and lit a stick of incense. Then he picked up a wavy-bladed dagger and saluted the four cardinal points, first north, then west, then south, then east. All the while he was chanting, but the thick glass muffled his words.

David frowned. When he'd been a member, the group had screwed around with Yoga, Kirlian photography, Ouija boards, and Rune cards, held séances and drawn their birth charts. But this was obviously something different, an attempt to perform actual ceremonial magic.

When he finished consecrating the circle, Carter tilted back his mask and raised a crystal goblet of white wine to his stained, jagged grin. Then he handed the goblet to Wally, who said a few words, drank, and passed it on. The cup was moving widdershins, counterclockwise, the direction associated with Satanic forces. A few weeks ago Wally wouldn't have tolerated any practice that smacked even faintly of diabolism.

When the goblet returned to Carter he took another fake sip, then whipped it down at the table; the bowl exploded in a puff of glittering dust.

Next he lifted a carved-bone cruciform wand over his head, shouted, and snapped it in two. And finally, still intoning whatever mumbo jumbo he'd deemed appropriate, he touched a pyramidal chunk of quartz to his forehead, mouth, and breast. When he set it back down on the table everyone started staring at it.

After a while the mortals tensed; some trembled. Liz flinched, then forced herself to look again. Whatever Carter was making them see, it wasn't any more pleasant than Steve Morales's bogus astral projection.

Eventually Kazuhide, looking prosperous and incongruous as ever in his three-piece suit, ripped off his golden-bearded Carnival mask. Swallowing repeatedly, his hand clasped over his mouth, he bolted for the bathroom.

After he fled the others unmasked and looked around. Either Carter had been ready to end the visions anyway or he'd done it to preserve the fiction that the intact circle had evoked them. When Kaz returned, eyes downcast and clearly quite mortified, Carter started talking to Liz, apparently quizzing her on exactly what she'd seen.

After she told him they all discussed it, probably trying to figure out its meaning. Carter had the last word, no doubt delivering the definitive interpretation.

They must all have seen something different, because

everyone got a chance to describe his hallucination, some diffidently and a couple nearly raving. Wally didn't say much until his turn came. His round face was sweaty and mottled, and he kept clenching his fists and squaring his shoulders; he looked like someone struggling to be brave. After he said his piece Liz started arguing with him, gesturing wildly and stamping her foot; she wouldn't stop until he shouted at her.

Wally turned his back and started unbuttoning his shirt; the dead thing put its mask back on and picked up an ivory-handled quirt.

David was moving before he realized he intended to. Vaulting over the iron rail, he splashed down in a puddle; pain shot up from his ankle into his twisted knee. He scrambled up the concrete stairs to Wally's front door, pumped the doorbell button, then yelled and hammered on the wooden panel.

As the latch clicked he realized he was still a ghost. Frantically he conjured up his new persona, a man his own age but a lot handsomer than he'd ever been, with bushy red eyebrows arching over bright green eyes and a lean, bronzed face framed by a neatly trimmed goatee.

Wally opened the door, his shirttail out and his buttons done up crookedly. He looked dazed, vacuous, and for a moment David wondered if somehow he'd remained invisible. But then his friend's eyes focused; he looked straight at him and said, "What is it?"

David took a deep breath. "Are you Wally Fulton?"

"Uh-huh."

"Great! I'm David White! I just moved to Tampa, and Becky Jordan told me I should look you up." Becky Jordan was the self-styled "Official Psychic of Philadelphia" and one of Wally's many correspondents.

Wally smiled slightly, a shadow of his usual jovial grin. "Oh. Becky. Well, any friend of hers—"

And suddenly Carter's brown, eyeless skull-face was sneering over his shoulder. "Excuse me, Wally, but shouldn't we return to our invocation? If Mr. White knows Becky I'm sure he'll understand."

David desperately wanted to turn tail, but he knew that if he did he'd never come back; besides, Carter was still holding the whip. "I understand, and I'd be honored if you'd let me observe. If it's Cabalistic or Wiccan maybe I could even help."

"Since you weren't here when we drew the circle you'd be unprotected; Please leave so you won't get hurt."

Liz crowded into the foyer behind him. "Jim gets sick, this guy tries to beat the door down—we've had too many interruptions. I don't think I could get back in the mood." Others quickly chattered their agreement.

Carter shrugged. "Ah. Well, if that's how you all feel, of course the majority rules. It seems we're not in the midst of any hocus pocus after all, Mr. White, so *do* come in and we'll all get acquainted."

David would have liked to wait for Wally to invite him in, but he didn't. He was already courting destruction; it would be crazy to provoke Carter any further.

The mortals scurried to snuff the candles and rearrange the furniture; it was as if they hoped to convince themselves that the ritual never happened.

"Nice to meet you," said Liz, holding out her hand; he froze for a moment, then grabbed it. Once he did, it was hard to let go.

"I'm Liz Yarborough. Would you like a drink or something to eat?"

"Uh, no, I had something right before I came over.

132

I guess I should apologize for spoiling your ceremony."

"Not as far as I'm concerned. Let's sit." She led him to the L-shaped sectional sofa under the framed aerial photograph of Tikal. Carter started to follow, but Sarah, still looking like a rotund and somewhat grizzled refugee from the *Summer of Love* in her paisley dashiki and granny glasses, intercepted him; she probably wanted to discuss her vision some more.

"What was the problem?" David asked. It was intoxicating to talk to her again; he wished he wasn't furious and scared half out of his mind.

"It—I should keep my mouth shut," she replied. "Maybe nothing's wrong *inside* the group, but bad things have happened outside and . . . you don't want to hear all this. Tell me about yourself; what do you do?"

"I'm just another perpetual student. If I picked a bad day to turn up on Wally's doorstep I wish you'd tell me."

"Maybe a new face will help take his mind off his troubles. His store burned down four weeks ago."

No! "That—Becky said that store was his life!"

"It sure was, and the big turkey hardly had any insurance. And that's not even the worst thing that's happened. It all seemed to start when the guy I'm dating had a scary out-of-body experience, but things got really terrible when a friend of ours died."

And Carter was involved both times, David thought, but of course the red-haired stranger couldn't point it out. "But what about *you?* Are you okay?"

She cocked her head quizzically, puzzled by the intensity in his voice. "I'm fine, thanks, except that I hurt when my friends do. And I guess I have some growing to do before I'll be comfortable with some of the things we've learned. It's funny, I

133

was so eager to advance spiritually, but—"

"You two are certainly talking up a storm. I daresay you've met before."

David almost screamed. He'd planned to watch Carter every second, but somehow, despite his immunity to illusions, he hadn't seen him cross the room. "N-no," he stammered, "of course not!"

"Oh, I'm sure you have. Doesn't he seem familiar to you, Liz?"

"I don't know," she said, frowning. "Maybe—"

"I swear to God I've never seen you before!"

"That's not true. You loved her. You worked side by side with her. I'm referring to one of your past lives, of course. I hope I didn't make you feel unwelcome earlier; my name is Carter Cavanaugh." He extended his frayed, withered claw and after a second, his guts churning with hate and revulsion, David shook it.

Chapter Twenty

When David rose to leave, so did Carter; he picked up the two leather suitcases into which he'd packed his masks and other paraphernalia and said, "It's past my bedtime too, so I'll walk down with you."

David suppressed a shudder. "Fine."

Liz stood up too; Carter glanced at her. Her face went slack, and she sat down again.

It had finally stopped raining, but the asphalt was still gleaming wet, a black mirror rippling with the street lights' glare. "I like slick pavement," said Carter, pausing on the landing. "Tell me, was it worth it?"

"I guess that depends on the price; are you going to hurt me? I had no way of knowing you were in there."

"Don't compound your offenses by insulting my intelligence You wouldn't have assailed the door in such a frenzy if you hadn't seen what we were doing."

"Okay, I did see, and it just . . . made me crazy. I'm sorry! But you said I couldn't live in your house; you never told me I couldn't see my friends."

"I believe I made it clear that *I* didn't want to see *you*."

And he bashed him with one of the valises. Thrown off balance, David grabbed for the rail but missed it and the next second he was tumbling down the stairs.

He hit the edge of every one and landed in a heap at the bottom. Sobbing with shock and pain, he struggled to stand; Carter was surely charging down to finish him. As soon as he made it to his feet he started punching, then saw he was facing the parking lot. Whirling, he lashed out again.

Nothing animate was on the stairs, just the two brown bags sitting at the top. Panting, giddy, he lurched around and around and around.

After about thirty seconds he calmed down enough to realize he wasn't accomplishing anything. He didn't understand how or why Carter had disappeared, but since he couldn't spot him and wasn't under attack he might as well try to steal away.

He took one step, then another, his shoulders hunched in anticipation of a paralyzing mental attack or a savage blow. But nothing happened.

Maybe Carter wasn't as angry as he'd thought. If he was truly furious he could have stayed at his side all evening, frightening and harassing him, but after that first attack he'd retired, it seemed, though David had been sure he'd been balefully observing him. Perhaps it was just his imagination.

By the time he'd limped a hundred feet unmolested he was so relieved that for the first time in weeks he felt like laughing. Apparently he was going to survive.

Something pulsed through the air behind him. His panic surging back instantly, he threw himself forward onto the grass. When he looked up, he actually did laugh; it was only an owl swooping low.

Carter's gone, asshole, he let you off with a warning. Instead of spazzing out at every little noise, you'd better get the Hell out of Dodge before he changes his mind.

As he pushed himself off the ground the sight of his gray corroding hands reminded him to check his veil. Sure enough, he'd lost it when Carter struck him; he was lucky the bird was the only one who'd seen him stumbling around out here without it.

The living David Brent was an easier phantom to conjure than the fictitious David White, but even so, the effort made him gasp. An instant later the night blackened.

He supposed it would serve him right if all his psychic abilities failed before he made it home. As his headache grew more and more intense, he'd known he was exhausting his magic. But he hadn't been able to tear himself away, and not just because he was afraid Carter would follow him.

He hobbled on toward the tennis courts, clubhouse, pool, and the boat trailers parked beside them. A squirrel sprang back and forth through the branches of a small tree, chittering furiously. Funny to see one bouncing around at night.

He wondered if it *had* been worth it, if it had really even been pleasant. It was exciting to talk to Liz but maddening that she didn't—couldn't—know him. He hated seeing the lost, defeated look in Wally's eyes. And fear rolled over him in gelid waves. What if Carter had actually unmasked him, somehow shown them all that he was really the fanged, rotting corpse of David Brent? He couldn't have borne it.

But even though he'd been terrified, frustrated, grieved, he'd also felt *connected,* a part of something that wasn't part of death.

Something scurried along under a line of parked cars, its tiny claws clicking on the pavement. A shadow skated across the sidewalk. He jumped, then smiled at his skittishness. Two more shadows glided after the first.

Regretting the loss of his night vision, he squinted at the sky. Except in nature documentaries he'd never seen so many wheeling bats; they'd probably come to eat the insects swarming around the lamp posts. Then sheet lightning flashed, glinting on talons, beaks, and feathers; was it natural for bats and birds to flock together?

Now something—no, several somethings were scuttling under the cars again; shrubbery rustled.

No, no, he reassured himself, this can't be what I'm thinking it is. Carter let me off the hook and besides, he told me vampires can't really control animals because you can't command a creature if you don't speak its language.

Right, like he told me I'd be able to read minds. Jesus Christ, I've got to get out of here!

The squirrel sprang out of the darkness onto his shoulder. He tried to knock it off; it darted across his back to the other one, and now its teeth were shredding his ear. He grabbed it, squeezed, felt it crunch, but before he could even drop it bats, owls, and pigeons were raining down, pecking, clawing, and clutching.

Bright slashes of pain danced across his upper body and his life-mask shredded away. He tried to become a ghost, but it didn't happen.

So he ran blindly, shielding his eyes with one hand and fighting with the other, trapped in a whirling chaos of living blades.

Now other beasts were tearing at his legs. He kicked away an orange cat, stamped on a toy poodle with a bow around its neck, then tripped over the corn snake that coiled around his ankles.

He slammed into a cloth-covered surface; he opened his eyes a crack. Blundering into the boat-trailer parking area, he'd fallen against somebody's runabout. There was a canvas cover snapped over the top; if he crawled underneath it would protect him!

He fumbled open a snap and then the tarp wriggled and heaved up out of his hand. A solid mass of squealing rats cascaded into his face.

Keening, nearly delirious, he ripped them off as he turned and staggered toward the swimming pool. The gate was padlocked; twisted prongs of wire snagged him as he dragged himself across the chain-link fence. For a moment he hung with half his body on either side, then toppled on over, crushing rats and sparrows when he smacked against cement.

He was too addled and in too much pain to stand up again. Brushing aside folding lawn furniture, he crawled the last few feet, his back carpeted with rending, snapping life. Something tangled in his hair scrabbled at his right eyelid, and then he was falling again.

His tormentors abandoned him when he hit the water. Scraps of flesh floated upward as he drifted down toward the drain eight feet below.

Thank God thank God. They weren't pursuing! His countless scrapes and gashes were on fire, but he didn't even care; he still had his eyes and he was—

—running out of air.

Which was crazy; a dead man shouldn't need any. But he still had a live man's instincts. There was a terrible pressure building in his chest, a voice in his mind yammering that he'd die if he didn't breathe.

But he wouldn't, and if he stuck his face out the animals would strip it to the bone. He could control his outmoded mortal reflexes; he *didn't* have to breathe, *didn't, DIDN'T*—

His breath exploded out and he sucked in water.

Instantly he was choking, strangling, *drowning!* A part of him understood that he wasn't blacking out, wasn't *really* dying, but the sensation was intolerable.

139

Floundering upward, he grabbed the edge of the pool and clung there helplessly retching.

Nothing attacked him.

When at last he was able to look around, the animals were gone. But Carter was lounging at a table under a green and yellow beach umbrella, his suitcases on the grass beside him.

"Was it worth it?" he asked again.

"Yeah. It was. I'll stay away from you, but I'll be back to see them. If that's not okay, you'd better call back the zoo."

"That won't be necessary. I've decided you may visit them whenever you like, even when I'm present. It will be amusing having you around."

Chapter Twenty-one

The blue Chevy pickup crept through the maze of narrow streets, past tiny Baptist and Pentecostal churches and sagging wooden houses with rusty kerosene drums mounted on their sides. Molly kept turning and doubling back—she didn't know anyone in this neighborhood—and David, crouched in the back under the tarp his father used to cover cargo, couldn't figure out where she was going. It wasn't until they passed Johnson's Klean-Kwik 24 Hour Laundromat that he realized his mother was looking for *him*.

He'd put off visiting his parents because he couldn't think of a way to begin insinuating himself back into their lives. But two nights ago longing and curiosity overwhelmed him and he'd returned home at last, resigned to simply spying.

He'd shivered when his one-story stucco house came into view. It looked strange, utterly familiar yet somehow wrong, like a mirage that didn't quite blend in with the surrounding landscape. Maybe it was just because the grass was several inches long; before he died his mother had insisted that he mow it every week.

Shrouding himself in his ghost-mask, he hobbled up the driveway. He hoped he could avoid looking through the windows; he'd more or less gotten used to being an outcast and a voyeur, but it would bother him to lurk outside his own house, peeping in. Besides, he wanted to hear their voices. Fortunately the door that led from the garage to the kitchen was unlocked.

He opened it an inch and saw no one, so he slipped on through and eased it shut behind him.

Once he was inside, the house seemed stranger still. Although he hadn't expected to find dirty dishes heaped in the sink, there wasn't an object in the room he hadn't seen a thousand times before, but now everything, the Audubon calendar hanging over the breakfast table, the checkered hand towel draped over the oven-door handle, and the crumb-covered plastic cutting board with the daisies emblazoned on it, seemed to loom and shimmer. He might have stood staring for hours if a blare of laughter hadn't startled him. Someone had switched on the living-room TV.

He took a single step, then almost bolted. He'd veiled himself hundreds of times, but for a moment he couldn't believe it was going to work. He couldn't be invisible to his mom and dad.

But of course that was nonsense. He took a deep breath, sharpened the image of absence transfixed in his mind, and goaded himself forward.

They were side by side in their accustomed spots on the couch. Stan, a Miller Lite in his hand and his bare feet propped up on a foot stool, was wearing one of the short-sleeved coveralls he bought at Ward's; Molly was dressed in her rust-colored robe and blue cotton nightgown and had her usual glass of Diet Cherry Coke sitting on the end table beside her. It would have looked like an utterly ordinary evening at home if she hadn't been slipping comics into plastic storage bags.

"Do you want to watch 'Night Court'?" asked Stan. "We've see this one, but it's funny."

"I don't care," she replied.

"I guess we could see what else is on." He pointed

142

the remote and started switching channels, jumping to a new one every few seconds. "Say, this looks like a winner: *Seven Sons of the Emerald Dragon!*"

She hated kung fu movies, but she only said, "Whatever."

Stan frowned for a moment, then stealthily sidled across the sofa cushions. Once he was in range, he lurched over into her lap. His face only inches from hers, he stuck out his tongue and curled it upward to touch his nose.

She hated that even worse than kung fu movies, or at least she said she did; once she would have squealed, averted her eyes, and proclaimed it the grossest thing she'd ever seen. Now she just sighed and said, "You'd better sit up."

"Come on, baby, give me a kiss!" He waggled his tongue like a demented rock star, then stuck it back on his nose again.

She took him by the shoulders and tried to lift him upright. "Please stop playing around; you have your elbow on some of the magazines."

"Sorry." He sat up and shifted back down the couch. "God forbid that I should damage any of our precious copies of *Doom Patrol.*"

"David always said they could be worth a lot of money someday if they were kept in good condition."

"You know, we have a lot to remember him by, our pictures and movies and all. We don't need his collection too, and I think he would have wanted it passed on to someone who'd really enjoy it. What do you say we sell it to another sci-fi fan and let *him* worry about keeping it in good condition?"

"Fine, when the time is right. But Wally deserves first crack at it, and he's in no position to buy it at the moment."

"I guess," Stan sighed. He took another swig of beer. "A couple people called the store today."

"Sergeant Stephens?" she asked quickly.

"Uh, no . . . well, actually, he called yesterday. It was just to say that there were no leads, so I didn't bother to mention it."

"He's a regular Sherlock Holmes, isn't he?"

"Well, he told us it would be difficult. Since most grave robbers are kids—"

"I wonder how he manages when he doesn't have you to make excuses for him."

"I only mean—Anyway, one of the people who *did* call was that John Lammers, to remind us that we still haven't picked out a stone."

"I suppose we'd better get right on it, hadn't we? God forbid that empty hole should go unmarked."

Stan picked up the remote, set it down, sipped, cleared his throat. David had never seen him look so nervous and uncertain. "I understand your point but . . . we can talk about it later. Gaston called too; he invited us down to Sanibel for the weekend."

"I'd rather not, but don't let that stop you. Go and have a *wonderful* time."

"You know, sweetheart, we have to go on living. We have to do the things that need doing, and eventually we even have to start trying to enjoy ourselves again."

"Oh, definitely," she spat out. "Why should we make a fuss, just because our boy isn't in his grave? It's so much easier just to stick a headstone over it and *pretend* he is. And let's get rid of his things as quickly as we can, so we can do something useful with his room. And by all means, let's have *fun;* God forbid that we should waste time mourning. With any luck it won't be any time at all before we forget that he ever lived!"

144

"Molly . . . we'll never forget and never stop grieving, but he *is* dead. I wish—"

She stood up and stalked off toward her bedroom. David and Stan both started to follow, and then neither did. David didn't know what he could do for her, and he guessed his father felt the same. Fleeing the house, he caught a bus back to Ybor City and spent the rest of the night lying in the attic, staring at the darkness.

He didn't want to go back, but he found he couldn't stay away. He couldn't just abandon them that way, his mother a shrew and his father lost and deserted. If he couldn't help, he owed it to them to at least bear witness to their misery. So tonight he'd returned.

He was just turning the corner when his parents' old Pacer backed out onto the street. His father drove by alone; there was probably a problem at the store.

If his dad had known Molly intended to go out, he would have left her the Pacer. But by the time David limped down the block to the foot of the driveway, she was climbing into the truck.

Oh God, what if she was sneaking out to commit suicide?

Usually she drove cautiously, but the pickup was accelerating rapidly before it even cleared the garage. Damn his father for backing it in; she wouldn't have to stop to take it out of Reverse. He dove as it sped by, caught his twisted foot on the side panel and slammed down inside on his shoulder. Certain that she'd felt the jolt, he checked to make sure he was still a phantom, but she never stopped to see what had happened.

For the next few minutes his guts churned and he wrung and kneaded the tarp. He was less than three feet away from her, but if she suddenly swerved

145

to crash he wouldn't be able to stop her.

But once she turned off East Hillsborough into the tangle of streets between Nebraska and Fifty-sixth, she slowed to a crawl. A collision at that speed wouldn't kill her, so maybe she wasn't suicidal after all. His dry eyes pulsed with relief.

But if she wasn't trying to destroy herself, what *was* she doing?

When he saw the laundromat, he understood.

Since the police couldn't find his body, she'd decided to search the area surrounding the cemetery until she found it—or at least the ghouls who'd supposedly stolen it—herself. She had to do it on the sly, because if his dad found out he'd think she'd gone crazy.

And oh God, she *had*. What if she never got better? She could spend her life driving up and down these streets.

The truck accelerated. Soon the squat houses and grubby little businesses gave way to a low concrete wall and the field of trees, slabs, and monuments beyond.

She parked a few feet from the wrought-iron gate. It was padlocked, but she had less trouble than he'd had hopping over the wall.

He didn't want to follow. How could he stand to trail her invisibly through a graveyard while she desperately tried to find him? But this was all his fault; if he just turned away he wouldn't be any better than Carter.

Silent as a specter herself, Molly made a long, meandering circuit of the cemetery until at last she arrived at his grave. They'd filled it in again, and if it weren't for his grandfather's marker he might not have recognized it. She stood staring at the oblong for a moment, then swayed and flopped down right on top of it.

146

A tear ran down her cheek, glistening like quicksilver in the moonlight; and she started picking idly at the grass. She plucked a single blade, paused, pulled another. Then several at once. Again and again and again, snatching them out as quickly as she could. At last she sunk her fingers into the soil itself.

For an instant he *knew* that if she kept digging she'd uncover his corpse, its eyes and mouth filled with dirt; he lunged forward and touched her shoulder.

She lurched to her feet and slapped him.

The blow snapped his head to the side; his David White mask began to shred away. Clinging to it desperately, he couldn't defend himself. She slapped again, clawed, kicked, punched, and then he was flat on his back with her knees digging into his chest and her fists hammering his face. "Where is he?" she hissed. "Where is he where is he *where is he?*"

When he was finally certain he wouldn't lose his shroud he grabbed her wrists. "Where's who? Who are you and what are you talking about?"

"Don't play dumb!" she snarled, struggling to tear herself free. "You must be one of the ones who took his body!"

"My God, lady, do you think I'm some kind of a grave robber? Look at me; I don't have a shovel! And I'm alone; how far could I carry a cadaver by myself?"

The blaze in her eyes began to dim. "I . . . I . . . then what are you doing here?"

"Just wandering around. I like quiet places; they help me think."

"Oh no." He let her go, and she climbed off him. "Oh no, I'm sorry. Now you'll call the police."

"Nah. There was no harm done," he said as he sat up. "Besides, I'm trespassing too. But I think you owe me an explanation."

"I . . . I guess I do. My son died several weeks ago. Three nights after the funeral someone opened his grave and *took* him."

"That's terrible."

"I thought so too, but apparently the police think it's a big joke, because they haven't done anything about it. So I decided to . . . patrol and try to catch the grave robbers myself." She smiled crookedly. "Go ahead, tell me I'm insane."

"I don't think that, but has it occurred to you that if you did surprise criminals in the act they might hurt you? Besides, you—I wish I knew how to put this delicately—you might be better off not knowing what they actually did to the body."

"I've thought of all that. I know I'm not equipped to deal with hoodlums and it would kill me to find out that devil worshippers cut him up or ate him or used him for sex—listen to me, I sound like someone in one of those stupid horrible movies, but *somebody* stole him for *some* reason. In fact tonight I started to open his grave myself, because just for a second I had the feeling that maybe somehow he was still in it after all and if I proved it I could stop acting like a lunatic.

"But don't you see, I just have to know! Because what if they picked *him* to dig up because he *wasn't* dead?"

"Now wait! That—that's impossible!"

"No no no!" She sprang to her feet and started pacing. "You see, he died under very mysterious circumstances! What if he was really only drugged?"

"But a doctor must have examined him! Someone . . . I'm sure someone embalmed him!"

"They *said* they did, but what if they were *in* on it? What if that Carter Cavanaugh paid them off?"

"Please—"

148

"He's a strange one, he is. He's got secrets and I intend to find out what they are!"

"No! Please don't try! You've got to forget all this craziness or you'll get in terrible trouble!"

"I don't care; if you ever have a baby, you'll understand. Now I can't waste any more time here, so good night."

"Please . . . wait . . ."

She didn't look back.

Stop, he commanded, *stop, stop, STOP!*

She froze.

It made him feel dirty. She was his *mother;* it was *wrong* to control her like a puppet.

But it would be even more wrong to let her continue as she was, wretched and obsessed. If Carter caught her snooping, he'd kill her. So he put his hands on her shoulders and stared into her eyes.

From this moment on, you'll never worry about what happened to David's body again. Your common sense will tell you that he must have been dead when they buried him, and instead of fretting over what became of his remains you'll think of him happy up in Heaven.

You'll always love him, but you won't be sad and lonely for him. You have me now and I'm going to fill the hole he left in your life. I love you, and we're going to be great friends.

She made a choking sound and started to collapse. When he clutched her to him she writhed in his embrace, saliva foaming from her lips.

Oh God oh God what had he done? *Don't,* he begged her, *please, I'm sorry, don't!*

Finally her convulsions subsided to twitching; her eyes blinked open. "What . . . happened?" she whispered.

149

"You had some kind of fit. Are you all right now?"

"Think . . . so." He tried to set her back on her feet, but she reeled drunkenly sideways and he had to catch her again. "Will you help me . . . go home?"

"Sure, but— I mean, I think you *should* go home, but don't you want to look around any more?"

Her whole body clenched and shuddered; for an instant he was sure she was going to have another seizure, but then she relaxed. "David's with God," she said dully. "I have to accept that and stop acting silly. I think I can stand up now."

"Okay."

"With God," she muttered. "With God" She took a faltering step and nearly tripped over her father's marker. "Great friends with God. I don't want to stay here any longer."

He took her hand. At first she stumbled along as unsteadily as he did, but by the time they reached the truck her gait was almost normal.

Chapter Twenty-two

They met in front of Banana Republic, under the dead glass eyes of the fake giraffe. With her corona of silky hair glowing in the lamplight, Liz looked like an angel. Although David had brushed his teeth even more diligently than usual, for some reason he could still taste blood; he had to keep reminding himself that she wouldn't.

"You're early," he said.

She smiled at him, but only for a moment. "I know; we finished sooner than Carter expected. Want to walk around for a little while before we go in the movie?"

"Sure." He started to reach for her hand, then snatched his own back and wiped it on his pants instead.

They wandered silently down the sidewalk, past couples eating blackened grouper under Campari umbrellas and windows full of dive gear, gowns, and Godiva chocolates. As David White, he'd always been glib and confident, but suddenly he couldn't think of anything to say.

She paused to inspect some diamond jewelry glittering on green velvet. "I used to love these stores." She sighed.

"Used to?"

"I guess maybe I still do, it's just—I don't know."

"Look, something's obviously bothering you, so why

don't you tell me about it. It's something to do with Carter, isn't it?"

"Not exactly."

"In other words, yes."

"Why are you so down on him?"

"I . . . I'm not, really, but—"

"I admit that he helped some of the group learn . . . *uncomfortable* things about themselves, but you don't blame the messenger because the news is bad."

He couldn't see a way to disagree, not without denouncing Carter or revealing that David White, who'd supposedly studied Wicca on the Isle of Man, Sufism in Alexandria, and shamanism on the Fort Berthold Indian Reservation, didn't believe in the New Age. "Well, maybe. How bad was your news?"

"It wasn't, it just—I guess I'd better tell you the whole thing from the beginning. In my private sessions I've been working on Tibetan overtone chanting, to—"

" 'To achieve mind-body resonance and tune the subtle body,' " he said, quoting Carter.

"Right, and I hadn't been doing very well at it. Carter said I was unconsciously holding back because I was afraid of having the same kind of experience some of the others have had."

"Then maybe you've got a smart unconscious."

"But we both know you have to open yourself up or you can't advance. Anyway, tonight Carter gave me a little glass of mead because he thought it would help me relax, and then we sat down on the carpet and started chanting.

"I guess the drink did help me, because before long I felt myself sinking into a deeper trance than I'd ever been in before. Energy flowed up my spine and my chakras popped and tingled one by one. The chanting became . . . independent of us. Instead of us making

152

it, it surrounded and suffused us, like the air.

"Then I started to leave my body."

"One second I was looking Carter in the face and then my point of view bobbed higher and I was staring down at the top of his head. I felt myself . . . slipping free, like the inside of my body had been greased. I'd never projected before and didn't expect to then, so I was scared. I tried to stay anchored, but it wasn't any use; a moment later I was floating free with a silvery cord running from one of my belly buttons to the other.

"I screamed, but Carter couldn't hear me. When I realized he didn't know what was happening, I got even scareder. Then I fell out of the world.

"I don't know how else to describe it. Suddenly the room was gone and I was plummeting down through black and yellow smoke with my cord streaming out behind me. The smoke stank like every phosphate pit and paper mill in the world all rolled into one; it made my eyes and throat burn. All around me I could hear huge machines roaring and grinding and pounding.

"I understood what had happened. Because I'd panicked, I'd fallen onto a lower plane, just like Steve did. I started chanting my mantra again, hoping it would control my fear, and after a while I got calmer and didn't feel like I was falling as fast. Maybe eventually I could have lifted myself out if I'd been left alone.

"But I wasn't. I heard metal clashing and then something swooped out of the smoke. It looked like a devil with flapping bat wings, like a Notre Dame gargoyle, but it wasn't flesh or even stone; it was made of a thousand jagged scraps of junk. Its eyes were cracked red plastic rectangles with something glowing behind them, like taillights. There was a Hawaiian Punch can

153

in the middle of its right forearm and a Georgia license plate in the center of its stomach. Its fangs were screws and bent rusty nails, and I think it was drooling and sweating oil." She shuddered, and he wanted to pat her shoulder.

"I went crazy with terror again. The thing flew over me, grabbed my cord, and started biting it, and when it did, pain ripped through me. I knew it was killing me, that if it cut my lifeline I'd be trapped there forever, but there was nothing I could do; I couldn't even hit at it because it was about ten feet above me."

"Jesus, I thought you said you didn't have a really bad experience!"

"I didn't, because just then a shaft of clear white light shone down from overhead. But it wasn't just a light; it erased the smoke and noise and left a clean silence in their place. The metal thing didn't dissolve, but it screeched, let go of my cord, and flapped away.

"Two beautiful naked people floated down." She was smiling now, her eyes wide and sparkling bright. "They *were* the light; it was shining from their bodies. The woman caressed my cord, and suddenly it wasn't frayed anymore and my pain went away. Then they drifted closer and, oh David, I saw that they were my *parents!*"

He knew they'd died in a plane crash when she was eleven. "Are . . . are you sure? Sometimes on the astral—"

"I'm sure. They were totally transformed, I mean, they were like Greek gods, but I could tell. Can you imagine how it felt to see them again, to see them like *that?* Happy doesn't say it; it was rapture! They each took one of my hands and we went flashing up, out of Hell and into the universe where they live now, so they could take me sightseeing.

"Their world is an endless deep blue sky with a flat green planet floating in the center. There are dragons sleeping in its caverns and mermaids frolicking in its oceans, and all the animals can talk. It's a clean world, with no pollution and no cruelty or poverty either, because the people are wise and kind and know how to use mind power to make the few things they need.

"The planet is so lovely that nearly everybody lives there—Mom and Dad live in a little cottage beside a beach with sparkling pink and amber sand—and some people spend all their time there, but the artists often work out in the void. Away from the commonage they're free to create anything they can imagine, and they build little island moons filled with marvels, games, and jokes.

"I wish I could tell you about every wonderful thing I saw, but that would take years and I couldn't do it all justice even then. So I'll just say that I felt like I was wandering through every beautiful poem and fairy tale that ever was.

"This will sound a little crazy, but being there with my parents was . . . intoxicating, so much so that I sort of forgot I didn't *belong* there. I was horrified when Dad told me I had to leave; there was so much more to see, and so many things I hadn't told them! I cried and begged, but it wasn't any use; Mom said they'd already bent the rules by keeping me with them as long as they had. They each kissed me and an instant later I was back in my physical body.

"Time runs differently when you're projected. It seemed to me that I'd been gone for hours, but it had really only been a few minutes; my body had never stopped chanting and so Carter never realized anything unusual had happened until that second, when I kind of wailed and toppled over.

"After that, of course, he was worried, but I couldn't bring myself to let him fuss over me or to explain what had happened; I needed to be alone to sort it out for myself first. I told him that, and did my level best to convince him I was all right, and finally he left.

"Actually, I wasn't all right; as soon as the door shut I started sobbing and couldn't stop for a long time. You told me you lost your mom and dad, so maybe you understand why. I tried to tell myself that I should be happy, not sad, because I'd been given a wonderful gift; how many live kids get to visit their parents in Heaven, even once? But I couldn't talk myself into feeling good because everything around me was so ugly.

"You see, once you've gotten used to a higher plane, earthly things don't look the same anymore. All the colors in my apartment were either dull and muddy or hideously garish; the green carpet reminded me of some kind of poison fungus, and the bright red *K* on my cereal box gave me an instant headache. My sketches and paintings were vulgar and pathetic compared to the treasures on the moon-islands and my Wyeth and Dali prints weren't much better. And when I caught a glimpse of myself in the mirror by the front door, I didn't see a spirit made of rainbows but a blemished animal that has to chew and snot and pee.

"After a while I couldn't stand my place anymore, so I took a walk, but outdoors things were even nastier. The air reeked of car exhaust, and the gutters were full of soda cans and McDonald's hamburger wrappers. Cars roared by and stereos howled; every sound was unbearably strident, and all the headlines on the newspapers in the vending machines were gloating over war and murder.

"All the foulness beat at me until I started feeling like I was going to throw up, and my head pounded like it was going to explode. I remember deciding there was really no difference between our world and the plane where the junk creature lived, and then I must have more or less blacked out.

"I came to sitting on a parked car. Apparently my mind had readjusted to being here, because things looked all right again. I remembered we were supposed to go to the movie and drove on down.

"But even though the world doesn't . . . *grate* on me like before, it's still not really okay. Everything seems kind of stale and hollow, and I'm not sure I want to live the same kind of life anymore."

"What do you mean?"

She turned to look at the diamonds again. "Up until now my life has had a spiritual side and a worldly side. I studied New Age, but I was also preparing for a career in commercial art. I planned to make a bunch of money and spend it on gorgeous clothes and vacations on the Riviera.

"But now I don't know if I care about success and material pleasures. Why should I, when I know there's a better world next door to ours, where every day's full of miracles and nothing's ugly and I could paint better than any artist on this plane ever has and be with my mom and dad? Studying New Age got me there once, and maybe if I do it full-time I can go back again and again!"

"So your idea is to drop out of school, drop all your friends and interests that don't involve the occult, and become some kind of cloistered New Age nun?"

"Well . . . yes, you could put it that way. I haven't

decided to, but I'm thinking about it."

He grabbed her hand. "Come on, run!"

"What? Why?"

Instead of answering, he lurched off down the sidewalk on his mismatched legs, tugging her along behind. Once she really started running it was a struggle to keep up with her; his dead muscles throbbed and the world rocked sickeningly back and forth. Their feet hammered the pavement, and strollers stepped out of their path and turned to watch them go by.

He didn't let her stop until they'd circled the entire shopping village. "Well," she gasped, her breasts heaving and her hair disheveled, "what was that all about?"

"Tell me everything you feel."

She knew how he wanted her to answer; Wally had done a lot of "body awareness" training in group. "Okay. My face is hot, and there's perspiration under my arms. Your hand's squeezing mine. My heart's pumping hard and I'm panting; my lungs burn a little as the air goes in and out. I'm thirsty, and my legs are quivering. I feel . . . exhilarated."

"Did you feel anything like any of that when you were with your parents?"

"Well, not really. I told you, it was like our bodies were made of light."

"Yeah. Look, Liz, I know there are wonderful things beyond the veil; that's why I study New Age too. But you have to remember that the world you visited is the world of the *dead*. Nobody there can suck down a Coke to quench his thirst or exercise a living, healthy, flesh-and-blood body until it tingles and aches. That's okay for the spirits that belong there; it's time for them to set aside those particular pleasures and move on to other things. But it's not okay for you.

"What I'm getting at is, don't you think God made

158

you alive for a reason? I mean, He's given you a chance to savor everything *this* world has to offer, and I can't believe He wants you to spend the rest of your time here sitting in a closet in the lotus position."

"I . . . I see what you're saying, and it does make sense. I don't *want* to hate life; I'm just worried that it's *spoiled* for me."

"Look at the moon. Look at those treetops swaying in the breeze and these peonies in this planter. This world's full of beautiful things too; if garbage is encroaching on them, that just makes them all the more precious. Enjoy them, and try to defend them when they need it; don't turn your back on them!"

"You're right; I should try."

"Damn right you should! Throw yourself into things! Eat, drink, dance, sing, laugh at Steve Martin! Kiss somebody!" He started to pull her close.

Gently but firmly, she pushed him away. "Please don't."

"Too soon?"

"No. Yes. I mean—did you think this was a date?"

"Well, yeah, I asked you—"

"I didn't realize you were 'asking me out.' I thought it was just friends getting together; I even invited Wally, Sarah, and Steve to meet us at the theater."

He stared down at the peonies. "Oh."

"I'm sorry, but I truly didn't understand. It never occurred to me that you'd think I was . . . available when you've heard me talk about Steve a million times."

Something flared inside him, and he grabbed her by the forearms. It was almost like being controlled by the thirst; he knew he shouldn't do it, but he couldn't stop. "No. I'm not going to let you turn me down! I

159

look good now—I mean, I look as good as he does—and I understand you and care about the same things you do!"

She squirmed. "You're hurting me!"

"Do you think he could have helped you the way I just did? We belong together, I know we do, I'll prove it!" He dragged her close again.

She slapped him. "Let me go!"

Shocked back to his senses, he released her. "Oh, God, I'm sorry!"

"You ought to be! Yeah, you did help me, but that doesn't mean you own me!"

"I know," he said, utterly abashed. "I don't know why I acted like that. I've never—ever—done anything like it before."

"I believe you," she said, less angry now. "And I still like you, and we can still be friends. But that's *all*. It might have been different if I'd met you first, but I didn't."

His eyes ached. "Sure. I understand. Whatever you say."

Silent now, they plodded back toward the theater.

Steve, Wally, and Sarah were standing on the brightly lit sidewalk in front of the box office. David discovered that he wanted to turn and stride away, to disappear into the night and never see any of them again, but he made himself smile, wave, and continue forward.

Sarah groaned, fumbled for Wally's arm, and collapsed, cracking her skull against the pavement.

Liz broke into a run. David instantly surmised that Carter was lurking nearby and had paralyzed Sarah with his mesmerism. His disappointment and humiliation displaced by fear, he peered wildly about, but the elder vampire was nowhere to be seen.

Wally stooped over the fallen woman. His arm slipped further out of his sleeve, exposing the huge black widow spider inked on his wrist.

Chapter Twenty-three

His headache and the grinding pain in his joints were worse than usual and the bus ride seemed to take forever. Maybe it was because he was so anxious to talk to his mother. To see his father too, if only he'd warm up to David White.

But he hadn't. When he answered the door he was glowering, his eyes bloodshot and his breath beery. "You might as well come in," he growled. "she's still getting ready for your *date*."

David knew he could probably change his dad's attitude with mesmerism, but he'd promised himself he'd win him over without it. "I wish you'd come along too."

"Really?" Stan flopped down on the couch and picked his can of Miller up off the end table. "I'm sure she doesn't. The times I tagged along, she barely spoke to me."

David sat down and crossed his legs, found that it made his crooked thigh hurt even worse, and uncrossed them again. "I hope it's not a problem for Molly and me to be friends. I'd like to be friends with *both* of you."

Stan grimaced. "I don't know if it's a problem. I can't tell if you're helping or hurting her."

"I'd never do anything to hurt her."

"No? Look, it's obvious what she sees in you; you

162

don't have to be Dr. Freud to figure out that she's using you as a stand-in for our son. But what do you see in her?"

"Well, for one thing, she's a great duplicate partner."

"Give me a break. When you met her you didn't even know a bidding system."

"No, but I'd always wanted to learn—Okay, that's bullshit. The truth is, I can't really explain why I like Molly so much. I only know that when I saw her sitting on your son's grave looking so pathetic, it touched something inside me."

"What a warm human being you are."

The temptation to use mind control came buzzing back like a persistent fly. "Do you think I'm going to try to get money from her or something?"

"All I know is this is a strange situation and you're a strange guy. How come you just happen to have the same name and the same friends as my boy and you just happened to run into Molly at night in a cemetery when she was in a bad way? How come such a dashing world traveler doesn't have a car? Why won't you show Molly where you live, and why don't you ever turn up until a couple hours after sundown?"

God damn it, he didn't need this! Not tonight, not when he was so sore and already had another problem on his mind. Maybe . . .

A door in the back of the house clicked open; footsteps came creaking down the bedroom hall.

"I think she's ready," David said. "Do you want to keep discussing this in front of her?"

"No; you know damn well I don't want to risk upsetting her. But remember," he continued, his voice dropping to a whisper, "I've got my eye on you!"

163

He smelled her a moment before she stepped into view; her perfume seared his hypersensitive nostrils. She was wearing a fancy red dress and high heels, with a gold bracelet on her wrist, pearls looped around her neck, and diamonds dangling from her ears; she looked like she was going to an elegant soiree, not a bridge game at a recreation center.

"Oh, David," she gushed as she rushed across the room to hug him, "you look so handsome tonight! All the other ladies will be jealous."

He usually liked it when she touched him, but not now, not with his father glaring; he squirmed free as soon as he could. "Uh, you look good too. I was just trying to convince Stan to come along with us."

She didn't even glance at his father. "Fine, if he wants to."

Stan snorted. "Forget it. I don't guess you *kids* need some old man following you around."

"Then let's hit the road," she said, taking David's hand. He wished she'd kiss his dad goodbye like she used to, or at least say goodbye, but all her attention was on him.

As usual, she asked him to drive. As he was backing the Pacer out into the street, she squeezed his forearm and said, "I always feel good when I'm with you! Can you come back tomorrow night?"

"Uh, no, I've got plans. Can I talk to you—"

"How about the next night? Please?" She sounded like a wheedling little girl.

"Yeah, okay, but only if you're sure it'll be all right with Stan."

It took her a second to answer; he had the crazy feeling that she was trying to remember who Stan was. "Oh, he won't mind."

"Are you sure? Before you came in tonight I got

164

the feeling he doesn't much like having me around."

"Damn him!" she exploded. "How dare he make you feel unwelcome! When we get home—"

"No, no, please. Don't be mad at him! He wasn't mean or nasty or anything; you're missing the point! I'm just worried that maybe he feels neglected."

"You're sweet to worry about someone who isn't even friendly to you."

"Look, I'm sure you're really nice to him, but maybe you should be extra nice for a little while, just to make sure he knows you still love him. He's probably still all torn up over your son's death."

"Well, as far as I've noticed, he's fine, but if you think it's a good idea, then of course I will."

He wondered if she'd really follow through. "Thanks. Could you do something for me, too? I need you to give me some advice."

"I'll be glad to! If you have a problem, I'll help you in any way I can!"

"I appreciate it. I can't be very specific about what's happening, but I'll describe it the best I can. I have some gullible friends who've fallen under the influence of a con artist. They could get burned pretty badly if he keeps on deceiving them. I could try to protect them, but it probably wouldn't help and it might really mess up my own life. Do you think I have an obligation to interfere?"

"No, absolutely not."

Just like that, no? Where was the woman who'd read him storybooks about the Apostles and the Founding Fathers? "But . . . why not?"

"Because your happiness is the most important thing in the world. If you made yourself miserable it would just about kill the people who really love you."

165

He turned his head. She was gazing at him raptly; in the darkness she looked like a mannequin with empty, ravenous eyes.

Chapter Twenty-four

The co-ed in the Burger King uniform sat slumped forward in her carrel, her head cradled in her arms and bracketed by stacks of books. Her soft buzz of a snore was nearly inaudible.

Not so Carter's voice; it reverberated across the hushed, brightly lit room like a gunshot. David winced even though he knew no one else could hear it.

"Now here's a serious scholar," Carter said. He pinched a strand of her dull blond hair between thumb and forefinger and lifted it aside to expose her nape; she twitched and shuddered but didn't awaken. "Attending classes all day, slaving away at a menial job in the evening, then burning the midnight oil till she collapses. Such industry rebukes the ants and honeybees."

Once again David tried to begin saying what he'd come to say; once again the words stuck in his throat.

"But she's not the most impressively ardent student in the room," Carter continued, sauntering away past a huge globe and rows of eight-foot bookshelves; David, limping hurriedly after, narrowly avoided a collision with a gangling black kid dressed in gym shorts and a university T-shirt. "For a textbook example of gallant determination in the face of adversity, consider this lad in the corner."

The boy sprawled in a motorized wheelchair. His limbs were as withered as Carter's and as twisted as

David's right leg; his head lolled to the left. It took his trembling fingers fifteen seconds to turn a page. When he spoke his voice was a strangled slur; his study partner couldn't understand him until he'd repeated himself twice.

"Who could blame this wretch if he spent his life on the dole?" Carter asked. "But he won't; he's driven to achieve, to become an inspiration to cripples everywhere. What a triumph when he's handed his diploma."

"Why are you talking this way?" David asked. "What are we doing here?"

"Shopping for my next meal; I'll be thirsty again in a few days. When I'm in a certain mood, I enjoy selecting appropriate prey in advance."

David turned away, gripped a gray metal shelf, and squeezed until it groaned; a girl with shiny black hair and wooden, pink flamingo earrings looked up, peered around puzzledly, then shrugged and returned to her reading. A moment later the words finally started stumbling out. "I . . . I have to talk to you about something."

"No, really? And here I thought you'd asked to join me on my peregrinations simply because you enjoyed my company."

"I want you to leave the people in the group alone; there are billions of other mortals you can play with."

"Yes, and when I deal with strangers I kill or maim whomever I choose whenever I please; my victim has no say-so in the matter. Our friends are considerably more fortunate: they needn't play my games if they don't want to and I won't lay violent hands on them even if they do. Some will even benefit."

"Give me a break."

"But it's true. Sarah's fat, so it will do her good to

168

fast, and once Wally's fully armored against evil spirits, it should do wonders for his self-confidence."

"You're turning him into a freak!"

"But with his full cooperation, which was actually quite easy to obtain. He knew the Burmese use tattoos as talismans, so when he saw himself under the needle in his vision, the idea didn't seem utterly bizarre. And after the fire, the burglary, and all his other trials, he was desperate enough to try anything."

"Look, I want to buy you off. With a secret. If I tell you something you haven't already thought of yourself, and if you agree it's valuable information, will you leave everyone I care about alone?"

"What an intriguing and unlikely proposition; I accept."

"Thank you. The secret is that I've found the perfect victims. Maybe it never occurred to you, but big modern cities are full of people who are brain damaged and terminally ill. Whenever I need blood, I kill someone who's suffering and can't really think anymore."

"Which makes you the first vampire vegetarian."

"You wouldn't laugh if you understood—"

"But I do. Because you're taking lives which you consider worthless, you don't feel guilty, and you think that if I did the same, I wouldn't either. You remember that I embraced wickedness largely because I knew I was fated to commit monstrous acts whether I wanted to or not, and by releasing me from that necessity, you're offering me the chance to become a virtuous fellow again."

"Well . . . yeah."

"I don't want it; even if I agreed that you aren't doing evil, I wouldn't emulate you. Cruelty truly is my only pleasure and my only solace; if I renounced it, I'd have nothing left but pain. I might even start repenting my past atrocities, and I suspect that if I did, I'd go quite mad."

"But—"

"Sorry, but I'm simply not interested. Now that I've spurned the carrot, would you care to brandish the stick?"

"I swear I didn't want to."

"If I were a fledgling confronting a master, I wouldn't either."

"Okay, we both know I'm no match for you. But there are humans crazy enough to believe that Carter Cavanaugh is a vampire. If I told them about you and they broke into your house during the day, you'd be in deep shit."

"Perhaps I should destroy you before you can."

"In a way I already have. I've written letters that'll be opened if I disappear."

"You needn't vanish just because I've killed you."

"Bull. Even if you knew the people holding the letters, you couldn't impersonate me because you don't know what David White looks like."

Carter laughed, his yellow fangs glinting. "Touché; you've grown a bit more clever since you died. I don't believe you'd speak or record my secret; you'd endanger yourself almost as much as me. But I confess I'm reluctant to bet my life on it. I wonder if we can work out a compromise."

"What kind of a compromise?"

"I don't know yet; let's wander back outdoors and stroll while I think about it."

Outside on the campus grounds they could talk without being overheard, so David stepped behind a pine tree to exchange his ghost-mask for the semblance of life. An instant later the world tilted and spun; Carter caught him just before he fell.

170

"Are you all right?"

"I guess so. I got dizzy and weak for a second, but it's going away now." He concentrated again; the effort made his head throb, but his veil dropped into place.

"I apologize; I'd forgotten how difficult it is for a novice to remain imperceptible for more than a few minutes. Tell me, how are you and Liz getting along?"

"Uh, okay, I suppose. I mean, I haven't thought that much about her since I . . . changed."

"Come now. I've already proven myself a good sport by accepting the possibility that your indiscreet correspondence actually exists. You mustn't expect me to swallow another whopper."

Another wave of nausea swept through David, his stomach churned and the moon lurched. After it passed, he said, "Even if I did still think of her as something more than a friend, do you think I'd tell you?"

"If you'd like to confide in someone, who else is there?"

"You must think I'm crazy. You made me a vampire, you hurt—Okay, look, I *will* tell you, just so you won't bug me about it anymore. I asked her out, but she wouldn't go. She said she's serious about Steve."

"Assuming that David White is handsome, I suspect that if you persist, you might change her mind."

"I don't want to. After she told me where I stood, I did a lot of thinking about what I'd been trying to do. I'd always figured that I couldn't keep her forever, but I thought that for a while we could kiss and hold hands, spend time together and share things. Now I see that it would have been selfish and mean to sucker her into a relationship that could never grow into what she expected it to. It would have been unfair to her and frustrating for both of us, and when she fi-

171

nally left, it would have torn me apart."

A lithe, grinning girl on a bicycle whizzed by, her cut-off jeans stretched tight over her bottom and her bare legs pumping; Carter turned to watch her recede into the darkness. "My poor, naive boy. You need an advisor so desperately, I almost regret not allowing you to share my home. You could give her more than any living man."

"That's nuts."

"Far from it. If you hadn't died a virgin, you'd realize you could bring her to climax with your mouth or hand just as well as with a functional penis."

David snorted. "I'm not so virginal that I don't understand *that*, but the woman expects the man to get hard and penetrate her, doesn't she? If he doesn't, the experience isn't complete for her and she knows that something's wrong with him."

"But she'll perceive an erection if you will her to, David. She'll discover a cock like Hercules's between your thighs if that's what you choose to show her. And when she feels it thrusting inside her, and you heighten her passion and sensations with your mesmerism, she'll go absolutely wild.

"The curious thing is, so will you. Male orgasm only lasts a second and it's a relatively insignificant part of the pleasure of lovemaking. The greater ecstasy derives from one's awareness of the female's loss of control, from the intoxication of mastery as you drive her mad with desire, and you're better able to do that now than you were when you were alive."

David felt faint and hot; he brushed his fingers across the parchment-dry skin of his forehead half expecting to find it slick with sweat. He vaguely suspected there was something fallacious in what Carter was telling him, but he couldn't make out what.

172

"Okay, maybe, but . . . but she doesn't want me."

"*Make* her want you."

"I couldn't, not Liz."

"You're already warping her perception; what's the difference between that and another form of mind control? Our mesmerism's just a more efficient form of the deceptions and manipulations the living practice on one another all the time anyway. But if you're squeamish about tampering with her emotions, there's another way. Turn Steve into someone who no longer desires her. Or make him behave boorishly, so she'll discard him. After all, he humiliated you."

A part of David didn't want to do it, but there was a bitter, lonely, aching part that did. Hadn't he thrown away life itself because Liz scorned him when he was human? Didn't that give him a right to claim her? What would be the harm, if he really could delight her more than any mortal lover?

"I don't know," he mumbled after a time. "Maybe it would be all right; I'll have to think about it."

"Well, I wouldn't think too long. If she continues to achieve such spectacular results with her chanting, she may eventually become unavailable."

David's muscles tensed; pangs lanced up and down his body. "What's that supposed to mean?"

"My precognitive powers tell me that Liz will continue to visit her parents in Paradise and that communion will soon become the most important thing in her life. But after a few weeks, she'll lose the ability to astrally project herself. Devastated, she'll find herself willing to try absolutely anything to return to Heaven. Perhaps I'll reveal myself, and then she'll become an Olympian, since godlike beings such as ourselves can leave their bodies at will, or perhaps she'll simply commit suicide so she can take up residence in Mom and

173

Dad's cottage permanently; I haven't decided yet."

"*No!*" He grabbed Carter's shoulder and spun him around. "You leave her alone, she's mine!"

Carter dissolved out of his grasp. "I suggest you keep your hands to yourself."

"Listen to me: I won't let you hurt her."

"But the melancholy truth is you can't stop me; I'm more experienced and thus more powerful than you. And if you actually managed to mobilize a human posse, they probably couldn't stop me either; I've been eluding mortal hunters since the night I emerged from my grave. But since I'd really rather not have to bother, and since you're obviously more concerned about Liz than about any of the others, I think we can negotiate that compromise I mentioned."

"What do you mean?"

"Well, you must understand that I allowed you to resume associating with our friends so I could watch you squirm as I tormented them, and I'm not willing to relinquish that pleasure altogether. But I *am* willing to stop molesting Liz, if you'll agree not to interfere when I toy with Wally, Sarah, and the others. Is it a deal?"

"I . . . I don't know . . . I mean, how can I just stand by—"

"If you don't agree, *no one* will be safe, including the insolent puppy who threatened me and his own true love. Would you find that preferable?"

After a moment, his dry eyes burning, David shook his head.

Chapter Twenty-five

The round, mournful face in the lithograph was blue on one side and yellow on the other; David flinched and tore his eyes away.

". . . these over here are mine," continued Liz, waving at the sketches, oils, and watercolors hanging above the TV and stereo. "And I guess that concludes our tour. Shall we sit down?"

She hadn't shown him the bedroom; she said it wasn't picked up.

"I like your work," he said as they stepped around an easel with an unfinished seascape on it on their way to the couch. "I wish I had the talent to be an artist."

"You might not, if you knew how frustrating it can be. A lot of my stuff turns out crappy, and even when something's halfway decent, like those, I'm never really satisfied."

"But you must like it, or you'd quit." He gingerly extended his arm along the back of the sofa; she didn't pull away.

"Oh, sure. Even when I was little, I knew it was what I wanted to do. How about you? Are you going to spend the rest of your life bumming around the world studying metaphysics?"

"I hope so. But lately I've been thinking I ought to

make a career out of it like a grown-up. Do you think I'd make a good anthropologist?"

"Sure! You could probably write the definitive book on witches or the Sufis."

He realized he didn't know what to say next; he was sick of spinning lies about Egypt and the Isle of Man. He really wanted to stop talking and make love, but he didn't know how to ask. Well, her dark eyes were sparkling and she was sitting close, so maybe he didn't need to ask in words. He started to enfold her in his arms.

She pushed him away.

He tried to keep his tone light. "You're not going to tell me this isn't a date, are you?"

"Of course not, but it's our *first* date. You know, I can't figure you out. When we talk, you're so charming and considerate but when you decide to get physical, you just sort of grab me and pounce. Why are you in such a rush?"

"I just like you."

"I like you too, but can't we take things a little slower?"

"I . . . sure."

"Great. Want to listen to some music?" He shrugged and she went over to the stereo. Fidgeting, his fingers drumming on his thighs, he looked restlessly around the room until his gaze fell on the lithograph again.

No, damn it, he couldn't take it slow, because after tonight Wally's face would be painted with outlandish colors too, and if he hadn't taken Liz to bed, he'd feel as if he'd allowed it to happen for no reason at all.

Besides, how long was he supposed to let her tease him?

He truly didn't want to force her; he hadn't even enjoyed turning Steve into a crude, gluttonous drunk.

176

But she did like him, she'd said so herself, so he wouldn't really be controlling her, just nudging her to do something she already wanted to do anyway.

When you turn around, he told her, *you'll realize that David White is the sexiest man you've ever seen. You'll* need *him to make love to you, need it tonight; you'll want him more than you've ever wanted anyone before.*

She went rigid, then swayed. For one awful moment he was afraid she was having a seizure, but she recovered her balance by clutching at the easel; the canvas fell off and landed facedown on the carpet. Ignoring it, moving tentatively at first, she selected and loaded a Heart CD, then turned and stared at him blankly.

After a few seconds she began to smirk. She pulled her sweater over her head, then unhooked her lacy white bra. Her breasts were almost as white, with wide brown nipples.

He sat paralyzed. He hadn't imagined it could happen so fast, or that she could seem so brazen.

When he didn't move, her smile began to wilt. She opened her arms beseechingly.

He shot up off the couch and stumbled toward her. "Yes, yes, I want you! You just caught me by surprise." Grinning again, she took his hand and led him to the bedroom.

The room was hung with more of her pictures, many of them unmatted and unframed, and it was as messy as she'd intimated, with paperbacks, sketchbooks, and discarded garments littering half the waterbed. She flung up the comforter and tumbled them to the floor, then kicked off her shoes and unbuckled her belt. She giggled when he turned his back to undress.

He always hated baring his corpse's body, and never more than now; when he opened his shirt, his stench ballooned up and flakes of gray flesh fell out. What if he got so excited he forgot to maintain his shroud, and she suddenly found herself embracing this twisted, festering thing? He should leave right—

Her fingertips glided down his ribs. She pulled down his jockey shorts and fondled him.

Trembling, his mouth hot and gritty, he turned. She was as beautiful as in his dreams; if only she'd speak . . . and smile like she'd smiled at Steve instead of leering.

But it didn't really matter. He pulled her close and kissed her.

She ground his shredded lips against his fangs; he gasped and shoved her away.

"I, I'm sorry," he stammered quickly, "cold sore, I'd forgotten it was there, don't kiss me on the mouth tonight, okay?" She nodded and drew him down on the bed.

She blew in his ear, then licked and nibbled her way down the mottled length of him; her tongue slid along the sutured fissure in his neck, then over skin like peeling paint and little pits of rot. When she lifted her head to smile at him, her mouth was smeared with slime; his guts churned and he had to close his eyes.

She kept hurting him. He asked her several times to be gentle, and he supposed she was trying, but still he twitched and winced at every touch. He knew his flesh was hypersensitive, but it was still hard to believe she couldn't make him feel good if only she weren't so damn clumsy!

The rawness in his mouth was creeping down his throat.

She took his shriveled, pustulate cock between her lips and squeezed; a bolt of agony drove up deep into his belly.

178

When the pain subsided, he realized he'd screamed and kicked her away; she was kneeling at the foot of the bed, crying. *Calm down,* he commanded, *everything's all right.* "God, I'm sorry," he growled aloud. "Sometimes when I'm really excited, I get ticklish. It'll go away in a minute; in the meantime, lie down and let me do you."

Obediently she flopped down on her back, and he started fumbling at her. He felt ignorant and awkward, risible, but he kept silently telling her he was the most beautiful, passionate, skillful lover she'd ever had, and she squirmed and wailed like an actress in a porno movie.

But for him it was no more exciting than cranking a meat grinder. He felt alienated, dizzy and queasy, and his mouth was on fire. He loathed the soft, useless blob jiggling between his thighs, the leprous fingers pumping in and out of her cunt; and he suddenly despised virile, handsome, *living* David White.

He despised the woman whining and bucking beneath him, too. He'd given up everything to have Liz, but somehow he'd been cheated because this slut certainly wasn't her. The Liz he loved would never have degraded herself by doing things that hurt and revolted him; she would have been sweet and tender and made him feel like a man.

He hated this bitch and he was thirsty.

He lunged forward, pinning her, grabbed her hair and reared up to rip her throat and—

He was staring into his mother's pale blue eyes.

He shrieked and recoiled. Her face, framed by chestnut hair and set atop tanned, youthful shoulders, gaped in shocked dismay; Liz's arm reached out to him. He lurched backward again and fell off the edge of the bed.

179

He curled up on the floor and shuddered until she stroked his arm; then he sobbed, clenched his fists, and made himself look at her.

She had Liz's features again.

He started to babble: "I'm sorry, oh God, please forgive—"

Single-minded as a machine, she smiled and reached for his crotch.

STOP! he roared, and she froze. *You don't want to have sex with David White anymore; right now you don't want or feel or think anything at all. In a second you'll go brush your teeth and take a shower, and then you'll go to bed and sleep. When you wake up you won't remember anything that happened tonight.*

Her face slack and, eyelids drooping, she rose and walked into the bathroom; a moment later, the faucet started hissing. Seething with rage and shame, he pulled on his clothes, stalked into the living room, and rummaged in her purse for her keys.

Chapter Twenty-six

David turned the corner a moment after the light turned red. When he looked down the crooked brick street, he slammed his fist down on his thigh, though underlying his frustration was a guilty pang of relief. Neither Carter's red Sentra nor Wally's blue Pinto was parked on this block, and if they hadn't come to the tattoo studio beside the skinhead bar, he had no idea where to find them.

But maybe they'd left their car elsewhere and walked here, just as he and Carter had an eternity ago. He swerved into a parking space behind two Harley David-sons and in front of a pawnshop with grilled windows full of shotguns, ghetto blasters, and saxophones; he switched off the ignition, and the Mazda chugged and shuddered into silence.

As he limped across the street, he started shivering again. He thought of what he'd done, and almost done, to Liz, then stepped up onto the curb and jerked open the door.

The front of the building was a tiny waiting room. Samurai, orchids, dragons, mermaids, and falcons, Flash designs rendered in vibrant colors, blazed across the walls. The linoleum was gritty with ash; the air smoldered.

The smokers slouched in molded plastic chairs. One was the Stoogeaphile, looking apelike as ever but now sporting long-tailed, intertwining comets down the length of one bare arm; some burned crimson and yellow, but others were only black outlines waiting to be filled in. Beside him sat a skinhead David hadn't seen before, a lanky, pimply kid with fingerless black leather gloves and handcuffs clipped to his belt, and across from him was a big-bellied giant in a biker's worn denim vest. He had tangled, shoulder-length hair, a Rasputin beard, and a picture of Marilyn Monroe kneeling naked in chains on his chest.

They all stared; no doubt clean-cut David White in his college-boy clothes looked out of place.

Stepping over their out-thrust legs, nearly tripping once, he hobbled quickly toward the curtained doorway in the far wall. Handcuffs sat up straighter and said, "Hey, you got to wait your turn," but he told him he was only looking for someone and pushed on through.

Wally sat trembling in an adjustable seat like a barber's chair. Leaning over him, stroking her fingertips down his pink, sweaty, *unmarked* face, was a thin young woman with feathery magenta hair; her arms were mazes of intricate floral patterns and her forehead and left cheek were emblazoned with Japanese calligraphy. Carter, a rotting scarecrow in a Brooks Brothers suit, sat on a doctor's examination table gazing out the window, one foot swinging.

After a second his head slowly twisted toward the doorway; as always, it was impossible to read any expression on his withered, eyeless face.

The others were peering at him, too. "D-David?" Wally asked uncertainly. Despite the choking haze of cigarette smoke, David could smell the alcohol on his breath. "What're you doing here?"

He thought again of Liz and managed not to falter. "I'm taking you home."

182

"What the hell's your problem?" the tattooist demanded.

"My friend doesn't know what he's doing."

"Bullshit; he's been here a dozen times before. Look, asshole, you don't just come barging in here and bother my customers. Get out *now.*"

"I would, if I were you," Carter murmured.

"I will, but I'm taking him with me."

Wally shook his head. "I can't leave; I've got to finish the ritual."

"Listen to me: the spirits don't want you to do this. He only made you think they do, as a sick practical joke; he wants you disfigured for the rest of your life!"

"Disfigured!" the tattooist screeched. "Okay, last chance: haul your ass out of here while you're still able."

Wally raised his hand. "Please, Kathy, let me handle this. David, I *know* I have to go through with this; my Sahu told me so. And Carter wouldn't hurt me; he's stood by me through all my troubles, and he's going to loan me the money to rebuild Illuminations. Now if you want to stay here and see me through my ordeal, that'd be great. But if—"

David lunged forward, brushing Kathy aside; she staggered back into a poster that read THIS MONTH'S SPECIAL—ALL PAIN ABSOLUTELY FREE! Ignoring Wally's fumbling attempts to push him away, he grabbed his shirt and ripped it apart.

Wally flinched. "The Sahu said it was the only way to control the forces that have been tormenting me. He said it would be a mortification—and purify me. *I was going to keep my shirt* on!"

In the center of his chest, Aradia, goddess of the Wiccans was writhing in the carnal embrace of six hideous demons; the Horned God, her consort, hung blinded and castrated, from an inverted cross. Behind him, other devils were torturing angels and bodhisattvas. There were skulls and infernal pentagrams on Wally's shoulders, and spiders, scorpions, snakes, flies, and rats crawling down his arms.

He'd turned his body into a billboard for satanism, a blasphemous mockery of everything he believed.

"If you put that garbage on your face, none of your old friends will have anything more to do with you," David told him. "You won't want anything more to do with yourself, either. Now, are you going to walk out of here with me right now, or do I have to carry you out?"

"I warned you," Kathy said. "Doug, Brad, Jim, get in here!"

"No, wait—" Wally began.

Out in the waiting room, chair legs scraped the floor and boots creaked. A moment later, the skinheads and the biker pushed through the curtain.

"This little shit bounced Kathy off the wall," Carter said; David realized that, although Wally saw the pale, elegant aristocrat he'd always known, the others must be seeing their skinhead buddy. "Maybe you guys should show him how we feel about that."

"No, please, he didn't mean any harm!"

"I don't give a damn what he meant," said Handcuffs. "Not if he put his hands on a lady. He needs a lesson, and you'd better stay out of it or you'll get one too!"

Wally opened his mouth to protest again, started to stand; Carter stared at him and he jerked and slumped back in his chair.

David started backing toward the wall, panic yammering in his mind. He doubted he could even beat the three mortals; his powers were too weak and unreliable. And if Carter got up off his padded table and joined the fight, he'd have no chance at all!

Something buzzed.

He spun around; Kathy had picked up an electric needle. "After they're done, I'm going to give you a little something to remember me by."

She thought she could spoil his pretty corpse's face! The absurdity of it somehow blunted his fear. He giggled crazily—and then they rushed him.

The biker reached him first, his huge fist looping around in a haymaker. David ducked and punched him in the stomach; he grunted.

Then Handcuffs was on his right, pummeling his ear and cheek, bashing his head to the side. The Stoogeaphile danced back and forth, waiting for an opening.

David's head was exploding with pain, his vision blurring. He swung twice, missed both times; the biker kicked him in the knee and he fell.

His veil began to dissolve. He clung to it desperately; whatever else happened, he *wouldn't* let these animals strip him naked!

Despite the kicking, stamping boots, somehow he managed to refocus the image in his mind. When he was sure he wouldn't lose it, he grabbed the biker's calf, dug his fingers into it as if it were wet clay, and ripped.

Blood showered; the giant squealed and stumbled back. Lurching to his knees, snarling, lashing out viciously, David drove the others back as well, then sprang to his feet.

The biker roared and lunged at him again. He silently shouted, *STOP!* But it didn't work.

So he blocked a punch, grabbed him by his crotch and neck, and swung him over his head. The other

185

mortals gasped and gaped; Carter, still lounging on the table, patted his mummified hands together in ironic applause. Then David threw the biker against the wall.

He hit with a boom, rebounded, landed in an inert, bleeding heap; framed photographs of tattooed men and women crashed down around him.

"Jesus!" said the Stoogeaphile. He tugged on his belt buckle; it came loose trailing a blade. Handcuffs pulled a blackjack out of his pocket.

David pivoted and snatched up a table; jars of ink and alcohol spun off and shattered. He tried to throw it —

—and a horrible, crushing pressure swelled inside his brain. The table slipped out of his bloody fingers and he fell back onto his knees in a puddle of pigment and broken glass.

Grinning, no doubt convinced they—or the biker— had seriously injured him, the skinheads closed in.

Get out, David screamed, *get out. I hate you. Freeze, hurt, DIE!* For an instant the paralysis abated. He started to lift his hands, but then Carter's power surged back full force and his body crumpled once more.

Handcuffs grabbed him by the hair, tilted his head back to expose his face, and started beating him. The first blow split open his cheek.

But then the pressure vanished; he could move again. He caught the descending arm, twisted it until it snapped, then flung his tormentor away. The Stoogeaphile's knife plunged into his shoulder, a white-hot piercing. He tackled him, threw him down, and pounded his skull against the floor.

Kathy dropped the whirring needle, wailed, and bolted, only to fall unconscious halfway through the curtain. Then Carter glanced at Handcuffs cowering in

186

the corner, laid his hand on Wally's shoulder, and they fell asleep too. "Would you like to kill anyone?" he asked.

David struggled to rise. His stressed, battered body was on fire, and he knew Carter knew it, but he tried not to let it show; he didn't want to look weak. "Just you. Why'd you release me?"

"Oh, I don't know; suddenly your brawl just seemed tedious, and I decided I'd rather talk than watch them maul you. Tell me about Liz. How did you feel when you recovered your senses and realized you'd converted her? Did you destroy her body, or is she going to return?"

For the first time in their association, David had the upper hand; at last *he* was the one who knew something the other didn't. It was too sweet a moment not to savor.

"I . . . I still can't believe it," he said with what he hoped was a convincingly anguished quaver in his voice. "Oh, God, if only I'd realized you were mesmerizing me that night outside the library! But I never dreamed that even you could be mean enough to make me kill the girl I loved!"

"Actually, I influenced you to accept my shameful bargain, and I fanned your lust, but I didn't make you go mad and take her blood. That's simply what happens whenever a vampire is foolish enough to essay unchastity."

"Really?" David asked, smiling despite himself. " 'Whenever?' Every single time?"

"In my experience." Carter cocked his head to the side. "You don't seem as . . . grief-stricken as you did a second ago."

"Because I *didn't* kill her, you son of a bitch! There was a part of me that didn't go crazy, and it found a

187

way to snap the rest of me out of my trance!"

Carter peered into his face for a few moments, then sketched a bow. "My sincere congratulations. Whoever could have imagined that *you,* out of all of us . . . Come live with me, David. Be my student and my friend."

"No way. I understand you now, Carter, so I know you'll never wish me anything but harm."

"Well, it was worth a try. I suppose we'd better decide where we go from here."

"Like I said, I'm taking Wally home."

"It won't solve anything. He'll still believe he needs his face marked."

"Convince him otherwise."

"Or else what? My dear young friend, you forget yourself. I admit you've grown a backbone, begun to develop your powers, and even, through some extraordinary fluke, won a tiny, transient victory over the thirst. It's all quite impressive, but it doesn't make you a match for me. I can destroy you any time I please."

"So go for it, if you can stand the thought of putting me out of my misery." He flicked a grain of broken glass off his blood- and ink-stained jeans. "I'd rather die than watch you hurt my friends again. But if you do, my letters will expose you."

Carter sighed. "Ah yes, your wretched letters. Perhaps I should have tried to mesmerize you into telling me whether they really exist when you first threatened me with them. But, as you may have discovered, subtly playing on someone's preexisting emotions, or even paralyzing him, is often relatively easy; compelling him to perform a blatantly self-destructive act such as disclosing a vital secret is immensely more difficult. Even mortals frequently resist that kind of nakedly injurious coercion, so it almost certainly wouldn't have worked

188

on you; the only effect would have been to alert you that I was tampering with your mind.

"I thought if you infected Liz, it would break your spirit and you'd stop opposing me. What a pity it didn't work out. But it hasn't, so I capitulate."

"What do you mean?"

"I mean that since you're willing to risk destruction and I'm loath even to risk inconvenience, you win. I'll stop molesting you and your associates. I'll even undo the damage I've already done—to the extent I'm able— just to prove I'm capable of losing graciously."

"You're giving in too easily; how can I trust you?"

The corpse-thing shrugged; its stained, jagged grin seemed to stretch even wider, but of course it was only a trick of the light. "I'll remain under duress, will I not? Besides, do you really have a choice?"

Chapter Twenty-seven

The gondola hung in a gulf of lights, white stars overhead and flashing multicolored bulbs and neon strips below. David could hear the barkers chanting, the rides clattering, balloons popping and calliopes moaning, but it all sounded faint and far away. The breeze and the slight rocking seemed to ease his headache and sore muscles, and for a moment he wished he could stay atop the Ferris wheel forever.

But if time froze and the ride never started revolving again, sooner or later Carter would slither out of *his* gondola. Crawling along the girders like a great brown spider, he'd climb from one car to the next, killing. He'd—

"You're clutching that bar for dear life," Sarah said. Oblivious to his unhealing lacerations, she put her hand over his. "You shouldn't have come up here if you're afraid of heights."

"I'm not, usually; it just sneaks up on me once in a while." Since he couldn't tell her what had really upset him, acrophobia was as good an excuse as any.

She nodded sagely, the midway lights sliding across her granny glasses; a strand of her graying brown hair slipped down her forehead. "I'll bet you had a terrible fall in one of your previous incarnations. I know a hypnotist who could regress you and help you work through the trauma."

190

"Hey, I'm not exactly like that guy in *Vertigo*."

"No, but I think you're more troubled than you realize."

"Gee, thanks."

"Now I don't mean you act crazy or anything like that. But you seem so jumpy all the time. Have you got any serious problems in your life?"

"Not really."

"Then it must be because of unfinished business from your past lives!" she said triumphantly. "Let me introduce you to Dr. Polk; you'll be amazed how much freer you'll feel after just a couple sessions."

"I'll tell you what: I'll think about it and let you know."

"That means forget it. Men! Even the ones who are supposed to be spiritually developed never ask for help or take advice until their problems get so bad they can't stand them anymore."

"That's because we're afraid we won't be able to sucker women into taking care of us if we look like we know how to take care of ourselves."

She snorted. "Well, you'd better take care of *yourself.* You're a jerk, but I've kind of gotten used to you." The wheel lurched and their car swooped toward the ground.

He wished there were someone who could help him relax. In the past month the various Sahus, ascended Lemurian hierophants, and deceased relatives had changed their tunes; and his friends' lives had more or less returned to normal. Wally was happily stocking the new Illuminations. He planned to have his chest and arm tattoos removed with laser surgery. It was going to be horribly expensive, but at least he wouldn't hate himself—or outrage his friends when he took his shirt off. And Sarah had stopped fasting but was dieting

191

sensibly and persistently for the first time ever; apparently Carter had bolstered her willpower with his mesmerism. In fact it was to celebrate their liberation from supernatural strictures and torments that the group had canceled their regular meeting in favor of an excursion to the fair.

But even though the elder vampire had proved as good as his word for once, David still couldn't bring himself to trust him; it seemed inevitable that Carter would attempt to destroy him if he ever ascertained that his letters and network of potential vampire hunters didn't actually exist.

But apparently Carter hadn't found it out, not yet, and maybe he never would. Perhaps one day he'd grow bored with trying and relocate to another city, where he could toy with mortals without any interference, and then David could finally feel secure. In the meantime, he guessed he'd just have to get braver or get better at covering up his fear.

The gondola whirled to the top of the wheel again, and from this lofty vantage point he saw Stan and Molly strolling down the midway arm in arm, grinning, chattering, eyes shining, enjoying the fair as they had every year he could remember. His dad was wearing an outsize cowboy hat, and his mom clutched a green-and-white, stuffed penguin.

The sight brought a lump to his throat. He wished he could greet them, but he wasn't a part of their lives anymore. The night after he'd carried Wally out of the tattoo studio, he'd relieved his mother of her unnatural affection for David White. He'd been afraid she'd become bitter and obsessed again, but instead she'd realized how badly she'd been treating Stan, and, horrified, had resolved to make amends. Stan had been eager to forgive her, and they'd set about rebuilding their marriage. Spying on them, David had been sure that one day they'd outlive their grief and be happy together.

Twice more around and the ride was over. David and Sarah were the first New Agers off; they waited outside the low metal fence for the others.

When Liz came through the gate, he gave her David White's most charming smile. "That view was fantastic. Anybody want to go again?"

She tried to meet his eyes, but couldn't. "Maybe later," she mumbled, then ducked behind Wally, interposing his body between them.

David swallowed and blinked away the pulsing in his eyes. She'd loathed him ever since the night he'd forced her into bed; she didn't remember it, but on some level she hadn't entirely forgotten it either, and now they couldn't even be friends.

"It needn't be this way," Carter whispered. David jumped; he hadn't realized the corpse-thing had even gotten off the Ferris wheel yet, let alone sauntered up beside him. "I'll rekindle her affection if you'd like."

"Forget it." He wouldn't have agreed even if he'd trusted him; he'd vowed he'd never tamper with anyone's emotions again unless he had to to survive. Which meant she'd despise him forever, but at least the knowledge he'd freed her from Carter's bondage would console him; he was looking forward to watching her lead a long and joyous life.

"Her existence would be more pleasant if your proximity didn't unnerve her."

"You promised to leave them all alone!"

"I promised not to harm her, and I was offering to help her, but of course I shan't meddle without my blackmailer's permission." He raised his voice so the mortals could hear. "Come along, my seers and

193

shamans, let's see what's down this way."

They ambled past a rumbling Himalaya and a snapping shooting gallery, then a funnel-cake vendor, a pizza stand, and a Mac and Ivy's Italian Steak Sandwich trailer. Sniffing the piquant, smoky air, Sarah started to open the voluminous paisley carpetbag that served her as a purse, then grimaced and snapped it shut again.

Beyond the refreshment stands, the midway suddenly seemed shabby. The crowd thinned out considerably, though plenty of crushed Coke cups and stained, crumpled paper napkins littered the ground. Floating in pools of shadow, green and yellow lights buzzed and flickered fitfully. A sloppily hand-lettered poster in front of the nearest attraction promised a look at a six-legged goat.

Overdressed and thus uncomfortably warm as usual, Kazuhide dabbed at his brow with a Kleenex, then opened his blazer and tugged at his tie. "I don't think there's much down here," he said.

"Ah, but you're mistaken," Carter replied. "This is the corner where they tuck away all the unique diversions that make an American carnival what it is. I'd never forgive myself if I permitted you to miss it."

As they set off down the lane, David shivered; suddenly he didn't want to follow. But he didn't know a reason why he shouldn't; it was just another anxiety attack, he told himself. Disgusted by his own timidity, he sucked in a deep breath and made himself hobble after the others.

Carter led them past the goat, the world's smallest horse, and a Haunted Mansion ringing with tinny shrieks and fiendish laughter. Beside it stood the Mirror Maze.

A teenage girl wearing clown makeup and a tiny

purple plastic derby sat in the ticket booth. Carter handed her a twenty. "This should pay for all of us," he said.

"You shouldn't," Kaz protested.

"Please, I want to. Come on, everybody! Mirror mazes are wonderful! I've loved them ever since I was a lad."

Obediently they began to file inside. Sarah took David's arm. "Let's make sure we stay together. It's no fun getting lost by yourself."

When they entered, David gasped.

"What is it?" she asked. "Don't tell me you're claustrophobic too."

"No, I just had a little stomach cramp for a second there. Too much cotton candy, I guess." Actually, he hadn't been prepared for the sight of twenty dead gray faces with sunken eyes and tattered lips staring at him, but damn it, he wasn't going to let it freak him out! He wouldn't give Carter the satisfaction; if his enemy could stand the mirrors, so could he. He pried his eyes open and strode forward.

For the next fifteen minutes they groped their way down coldly gleaming corridors, surrounded by an army of their twins. It was astonishing how a structure that looked so small from the outside could become so vast and disorienting once they were within. Repeatedly they met their friends, greeted them, and only then realized they were talking to reflections; twice they found themselves back at the entrance. Each time David wanted to run out but plunged back into the labyrinth instead.

Five Wallys grinned, waved, and vanished; David reached out, sure there was a mirror beside him, and found the space was empty after all. So he ushered Sarah through and they started down the next aisle. A moment later, Carter appeared behind them.

As usual, he stepped out of nowhere. Somehow even the mirrors had failed to betray his approach; his leering skull-face burst inside them all at once, as if they were shattering.

"Found the room in the center yet?" he asked.

"I thought the idea was to find the exit," Sarah replied.

"Ultimately, yes, but you wouldn't want to miss the curved glasses in the middle. They make one look delightfully grotesque. Although I'm afraid there are a few of us—prissy, aging bachelors and such—who don't need any help in that regard."

Sound bounced through the maze almost as unpredictably as light. For just an instant, beneath the whoops and giggles, it sounded like a child was crying.

"I wouldn't call a grown-up who still loves fun houses prissy," Sarah said.

"To the tell the truth, I lied about enjoying them when I was small. I'm sure I would have, but they hadn't been invented."

"I thought they had them way back before the turn of the century."

"They did, but I was born long before that. You see, I'm a vampire."

For a few seconds, David could only stare. Somewhere off to the left, someone was talking excitedly.

"That—that's kind of a silly joke," he stammered at last.

"Yeah," Sarah said, "and you sure picked the wrong place for it. Everybody knows vampires don't cast a reflection."

"But like so much of what 'everybody knows,' it isn't so," Carter replied. "Just as it isn't so that we possess an eerie alabaster beauty; we're actually walking carrion, nearly as decayed as if we'd remained quietly in our graves. We cast a sort of spell that prevents mortals from seeing us as we really are.

"And that's why we occasionally do have a problem with mirrors. The human mind resists our glamor, and the more complex and comprehensive the illusion, the more easily you penetrate it. Thus, weakened and maladroit undead have been known to fumble the task of shielding both their images and themselves."

Somewhere behind them, Wally yelled.

"Of course, even fledglings generally acquire enough psychic power to cope with a single glass fairly quickly," Carter continued. "They couldn't survive in the modern world if they didn't. But it takes a master vampire to veil himself and his myriad reflections for very long in an environment *made* of mirrors, such as this."

David started to shake. *"You bastard."*

"I warned you not to defy me. Now I'm going to take away everything that makes your existence bearable."

Sarah shook her head. "This is about the dumbest scam anybody's ever—" She turned white. "No. I was at your funeral."

"Please," David whimpered. "I—I promise I'm still the same inside."

"I was at your funeral!" she screamed.

Carter grabbed her arm and jerked her to him. "She's only the first," he said.

David sprang, felt his strength drain away, fell and cracked his head against a mirror. Sobbing, he pounded madly at the crippling alien presence in his mind. And after just a moment, it seemed to lose its grip! Thrusting himself up from the floor, he raised his eyes and—

Too late! A torrent of blood was already pattering down from a throat like soggy, shredded paper. Carter spat out a mouthful of meat and let the body drop. "They all saw *you* do this," he said.

David snarled, began to lunge again—

—and Liz stepped through the gap between two mirrors. Wide-eyed and trembling, stammering a Wiccan incantation, she shuffled toward him, a nail file clutched in her right hand.

He wailed, threw up one arm to hide his face and swept her aside with the other. Bolting past her, he blundered blindly through the maze, caroming from one row of mirrors to the other, his treacherous reflections slipping on ahead. He passed an elderly couple with their tiny, golden-haired granddaughter, Wally, Kaz, three boys in Brandon High School letter jackets—everyone recoiling, everyone's face contorted with terror—and then he burst into the central chamber.

Where his mom and dad were, grappling viciously, writhing and rolling on the steel floor. Her eyes blazing, Molly was struggling to worm closer to the doorway. "Baby!" she shrieked. "Sweetheart! Come to Mommy!" Stan, his shirt torn, his hands and face livid with scratches and bites, began to hit her.

Now that it was too late, David realized it was no coincidence that they'd come to the fair the same night he did. Carter had compelled them to come with his mesmerism, had commanded them to enter the Mirror Maze at a preset time.

He lurched on toward the opening in the opposite wall; Molly's cries stabbed after him like daggers. Dwarf Davids, pinhead Davids, Davids with elephantiasis oozed along beside him, none of them more hideous than the original.

Once through the doorway, he found himself in another silver hallway leading nowhere, his own dead, gashed features mocking him from every panel. The maze resounded: screams, shouts, the thunder of running feet. His mother calling him and his father's fists smacking her.

He punched his reflection; pain jolted up his arm. *Where was the exit?* Whirling drunkenly, he killed himself again and again. He had to get out—right now!—because he *couldn't stand this.* . . .

Afterward, he knew he'd lost himself again for a little while. When he came to, he was crouched, cowering, in the dark space between the floor of the maze and the ground. Hours later, long after the commotion had died down, he finally managed to don his ghost-mask and creep away.

Chapter Twenty-eight

Three stooped old women in shabby dresses stood swaying and wailing over the inert husk of a fourth. They were praying, but they looked and sounded like demoniac hags gibbering incantations. In the bed nearer the door, a chubby middle-aged man was trying to watch TV; he winced and rolled his eyes whenever the screeching got particularly loud.

It didn't look like the prayer meeting would break up before visiting hours ended. David stepped away from the doorway and resumed pacing the corridors.

He almost didn't mind waiting, almost relished the burning in his throat. Somehow it seemed only fitting that his body should be as anguished as his mind.

As soon as he'd awakened, he'd rushed out to buy a *Tribune*. The front-page story was like something from a supermarket tabloid. It didn't quite say that an undead abomination had murdered Sarah, but it made much of the fact that the killer David White had turned into an uncanny facsimile of a cadaverous David Brent, whose corpse had mysteriously vanished from its grave, and of Sarah's involvement in the occult. The police were searching for both Davids. Baffled by his sudden disappearance from the maze and suspicious about his parents' presence, detectives had grilled his dad for hours, but they hadn't had a crack at his mom yet; she'd been committed for psychiatric evaluation.

Deep inside, he'd always known that someday the world would find him out. Now it had, and everything was even worse than he'd imagined.

A slim, ginger-haired girl of about his own age, her neck wrapped in a bulky beige brace, hobbled past him toward the pay phones. Her body smelled of soap and deodorant, emanated warmth; he couldn't help staring at the strip of skin bared by her open-backed gown. Her heart pulsed strong and steady . . .

He closed his eyes and clenched his fists so tight they throbbed. As she moved on down the hall, his head cleared.

He shivered; he hadn't come that close to losing control in a long while. No matter how wretched he felt, he mustn't let the thirst edge him into delirium. He mustn't become the creature Carter intended him to be.

He made four slow circuits of the ward, then sat down in a waiting area when his muscles started twitching and his vision blurred. He kept glancing at his watch, willing the numbers to change faster. Just ten more minutes, he told himself, the old ladies will be gone in ten more minutes.

"Excuse me," someone said.

David jerked his head up. Before him stood a skinny, balding man wearing black-rimmed glasses and a lab coat with a Monster Trucks Marathon T-shirt underneath: Frank Pruitt, one of the nurses. Frank was a jovial amateur comedian who seemed to spend most of his time wisecracking and doing bad impressions of Reagan and Stallone; David had never seen him scowl before.

He hastily checked his shroud. It was intact; Frank was seeing a nondescript hospital maintenance worker in light brown coveralls. "Hi. What's up?"

201

"That's what I'd like to know; I've been sitting in the nurses' station watching you tramp around in circles. If you aren't working, you shouldn't be on the floor."

"But I was; I was looking for your bugs."

"Bugs?"

"Hell yes. The day guys reported you've got moths or termites or some damn thing swarming up here, only I couldn't come before the shift changed and now I can't find them. Do you know where they're supposed to be?"

"No; I haven't seen them or heard anything about it. I think you'd better come back tomorrow."

"Can't. According to my boss, Infection Control is really torqued; he said I can't go home until I spray."

"But if you can't find them—"

"I'll find them if you'll let me keep looking. I'm just trying to do my job, so why are you giving me a hard time? I always heard you were a nice guy."

Frank flushed. "Look, normally I don't give people the third degree, and I really don't want you to get in trouble, but . . . Just sit right here, okay? I'll make a couple phone calls and we can probably get this all straightened out."

But you know damn well everything's okay, David told him. *If you call, you'll just make yourself look like an officious jerk.*

Frank turned and strode toward the nurses' station.

His stomach queasy and his head pounding, David struggled to focus his will. Finally the nurse stumbled.

When he turned back around, his eyes were glazed and he was smiling sheepishly. "Hey, I'm really sorry; you must think I'm a prize tight-ass. Go ahead and do whatever you have to. Just check with me before you spray in a patient's room, okay?"

202

"No problem."

As he watched him walk away again, David wondered what had happened to make someone who was usually so easygoing so suspicious. Maybe the thirst had affected him more than he realized; maybe he'd been mumbling or staggering.

If so, then he'd better hurry and drink before he had a full-scale blackout. Fortunately, down at the other end of the corridor the old ladies were shuffling to the elevators at last.

When he reached his victim's room, he glanced around. No one was looking, so he became a phlebotomist with a wire basket of bottles, and needles in his hand.

The chubby man grinned when David stepped through the door. "Please, mercy, not again!" he moaned lugubriously.

"You're safe this time; I'm here to stick your roommate." He crossed the room and closed the curtain behind him.

You're feeling awfully tired. In fact, can hardly keep your eyes open. This show's boring anyway, so you might as well turn it off and go to sleep.

He repeated it over and over. Eventually the television clicked off and the light beyond the barrier went out. A minute after that, the snoring started.

And then it was finally time for poor, shriveled Mrs. Drake. Giddy and feverish, he wanted to pounce and rip, but instead he made himself take the time to gently turn her head and carefully position his mouth above her throat; when he struck, it was sudden and precise.

Sucking frantically, sick with the vileness of it as always, he didn't hear them until they threw open the curtain.

"It *is* Brent!" Frank squealed. For a moment the burly security guard looked like he was about to throw up; then he snarled and swung his billy club.

Frozen with shock, David just barely wrenched his head aside in time; the baton cracked down on Mrs. Drake's cheek. He snatched at it, grabbed it, tore it free trailing a strand of the dead woman's snow-white hair.

Frank was shaking the chubby man. "Get out!" he cried, his voice still shrill with terror. "She's gone and we can't stop him by ourselves!"

The chubby man lurched up. Scrambling backward, the guard fumbled for the walkie-talkie holstered at his side.

David tried to freeze him, but it didn't work; so he vaulted bed and corpse and lashed out with the billy club himself.

His second blow connected; the guard's forearm snapped and the radio went flying. He fell back onto the floor.

But it had taken too long; Frank and the patient were already running down the corridor shouting. David snatched up the walkie-talkie, leaped over the guard and out the door, and sprinted in the opposite direction.

Rounding a corner, he found a door to a stairwell. He dashed down two flights, then leaned, gasping and shuddering, against the wall. After a minute or two, when he felt a little less panicky, he managed to make himself invisible.

Now that he was a ghost, he didn't have any more trouble getting out, though twice security guards passed him on the stairs; the walkie-talkie warned him they were coming.

An hour later, listening to a news broadcast on his

Walkman, the taste of blood still foul in his mouth, he found out why he'd been discovered.

Earlier that evening Carter had veiled himself in David's image, slipped into a nursing home, and savaged four elderly residents in front of witnesses. During the process he'd demonstrated his ability to become a phantom and change his appearance. No wonder Frank had been so leery of strangers who seemed to have no business on the ward; no doubt he'd heard an earlier report.

Carter would keep doing it, too, until all the hospitals and nursing homes were fortresses with alarms, cameras, and squads of guards with guns protecting the hopeless cases.

If David continued to hunt his chosen prey, he'd eventually be destroyed; if he didn't, he'd become the devil everyone thought he was.

Chapter Twenty-nine

The house was dark and silent, the driveway empty.
Maybe Carter was off killing more sick people. If he
wasn't lying in wait.

Hastily, before he could chicken out, David redefined
his ghost-mask, shifted his grip on the cardboard box,
and limped up the front yard and around the side of
the house.

In back yards up and down the block, dogs were
snoring or snuffling, twitching at their dreams or pacing and dragging clinking lengths of chain. He tensed,
but none of them barked; as he'd hoped, he was a
wraith to animals, too.

He peered in a kitchen window, saw nothing moving,
set the box down on the dewy grass, and pulled the
foot-long stake out of his belt. Clutching it in his right
hand, he tried the door with his left. Locked.

When he tore the screen away from the window, he
found it was locked, too, so he attacked the pane with
his glass cutter and duct tape. As he worked, he kept
imagining Carter stealing up behind him, kept wanting
to snatch up his weapon and spin around.

The circle of glass pulled loose with the softest of
rattles, so soft a mortal couldn't hear it. But a vampire
might, even from another room. His skin crawled as
he reached through the hole to release the lock.

But nothing grabbed him.

He lifted the window slowly; it squealed anyway. He flinched, lurched backward, and Carter still didn't appear.

He swallowed, then pulled apart the curtains and climbed in.

Crouching motionless on the sill, he strained to perceive. One of the bathroom faucets was dripping and the air still smelled of lemon. No breathing or hearts beating, no cloth rustling or floorboards creaking, and only a vestigial whiff of rot.

Maybe Carter really *wasn't* here; if only he could accomplish his task and get away before he returned! He dropped to the floor, unlocked the door, and retrieved his time bomb.

He'd found the recipe in *The Anarchist's Cookbook*. Mix two parts Vaseline with one part gasoline, detonate electrically; a diagram showed how to hook it up. After he finished he'd wrapped it in towels and sheets of plastic until he couldn't smell it or hear it ticking anymore.

He hoped to hide it near Carter's bed, but it ought to kill him even if he couldn't. If the blast didn't get him, the fire would, and if that didn't, the firemen would find him and carry him out into the sunlight.

It *should* work; he didn't know why, now that he'd made it this far, he suddenly felt so certain that it wouldn't.

Well, it certainly wouldn't if he didn't get on with it. His shoulders hunched, still half-expecting Carter to spring up out of nowhere, he crept on into the living room.

The masks and books were gone. Propped against a candelabrum on the mantelpiece, an envelope gleamed like polished bone.

Eyes stinging and blurring, hands shaking, he fumbled it open. A snapshot and a folded sheet of stationery fell out.

The photo was of Kaz. He was lying in bed on wet red sheets, his amber face contorted and his throat a ragged absence. A fly was crawling on his lip.

The letter was typed and unsigned. It read:

I told you Sarah was only the first. Everyone you love is going to die.

As you've no doubt inferred, I've neutralized your threat of exposure by assuming a new identity. You can't dispatch mortals to trouble my repose if you no longer know my name or where I live.

I never dreamed I'd intentionally reveal the existence of vampires to the world at large; it's one of the most reckless things our kind can do. But I never wanted to crush anyone's spirit as badly as I do yours.

Please, do try to stop me. It will add to my sport.

David sobbed and slammed his fist down; the mantel cracked in two.

Chapter Thirty

David caught the stench as he started up the stairs; by the time he reached the top, he was nearly choking.

Someone had taped a folded piece of paper under the brass numbers and peephole in the center of the door. Cringing, certain it was another taunt from Carter, he pulled it down and opened it.

But it was only a warning from the landlord: he wanted the apartment cleaned by the end of the week. So just maybe, despite the ominous reek of corruption, Steve was still alive.

He rang the doorbell, waited, rang it again. Still no one came. But then, so faintly he half-suspected he'd imagined it, someone groaned.

Maybe Carter *had* attacked Steve but somehow he'd survived. Or maybe Steve had been attacked several nights ago and now he was waking up a vampire. Whatever was happening, he obviously needed help! Suddenly frantic, David started kicking.

The second kick broke the locks and the third ripped out the chain. Stumbling in his haste, he plunged inside.

Sony TV, VCR, and CD player and Goodwill furniture, travel posters aglow with blue water and bathing beauties and a plank and cinder-block bookshelf laden with textbooks, paperback science fiction, and copies of *Salt Water Sportsman, Skin Diver,* and *Playboy:*

once it had been a typical student apartment.

But now it was like the inside of a dumpster, with clear, green, and brown bottles, pizza boxes, ice cream cartons, junk food bags and wrappers, and styrofoam burger containers strewn everywhere; roaches skittered rustling through the refuse.

Still unconscious despite the noise of the break-in, his breath and sweat stinking of bourbon, Steve lay sprawled on the carpet. His new paunch oozed over the top of his leopard-print bikini briefs. His skin and hair were greasy, his heartbeat irregular.

Appalled, David sank to his knees beside him. This couldn't be his fault. Sure, he'd used his mesmerism to give Steve an insatiable craving for food and alcohol, forced him to eat and drink constantly, hour after hour, day after day, until Liz finally dumped him in disgust. But after that he'd wiped the compulsion away.

At least he'd thought he had, but obviously his powers had fucked up again. Christ, what if he'd never checked? Steve could have stayed like this for the rest of his life!

He still might, if David couldn't snap him out of it this time around.

David had never tried to influence an unconscious mind, and he suspected he couldn't. He grabbed Steve's shoulders and shook him. "Steve! Steve! Come on, wake up! Rise and shine!"

Still asleep, Steve tried to squirm away.

"Damn it, wake up! Come on, man, *please!* We have to do this now. With our luck, the cops are liable to nail me before I can come back."

He began to snore.

At last David started slapping him, hard, fast blows that popped like a string of firecrackers.

Eventually Steve started crying and whining incoherently; coiling himself halfway into a fetal position, he tried ineffectually to shield his face.

At least his eyes were open; David doubted he could beat him lucid. He lifted him into a sitting position and hugged him.

"It's all right," he said, both aloud and silently. "I had to hurt you to get your attention, but I promise I'll never do it again.

"Now listen: a while back I hypnotized you; I gave you an insatiable craving for food and alcohol so you'd eat and drink like a pig. It was a vicious thing to do and I apologize.

"But the important thing now is that I'm releasing you. From this moment on, you don't have any horrible compulsions; you're your old self again."

Dry eyes pulsing, he droned the last words over and over, until Steve lapsed into complete unconsciousness once more. Then he carried him to the bed and started cleaning the apartment.

Chapter Thirty-one

When Steve answered the door his cheeks were bruised, his eyes were bloodshot, and he had a bottle of Heineken in his hand.

He smiled crookedly. "Don't worry, I'm not drinking myself into another stupor. I just need to take the edge off my hangover."

"Thank God," David said.

"I feel too sick to beat you up, so you might as well come in. You want a drink? There's plenty left."

"No thanks." Steve led him into the living room, paused at the stereo to turn off a top forties' rock station, and then they sat down. "Apparently you remember last night."

"Enough. You said you turned me into a food and booze addict. But why? I don't even know you."

"Yeah, you do." He replaced the shroud he'd been wearing with the image of himself alive.

Steve stiffened for a moment, then slumped back in his armchair. "Well damn."

"I . . . I guess I'm glad you're taking this all so calmly."

"You want me to bug out my eyes, scream, and state the obvious? Okay." He thrust his head forward and goggled. "Eek, David, you're *dead*. Look, I spent the last few hours trying to come to terms with the fact that somebody reprogrammed my brain and turned me into a completely different person. Right now I'm kind of burnt out in the fear department."

"But what about the stories in the news?"

"The only story I heard was the one about your grave being opened. I'm afraid I've been a little out of touch."

So David told him everything, beginning with the night Carter took him to the Blue Cockatoo. Steve listened impassively to it all.

"And now I need a mortal partner," David concluded an hour later. "To do detective work that can only be done during the day, so we can uncover Carter's new identity and kill him in his sleep. And to fight, in case we can't.

"Like I told you, I'm no match for him alone. But if the two of us were well armed and caught him by surprise, I think we might be able to nail him."

"Why the hell did you pick me?"

"Carter hurt you with his illusions the night we met him, long before I was even dead, and you hated him for it. You avoided him afterward, and as a result he never had a chance to mesmerize you or charm you into thinking he was a nice guy after all. So I thought you might believe what I had to say about him.

"Also, he knows we were never really . . . close friends, so he probably won't expect me to turn to you. That means you'll be safer, and it'll make it easier for you to trick him or catch him off guard if we wind up having to take him out while he's awake."

"Swell, but what made you think I'd risk my life for you? You're damn right we're not friends; look what you've done to me. I lost my girl and my job. I blew my savings, and I'm failing all my courses. My landlord'll kick me out when he sees that door. My life's a total wreck, and it's all your fault!"

"You've got to understand, Carter *made* me—"

"Bullshit!"

"Okay, you're right; he influenced me, but he didn't really force me to do that particular thing—and if I were you, I'd hate me too. But you can't let him kill Liz just to spite me."

"She turned her back on me when I was in trouble."

"I don't believe you! There was no way she could know something had made you crazy, and she stuck it out with you for a while anyway. But all right, if you're pissed at her too, forget about her. Carter is going to kill a lot of people!"

"So's Khadafy, and you don't see me flying out to Tripoli to dispose of him. It's not my responsibility."

"Steve, *please*. Everyone in Tampa is scared of David Brent the Vampire Killer, and all the other people who know there's something magical about Carter are sure they saw me bite out Sarah's throat; I couldn't convince anyone else that he's the bad guy and I'm the good guy even if I used mind control. You're the only person I can ask!"

Steve smiled. "Okay, here's how it is: I've been yanking your chain a little bit. Of course I don't want to see Liz, Wally, or anybody else die. So I'll help you, but only on one condition: you'll have to tell me where *you* sleep."

"In other words, put my life in your hands."

"Right. See, I believed part of what you told me—that Carter's a menace. But that doesn't mean I'm

214

convinced you're any better. Maybe you do just as much harm as he does. Maybe you're planning to kill me once you don't need me anymore. I want to be able to eliminate you if I decide it's just as necessary as eliminating him."

"Maybe you've decided it already."

"No. Of course, I wouldn't tell you if I had."

"You know, if you insist, and I refuse, and your suspicions are correct, I'll kill you now."

"Which'll leave you without a partner. I was kind of expecting you to try to change my mind with—what did you call it?—mesmerism."

David snorted. "Why bother? It took me four nights to intensify your yen for food and alcohol when you didn't even suspect anything was wrong. I'm sure I couldn't zap you now that you're on your guard, and if by some miracle I did, it would probably either wear off or leave you crazy and unreliable. Besides, because I'm truly *not* like Carter, I realize now that it's wrong to screw around with someone's convictions and deep feelings except in an emergency."

"Yeah? Too bad for Liz, your mom, and my waistline that you didn't figure it out before. Well, what's it going to be? Are you going to put your faith in little old me or take on the big, bad master vampire all by your lonesome?"

"You're really enjoying watching me squirm, aren't you?"

"In my place, wouldn't you?"

"Probably. I don't suppose there's any point in lying."

"Nope. I'm going to take a tip from Ronnie and trust—but verify."

215

David massaged his temples; the pressure hurt his fingertips without making his headache any better. "All right," he sighed at last. "How well do you know Ybor City?"

Chapter Thirty-two

The four white mice cowered in the far corners of their cage.

David sat on the floor beside it, his back against the wall and a hunk of cheddar in his hand. When the pounding behind his forehead eased, he tried again, this time concentrating on only one mouse.

Come on, pal. You're hungrier than you've ever been before, and this cheese smells more delicious than any food you've ever eaten, so step up to the door and chow down. I know I'm ugly, and I stink, but I like mice and I would never hurt you.

The mouse didn't move.

David couldn't help grinning. He was used to his mesmerism misfiring, but this was pathetic; he'd matched his willpower against a rodent's, and it had won.

But of course willpower wasn't really the problem; the problem was that animals didn't understand English.

He was sure he didn't have a chance of beating Carter in a fight unless he overcame the handicap of ignorance and misinformation the master vampire had left him with, so he'd planned a series of exercises and experiments to further develop his powers and discover what his weaknesses actually were. But so far the results were unimpressive.

Jesus Christ, mouse, move your ass!

It shivered, but he didn't guess that counted.

Or did it? Perhaps the mouse had trembled at that precise instant because he'd made it feel his frustration. Maybe if he could code his suggestions in sensations and images instead of language he'd be in business!

He closed his eyes and remembered: his old Airedale Selma leaping to catch a frisbee, his Aunt Vivian's Siamese purring in his lap. Imitating a gibbon's call and the gibbons calling back; touching a dolphin's silky flank; rolling along high above everyone else on an elephant's back. He savored reminiscences of how marvelous it had all been, of all the delight and wonder animals had given him.

Next he imagined being hungry, not the nauseous fever of the blood-thirst but the belly-rumbling emptiness of a living creature. When he'd evoked a ghostly hollowness in his stomach, he opened his eyes and stared at the mouse, struggling to make it feel everything he was feeling, to show it his love of animals and infect it with hunger too.

After a few seconds the mouse raised its head. Nose and whiskers twitching, pink eyes gleaming, it scurried to the door and started nibbling the cheese. He stroked it with his finger, and it didn't recoil.

Once it had eaten its fill, he let it out. As it wandered around the base of the telescope, he fantasized that the instrument was actually Carter. Carter had paralyzed him, and now he was about to destroy him; his withered corpse-face loomed and his fanged jaws gaped. When he'd scared himself, he tried to broadcast that.

The mouse froze.

All right, the telescope was still Carter, but the unnatural vitality that had sustained him through the centuries was finally failing. Suddenly he'd lost his strength and abilities; in fact, he was crumbling into dust. At last David had him where he wanted him; at last it was time for sweet revenge!

The mouse sprang at the tripod, started madly snapping and scratching at one of its rubber-shod feet.

He tried to extend his control to the other mice. His night vision guttered out, his head throbbed so fiercely he nearly sobbed, but then they charged out to join the fray.

When he was able, he calmed them and returned them to the cage. He'd had to strain so hard that it was difficult to believe he'd ever be able to command a horde of animals the way Carter could, but no doubt practice would refine this particular talent just as it had his others.

Time to rest his mind and exhaust his body; he began driving himself through a grueling series of push-ups, sit-ups, deep knee bends, and squat thrusts. Then he ran in place. He knew even the most strenuous exercise couldn't make his decaying muscles any stronger, but he hoped to inure himself to pain so completely that it wouldn't hamper his movements anymore.

Agonizing as the calisthenics were, he didn't want to stop; he wanted to delay the remaining experiments as long as possible.

But after twenty minutes he had to stop or collapse; besides, he couldn't postpone the unpleasantness forever. After he caught his breath he lay down on the floor between the telescope and the cooler and tried to relax.

Damn it, he was a wimp to be so frightened. If other vampires could dissolve into shadows, so could he. In fact, he suspected he'd already done it; how had he vanished from the Mirror Maze, if not by slipping right through the floor? If he could do the same thing while he was in his right mind, maybe he could straighten out his leg.

He tried for several minutes, but he couldn't start the cold tingling dancing over his skin. Maybe he could concentrate better if he shut his eyes.

He realized he was afraid to.

He grimaced and forced himself to do it anyway. Alone in the darkness, he struggled again to transform.

And icy needles stabbed up his legs. But in that same instant, he suddenly *knew* he was still sealed in his coffin, that he'd be a severed head forever, that his fog-flesh was about to waft *apart* and—

He gasped and sat up.

No matter how many times he tried, the results were always the same. When his eyes were open, he couldn't begin the metamorphosis at all, but if they were closed, he panicked.

At last he conceded he couldn't learn that, not tonight, anyway. Scowling, he turned his attention to the implements laid out on the window sill and the bundle on the floor beneath it.

He doubted an air bubble would hurt him, but he squirted the hypodermic anyway. Then he pulled his sleeve up to his elbow, positioned the needle over a prominent vein, and, wincing, jabbed it in.

According to the *Physicians' Desk Reference,* he'd injected himself with enough thiopental to knock out a horse. After five minutes passed and he still didn't feel any different, he concluded that he was immune to drugs and poisons.

Next he picked up the sterling fork and pricked the back of his hand. It stung and pierced the skin, but it wasn't any worse than the needle had been. Apparently silver weapons were no more dangerous than any other kind. He'd suspected as much, since he'd handled silver objects without any kind of allergic reaction, but he'd wanted to be sure.

He scratched himself with a wooden splinter; it didn't do extraordinary damage or cause more pain than the syringe, either. It still might be true than a wooden stake *through the heart* was necessary or at least unusually effective for killing an undead, but he was inclined to doubt it. It seemed more likely that in ancient times mortals had invented a number of vampire vulnerabilities simply so they wouldn't feel so helpless.

And now, as long as he was sticking and gouging himself, he supposed he might as well get the serious cutting over with. He opened the jackknife, laid his little finger on the window sill, and set the blade against it.

Oh God, he didn't want to do it! But he'd already failed to overcome his fear once tonight; if he was going to cave in every time he faced suffering or danger, he might as well give up all hope of destroying Carter right now.

You can do it; those Yakuza guys do it without turning a hair. Just close your eyes and do it now.

Pain flashed up his arm.

For a while he just knelt there rocking and whimpering. Finally the agony abated slightly and he was able to bring himself to examine the stump.

A cross section of raw gray meat oozing pus; he wasn't growing a new pinkie.

But he could still feel the old one.

His hand hurt so terribly that he hadn't noticed at first, but somewhere beyond the pain pulsed a second one like a faint echo of the first. When he focused his attention on it, he could also feel a span of cool, flat surface.

He pinched the severed member between his thumb and forefinger and lifted it off the sill; the surface vanished, replaced by a double pressure.

He lined up the wounds and pressed the finger back into place.

And then he moaned and keeled over; reattachment was as excruciating as amputation. Within seconds tendrils of putrescence seeped up and down across the gap, fusing to form a bulging, green-black ring.

As he gingerly opened and closed his hand, almost expecting the finger to fall off again, he wondered what would happen if he cut if off a second time and tried to stick it back on rotated halfway around. He quickly decided he wasn't curious enough to find out.

How strange that he'd been right all those nights ago, when he'd conjectured that he might be able to recover from crippling injuries even though his lesser ones never healed. It really did seem to imply that some sadistic supernatural intelligence had designed vampirism, that the undead were damned, each and every one condemned to suffer and do evil forever.

But he didn't *know* that was true, so screw it for now; he'd have plenty of time to brood about his position in the scheme of things if he survived his present difficulties. He began tearing open the bundle.

Steve had procured and wrapped the items inside; David hadn't wanted to see, smell, or handle them until he was alone for fear he'd lose his shroud. But now that he knew wood and silver didn't have any special power over him, he seriously doubted that this stuff would either.

Breaking strips of tape and folding back layers of

222

newspaper, he uncovered the garlic. Six bulbs of elephant garlic, in fact; maybe Steve hoped to make him thoroughly miserable.

If so, he was in for a disappointment. When David touched them, they didn't burn, and when he raised one right up to his nose, it just smelled like what it was; he didn't retch, choke, or even sneeze.

The second package was flat and rectangular. Now almost certain that the contents wouldn't harm him, he ripped into it.

An explosion of heat and glare hurled him backward. In the endless, blazing moment before he hit the floor, he wondered what had finally made Steve decide to destroy him, and what book he'd consulted to construct his bomb.

Chapter Thirty-three

"If I kill you I'll just chop you up while you're in your coma," Steve said sourly.

"I realize it wouldn't make sense for you to slip me a bomb," David replied. His joints were aching fiercely; hoping to ease them, he got up off the cooler and started pacing. "I'm just telling you that the . . . flare affected me so powerfully that for a second I thought it had to be a bomb.

"For about five minutes the heat, the blinding brightness, and the waves of sickness and wrongness pouring out of it were so overwhelming that I couldn't have approached it if my life depended on it. But finally the glow got cooler and dimmer and I managed to crawl over and cover it up again.

"It's funny; the more I learn about vampirism, the more mysterious it seems. Why did a cross hurt me when Liz's Wiccan spell didn't? Because Christianity is a valid religion and witchcraft isn't? Because my parents raised me to believe in Jesus and deep down, I still do? Or just because the supernatural being who wrote the undead rulebook decided that was how it was going to be? Beats the hell out of me.

"And another thing: I suspect that sometime during the last few months I must have passed near and glanced at a cross, even if I didn't notice it consciously. So why didn't it blast me? Maybe somebody would have had to deliberately shove it in my face to activate its power, and when I unwrapped this one, that's what I was doing to myself.

"At any rate, the important thing is that it repelled me—and the holy water did too. We've found magic you can use."

Steve scowled. "Neato."

David blinked in surprise. "You may decide it is if it winds up saving your life. What's bothering you, anyway?"

"If you were even a little bit human, you wouldn't have to ask. Carter keeps on raiding at least one hospital or group home every night; tonight he butchered two retarded kids at MacDonald Training Center. Plus, another of Wally's New Agers has disappeared. I—"

David winced. "Who?"

"Virgie. And I know who's responsible, I know another dozen people who're scheduled to have their throats torn out, but I haven't told anybody!"

David sat back down so he could look him in the eye. "I understand how you feel, but we've discussed this before; talking wouldn't accomplish anything. People *see* me commit the murders and they *think* you're a drunk: nobody would believe you. And if Carter found out, he'd come after you."

Steve glared at him. "All right. But if we can't warn people, we should be out there protecting them."

"Out where? With Liz or my mom and dad? Trust me, Carter'll kill them last, as the grand finale, so they're safe for the moment. Should we be watching another New Ager or one of the treatment facilities? Which? There're too many possibilities; we'd almost certainly wait a long time before he showed up, and meanwhile, since I can't stay invisible all the time or make you invisible at all yet, somebody would probably notice us staking the place out and sic the cops on us."

"As long as your 'pet' humans are safe, you don't care what he does to anyone else, do you? Hell, why would you? You bleed someone every night yourself."

"It's not the same and I *do* care!"

"Bullshit. If you did you would have tried to destroy him as soon as you discovered what he really was."

David turned away and stared out at the night. "I wish I had," he said at last. "God knows I fantasized about it. I keep asking myself why I didn't.

"I think it was because I was so much in awe of him. He seemed so cunning, so potent—so satanic—that I couldn't imagine anyone could ever destroy him by any means whatsoever. I sure didn't feel like I could; I was having enough trouble just holding onto my sanity and surviving.

"But there was even more to it than that. Crazy as it sounds, I think I hoped he might still decide to be my friend. I was so lonely that I would have embraced any confidant, even the bastard who cut me off from the rest of the world in the first place.

"And, last but maybe not least, I think I felt like I didn't have any right to kill him and then go on existing myself, because I suspected I was really just as foul a monster as he was.

"So first I obeyed him and stayed away from him, and then I bluffed and bargained, when I should have been plotting his execution, and my hesitation's killed a lot of people. And I'll tell you something: I'm still in awe of him. He *still* terrifies me. Every night I want to run away to another city, but I don't. Every night I pray we'll find his new house so you can destroy him by daylight, but if you figure out where he'll strike next, I'll be there waiting. He won't kill anyone else if

I can stop it!"

"I shouldn't have shot my mouth off," Steve said softly. "I guess you do care, at least a little, and I guess you're doing everything you can. The thought of all these deaths, night after night after night, is driving me crazy. I'm supposed to prevent them and I'm fucking up."

"You're doing everything you can, too."

"I didn't feel like James Bond the days I spent hitting my dad up for money and moving into the duplex."

"You have to do what's necessary to live, just like I have to start every night . . . doing what I do."

Steve's mouth twisted. "Right. I suppose you want to hear about my day?" David nodded. "Okay, it won't take long. The certified letters came back marked 'Moved—No Forwarding Address' as usual. I worked the banks some more, but I still haven't found out which one he used, let alone what happened to his money."

"He wouldn't just abandon it."

"No, but that doesn't mean I can find it."

"Did you check with that art dealer?"

"I called him two days ago, at which time he hadn't had any recent contact with Carter or anyone else interested in masks. I can't bug him every day or he'll stop talking to me."

"What about the Sentra?"

"I haven't had a chance to look for it yet."

"*Still?* If it's on a used car lot, they could sell it anytime!"

"I'm doing the best I can, remember?"

"Sorry."

"I did identify the people you saw in the library. The Burger King girl died last month, but the guy

227

with cerebral palsy is still alive. His name is Ken Dumont and he's an honors student in pre-law."

"My God, actual information! Why didn't you tell me this before?"

"Because I don't see what difference it makes. Carter's devoted himself to making your life miserable; I doubt he even remembers Dumont anymore."

"That's because you still don't understand how arrogant and malicious he really is. Once he's selected a victim, he considers it a point of honor to follow through and claim him, especially if he's announced his intentions to someone else.

"And remember: hunting him is a full-time job for us, but punishing me only takes him a couple hours a night. He's got plenty of time to pursue other interests, too."

"But you said he told you he planned to kill Dumont for his blood. At the moment he's getting more blood than he could possibly need."

"No, he isn't. If you study the eyewitness accounts and the photos of the bodies in the newspaper, it's obvious that he kills and moves on without pausing to drink. It isn't safe for him to linger, and I think he's emphasizing the fact that the people from the group and all these poor invalids are dying *only* because I defied him."

"Okay, let's say we know Dumont is marked for death at some point in the future. How does that help us? It's the same thing we already knew about Liz and the others."

"It's close to the end of the semester, isn't it?"

"Don't remind me. Finals are the week after next; I don't suppose there's any point in me showing up to take them, even if this mess is over by then."

"Look, I'm sorry. I swear that if we survive I'll find

a way to make it up to you. But anyway, what if we write a press release announcing that Dumont has won some special scholarship and will be spending the next couple of semesters at Yale? We'll send one to the *Oracle* and the *Trib* and St. Pete *Times* too. You'll locate the appropriate editors, and I'll mesmerize them to make sure they run the story and forget to print a correction if they receive one. When Carter reads it, he'll come after Dumont right away to make sure he doesn't slip through his fingers, and that'll be ambush time!"

"You're talking about using a human being for bait!"

"I don't like it either. But remember, Carter's planning to attack him eventually anyway. This way, Dumont'll have us there to defend him."

"But he's crippled! He won't have a chance in hell if we screw up!"

"There's no one else we can use. Even if we could get a news story published saying that my dad or one of the group was leaving town, Carter would be sure to smell a trap. He still might, but with Dumont at least we have a chance."

"Forget it! I'm not dead, and I can see it's wrong!"

"This is the first and only idea—listen!"

"What? I don't hear anything."

But David did: footsteps creaking, breath rasping, and hearts pulsing on the first floor.

Chapter Thirty-four

". . . slow . . . don't split up."

". . . don't like . . . we could get charged with mur—"

"You bag the Vampire Killer . . . fucking medal . . ."

David spun back to the window; flashlight beams lanced through the darkness below. "Damn!"

"What is it?" Steve asked.

"Keep your voice down! It's vigilantes hunting me."

"Are you sure?"

"Yes! They're whispering about it. My hearing's fading, but I caught enough."

"How do they know you're here?"

"They don't. They must've decided to search all the abandoned buildings in the area, probably because they've heard that David White visited the neighborhood tattoo parlor and that a guy who was scared of demons got himself murdered just a couple blocks away." At the bottom of the staircase, risers groaned. "Look, we can play Twenty Questions later. Right now we've got to get out of here!"

Steve grinned nervously. "What do you mean 'we,' white man? Just kidding; what's the plan?"

"I'll become a ghost and walk right past them.

You'll have to talk your way out. If they believe the stories that the Vampire Killer can change his appearance, it might not be easy. But I'll try to mesmerize them if you have trouble."

" 'Try' being the operative word here, since it usually doesn't work on people who are tense or suspicious. Wonderful. Let's get on with it."

"I think you'll still be able to see me, since you already know I'm here."

"Whatever; just *do* it!"

David pictured himself standing in the bare, high-ceilinged room, then began to erase his image from the scene. A spike of agony rammed through the space between his eyes; he grunted and dropped to his knees.

"What's wrong?" Steve asked.

"It didn't work! I wore myself out messing around with the mice and the cross and the holy water, and now I can't do it!"

"Sure you can. Think about it: you're projecting a shroud right now."

"The easiest one; invisibility is hard."

"Then don't be invisible; be somebody besides David Brent or David White and we'll both talk our way out."

"Okay, I'll try." He closed his eyes, concentrated, but only produced another burst of pain. "No good. So here's Plan B. You hide in the attic, and I'll go downstairs and attack them. Maybe I can run them off. If not, I'll run and they'll chase me. Either way, you come out when the coast is clear."

Steve unzipped his windbreaker, exposing the butt of the Browning High-Power stuck in the too-tight waistband of his jeans. "No."

231

"Oh, come on. Maybe my psychic powers are shot, but I'm still as strong as a gorilla and a lot harder to kill. You're the one who's in terrible danger, so why don't you let me deal with these assholes and save your heroic impulses for later."

"Because they're not assholes. They're innocent people trying to do the same job we are. You can't hurt them just to keep me out of danger."

"I won't hurt them any worse than I have to."

"You hide in the attic. I'll try to persuade them they should go search someplace else."

"It's too risky. If they look up there and spot me, they'll know you're on my side and kill you."

"Well, that shouldn't make your chances of slugging your way out any worse."

"Damn it, I *need* you! Liz needs you!"

Disks of light slashed across the hall ceiling; the stairs creaked again.

Steve stooped and snatched up the newspaper-covered cross; despite the wrapping, the air grew warmer. "Get up there now, or I'll help them catch you." David jumped, caught the edge of the opening, and dragged himself up.

Then he realized he was in a box.

What if Steve betrayed him? Unveiled the cross and led the posse up here? Already weakened, trapped in the debilitating corona with the only exit blocked, David would be easy prey.

But, of course, Steve wouldn't do that. Or would he? After all, he was the same guy who'd said: *What made you think I'd risk my life for you? . . . You're damn right we're not friends; look what you've done to me . . . Maybe you're planning to kill me once you don't need me anymore . . . If I kill you— . . . If*

232

you were still even a little bit human— . . . I'm not dead. . . . What do you mean "we," white man?

David lay on his stomach peeking down, his flayed fingers biting into the floor.

Steve bent to the eyepiece of the telescope. *Zip your jacket,* David told him, not daring to speak aloud, *they're going to be suspicious if they see your gun!* But he didn't, and an instant later the vigilantes entered.

Two skinheads and two longhairs, each with a flashlight in one hand and a pistol in the other. The longhair in the lead, a pug-nosed young man dressed in a fashionably mangled denim jacket and a T-shirt with the message TOURIST GO HOME BUT LEAVE YOUR DAUGHTER on it, shouted "Freeze!"

"I'm froze," Steve said mildly.

Three of them swarmed across the room. Pug-nose held his gun at Steve's temple while the other two jerked him to his feet, relieved him of his Browning, and frisked him.

The remaining vigilante had shaved his head but cultivated a pointed black goatee. At least six and a half feet tall and as thin and wasted-looking as a poster child for famine relief, he wore a ring on every finger. After staring intently at Steve for a moment, he seemed to lose interest and began peering aimlessly about. When he raised his eyes to inspect the ceiling David flinched back into the darkness.

The other longhair was a teenager; he had tangled copper tresses, bright, darting copper eyes, three copper rings in his left ear, and an orange rag knotted around his left forearm. Twitching, hands trembling, he fumbled Steve's wallet out of his back pocket.

"Esteban Carlos Morales," he read from the driver's

233

license. "Bet it's not his; bet he took it off the last guy he drained!"

Rings turned and meandered back out of the room. The other skinhead, a man as squat, battered, and unprepossessing as an old garbage can, sighed and shook his head.

"If you think I changed my face, then you must be hunting the Vampire Killer too," Steve said. "Well, I can prove I'm not him. Unwrap those parcels and hand me what's inside."

"It's a trick!" Copper snarled.

"I got him covered," Pug-nose said. "We'll see what we're giving him before he gets hold of it. So what do you think he's going to do, assemble an H-bomb or something? Go ahead, Tom, let's see what he's got." The squat man set down his flashlight, put his pistol in his pocket, and picked up the bundles; Copper took two steps backward and leveled his gun again.

The cross and vial didn't flare, but they flickered. David held his breath until he was sure the mortals couldn't see it.

"I guess you have no way of knowing this is really holy water," Steve said as he unstoppered it and poured a little in his palm. "But you can see that's really a cross and those are really bulbs of garlic, and touching them didn't bother me either."

"Okay, that proves you're not a vampire like in the movies," Pug-nose said. "But it doesn't prove you're not the Vampire Killer."

"Get real," Tom growled.

"Yeah, why don't you?" Steve said; he sounded bored, not frightened. "Tom, would you please scratch my face?" Tom hesitantly raised his hand. "Harder;

234

break the skin if you want to. You're not touching anything but flesh, are you? All right, guys, now think about it: if Brent is supernatural, he can't face garlic or sacred artifacts; if he's an ordinary human, he can't disguise himself without makeup or a mask. Either way, I can't be him."

"But Frank says the stars are almost right again," said Copper. "The time of the dark lords is coming round at last, and the talismans of the Dead God are losing their power. If he's a powerful demon with plenty of blackfire in him, then he could handle the Host or a piece of the True Cross itself!"

"If I'd known you were anywhere near this crazy, I would've stayed home," Tom replied. "Will you fucking look at him? He's just a *person,* just another ignorant, superstitious motherfucker like you. Let's let him get on with his snipe hunt, and we'll get on with ours."

"Not until Frank says he's okay."

"You know, I was never much impressed with Frank's mumbo jumbo," Pug-nose said thoughtfully. "I'm not convinced this Brent guy is really a spook, and I don't see how our buddy here could be him. But this is a weird setup. If you thought you were stalking a real vampire, would you keep your protection covered up?"

Steve said, "I was afraid he'd sense it otherwise."

"Right. What are the mice for?"

"Early warning system. Supposedly, animals freak out any time the undead are close by."

"And the hypo?"

"Haven't any of you ever taken a little pick-me-up when you wanted to make sure you'd stay awake?"

"Cover him." Copper pressed his gun against the

235

back of Steve's neck; Pug-nose opened the cooler and stuck his hand in. "Your ice is all melted; water's not even cold. How long have you been camped out up here?"

"I found the cooler here when I started last week. I only use it for a chair."

"What's your point?" asked Tom.

"I don't know, but I think we ought to search the rest of the house."

"Once Frank finishes looking around this floor, we will have." Apparently, intent on capturing Steve, he hadn't noticed the opening overhead; maybe the other two hadn't either. "He's lost somewhere in the fifth dimension again, but I assume he'll notice the Vampire Killer if it turns up right under his nose."

"You want to know what I think?" Copper asked.

"Not particularly."

"I think this cocksucker is Brent's slave, man. I think he's standing guard over his master's turf."

"I think you should switch to a different drug," said Steve.

"I'll tell you what I'm going to do," Copper said. "I'm going to count to three, and if you haven't told me where your boss is by the time I'm through, I'm going to blow your head off."

No! David screamed. *He's obviously innocent; leave him alone!*

Steve turned to Tom. "You know this is crazy! Don't let him do it!"

"It probably is crazy," Pug-nose said. "But there's something funny about you, so maybe he's got the right idea. Even if he doesn't, this way you can't have us arrested for threatening you and we get to keep your piece and money. Sorry."

236

"He's looney tunes, but he's my partner," Tom said as he turned to face the window.

"One."

If Copper was startled his trigger finger would almost certainly clench. Sick with the foretaste of futility, David crouched to spring anyway.

"I can't tell you what I don't know!"

"Two."

"I'm on your side! We can work together!"

He began his leap—

"No need for that," said a new voice.

—and caught himself just before he plunged through.

Frank stepped back into the room. "The blood prince has never been here, and this wretch has never met him. Let's move on."

Pouting, Copper lowered his gun.

"How do you know that?" Pug-nose asked.

"Psychometry."

"Oh. Well in that case I'm sure you must be right."

"Hey, I'm for moving on, too," Tom said. "We looked for Brent and didn't find him; we tried to scare information out of Esteban here and apparently he doesn't have any. Whatever you think of psycho what's-it, it's time to check someplace new."

Pug-nose shrugged and sighed. "Sure, why not?"

Now if they'd only hurry up and leave without anyone else looking up!

"Will you go to the police?" Tom asked. "You don't know who we are, and it'd just be your word against ours, anyway."

"Hell, no," Steve replied. "There was no harm done. I could tell you didn't really mean to kill me, and I meant what I said about working together."

"We don't need you or your pallid, decrepit magic," Copper sneered. He spat on the cross, then ground it under his boot. "We're warlords of the dusk; the flame of primal chaos sings in our veins."

"Yay, team," said Tom.

"Well, can I at least have my gun and wallet back?"

"You wish," Copper said; Frank raised an eyebrow, scowled, and set them on the floor.

Pug-nose was the last one through the doorway. He paused for a last, slow, narrow-eyed look around, and David was absolutely certain he was about to tilt his head back and see the opening at last but then he said, "Watch your ass, buddy" and followed his companions down the stairs.

Steve sank down on the ice chest and sat there staring. David waited until he heard the front door close, then dropped into the room. "Are you all right?" he asked.

"It all happened so fast," Steve said dazedly. "One minute they were just questioning me, and even though they were pointing their guns at me I wasn't all that scared, and then that bastard—God! Do you think he really would have shot me?"

"I did for a second; I was about to jump down and attack him when Frank came back. Thinking about it now, I just don't know. The others wouldn't, but the redhead was crazy.

"You know, I realized too late that I shouldn't have left the cross and holy water down here. If they'd had a chance to use them against me, I could have been in really deep shit. So, uh, thanks for not giving me away."

"Forget it; at that point I was just trying to protect

238

myself the best way I knew how. I figured my chances were better playing dumb than admitting I was your accomplice, no matter what they said."

"Well, anyway you kept your mouth shut. Most people would have cracked under the pressure; I'm impressed that you didn't. And I guess the important thing is you prevented four fine, upstanding 'innocent people' from falling into a violent situation."

Steve grinned. "They weren't innocent people; they were a bunch of assholes.

Look, this hideout obviously isn't safe anymore. You'd better come stay with me."

David cringed. Sometimes, to make sure he was still sleeping where he claimed he was, Steve stayed with him until the end of the night, departing just before daybreak so no one would see him sneaking around the property. But if they lived together he could easily examine David while David was unconscious, could see and smell him as he really was. "I . . . I'm not sure that's such a good idea."

"Sure it is; it would be even if this house was secure. Now that we're going to be guarding this Dumont guy, we can't afford to waste time linking up."

"I thought you thought that plan was wrong."

"It's horribly wrong, but we've got murders every night and bands of trigger-happy lunatics hunting the killer through the streets, so I guess we really do have to try something, don't we? But if we're going to do it, we can't do it half-assed. I'll need to give you the day's intelligence and plan strategy with you first thing every evening. And I'll have to do it in north Tampa, so I can get to campus and start watching Dumont just a few minutes later."

"All right, I'll move in with you if you're sure you

239

want me to. But it means you'll be around me when I'm thirsty."

"Believe me, I'm familiar with the feeling."

Chapter Thirty-five

Just inside the automatic door, at a table with a sign that said VISITORS MUST SIGN IN AND SHOW PROPER I.D. on it, stood a security guard wearing a tiny gold cross as a tie clasp. He couldn't see anything amiss, so it didn't blaze unbearably, but apparently he'd put it on to ward off vampires because it pulsed and David's head throbbed in time with it. He waited three long minutes, afraid every second that his ghost-mask would shred away, until finally someone else walked up and activated the door, allowing him to slip inside unnoticed.

He limped quickly past the gift shop, the coffee shop, and the automatic teller machine toward the hospital information desk and the elevators and corridors beyond. As he crossed a lounge area, the television caught his eye. According to the reporter on the screen, an occult bookstore owner named Wally Fulton had invited "spiritually awakened" Tampans of all persuasions to assemble on a field at the outskirts of the University of South Florida campus. Several hundred – Pentecostals, Neo-Pagans, Hare Krishnas, Spiritualists, and Shintoists among them – had heeded the call and were busily praying, chanting, singing, dancing, meditating, and performing various rituals,

241

all of them intended to "exorcise" the Vampire Killer.

I wish it was that easy, David thought. Another surge of thirst goaded him on.

The sign taped to the door to the stairwell said EMERGENCY USE ONLY – ALARM WILL RING IF OPENED, so he hobbled back to the elevators. Fortunately, the one he boarded didn't get crowded before he reached his floor.

When the doors opened, he almost stayed inside; they'd installed security cameras in the hall. The black, staring boxes still bothered him, even though he'd determined through wary experimentation that the people watching through them must see only his shrouds. He was afraid that if he let the lenses peer at him too long, the monitor screens would eventually betray him, just like the glasses in the Mirror Maze.

So he hurried to the nurses' station. When he looked in the window, he snarled.

It hadn't taken the authorities long to realize that the Vampire Killer preferred victims who were incurably ill and severely handicapped, and now they'd obviously guessed that he peeked at hospital records to identify them, because someone had padlocked a sort of steel cable net around the rack containing the patients' charts.

No point going to another floor; they'd take the same precautions on every ward. Even driving the Taurus Steve had rented for him, there was no time to travel to another hospital or a nursing home; he was already getting light-headed.

He couldn't put on his medical student mask and ask to have the net unlocked, not when everyone was on the lookout for a murderer who was a master of disguise. But there were half a dozen folders outside the rack, the folders on which the nurse, the intern, and the ward clerk were actually working. If he could distract them long enough and thoroughly enough to sneak a look, perhaps he could still find suitable prey.

The intern was a skinny, stoop-shouldered guy, not bad looking, with limp strands of mousy brown hair dangling down his forehead, a stethoscope and a loosened knitted tie hanging around his neck, and blue ink stains on the edge of his writing hand. Frowning, squinting through the wire-rimmed glasses that kept slipping down his long nose, he stood beside the medication cabinet scrawling notes. The nurse was a willowy redhead whose unnaturally luminous turquoise eyes were probably the product of tinted contact lenses; the ward clerk, a short, buxom, curly-headed blonde fashionably dressed in tight, stone-washed gray jeans and a matching jacket. All three appeared to be in their twenties and none of them was wearing an engagement or wedding ring.

Your back aches, your eyes sting, and your vision's a blur, David told the intern. *They've worked you so many hours you're exhausted; you can hardly stand to write another line. If you don't take a break soon, you won't be able to keep going later, so you might as well take one now, while you've got two pretty girls to take it with.*

Look how beat this poor guy is, he said to the women. *The hospital works the interns like slaves, and you can tell he's the conscientious type who'll keep grinding away until he drops. He's liable to get sick if somebody doesn't make him unwind a little bit. So be a friend; after all, he is kind of cute.*

The intern closed the record he was holding, grim-

243

aced, and stretched; his back popped.

"Why don't you sit down and we'll all take five?" the ward clerk said. "I don't think any of the patients will croak if we put off the rest of our charting for a little while."

The intern removed his glasses and rubbed his eyes. "I really wish I could, but I can't. After I finish here, I have to check on the tenth floor to see—"

"You look dead on your feet, and the tenth floor's not going anywhere." She leaned sideways, grabbed another chair, and pulled it up beside hers. "Come on, park it."

"Well, okay, but just for a second."

"Are you going to Sally Bernstein's party Saturday night?"

"I don't know. See, I've got to give this presentation . . ."

The nurse listened and smiled, but she didn't say anything or stop her writing. Maybe she was resistant to mesmerism. Maybe she had a steady boy friend even though she didn't have a ring to prove it. Or maybe she was a dyke or a workaholic.

Whatever the problem was, all the blue plastic folders were right in front of her. Despite the pounding in his temples and the increasing fragility of his ghost-mask, David had to try again to distract her.

Also sitting on the desk before the nurse was a lidless forty-four-ounce Circle K Thirstbuster cup; she'd nearly emptied it.

This time he tried to influence her the way he would an animal. He remembered one of the few discomforts that no longer troubled him, the sensation of a swollen, aching bladder, and when he almost felt the urgent pressure, he struggled to make her feel it too.

Look at that huge cup, he told her after a while. *It was full, and now all the liquid that was inside it is inside you. It's got to come out* right now; *run to the bathroom before you wet your pants!*

"Excuse me!" she yelped, then shot up out of her chair and scurried to the restroom door.

The ward clerk and the intern barely glanced at her. "Yeah, Bon Jovi's great!" the blond woman said. "Did you see them when they played the Sun Dome?"

David started leafing through the charts. He had to hurry; the nurse wouldn't stay in the bathroom long! But he also had to turn the pages carefully, silently, when he was sure the others wouldn't see, and the nearly illegible handwriting and esoteric medical terminology slowed him down even more.

A middle-aged woman with a mild heart attack. A high-school kid with a collapsed lung. Suddenly he was sure that none of the six would be sick enough to kill. His mouth was dry and gritty; the room began to tilt, and he drew a deep breath and clutched the desktop to steady himself.

A man in his seventies who'd recently begun having seizures. It took two precious minutes to determine that he was still lucid.

The toilet flushed.

Only time for one more! He snatched for the next folder, knocked it off the stack and toward the edge of the desk.

He slapped his hand down, caught it, froze; they hadn't heard. Trembling now, he fumbled it open to the admission note.

This one was perfect.

Another geriatric patient, this one in his eighties.

Severe alcoholic deterioration: agitated, combative, and incoherent, diabetic, dehydrated, heart, kidneys, and liver all failing. Keep comfortable and sedated; DNR.

The poor old guy even had a private room.

The restroom faucet stopped hissing. He hastily re-stacked the folders and crept back outside. Despite the hot pain in his throat and the sight of yet another glowering security guard prowling the halls, he was smiling as he hurried toward his prey.

He stepped into the room, started to shut the door, then realized just in time that the person watching through the nearest camera might see it move. He was getting dangerously clumsy and muddled; thank God it was time to drink at last.

Fortunately, floor-length beige curtains surrounded the bed; he didn't need the door to hide behind. The old man was completely cocooned in tangled sheets and blankets; not even the top of his head showed. For a moment David fancied that his victim was already long dead, that when he pulled down the covers he'd see green corroded pennies sealing sunken eyes.

Certainly there was *something* strange . . . The thirst welled up and he was lost for an instant. No, of course nothing was wrong. The old man just looked creepy all wrapped up, like Frankenstein's monster lying on his slab. Ridiculous that, after all he'd been through, something so trivial could still unnerve him. He drew away the sheet and, sure enough, squashed against the pillow was the slack, wrinkled face he'd expected.

The bloodlust pulsed again and his ghost-shroud finally dissolved. He carefully positioned himself—

—and the old man's hands struck like cobras, snapped a shackle tight around his wrist.

David recoiled in shock, wrenching his arm when he hit the end of the chain. Nimble as an acrobat, the old man rolled off the opposite side of the bed, whipped aside his gown, and pressed a button on the belt underneath; a siren began to shriek.

Now that it was too late, David realized what he'd been too dazed and avid to consciously notice a moment before. His quarry didn't *smell* like a dying old man; in fact, he had a strong young heartbeat!

Panic set his own heart racing. He pulled the chain but it wouldn't come loose from the bed frame; he tried to pick up the whole bed and found it was bolted to the floor.

Safely out of his reach, the cop paused to peel off his wispy white wig and latex appliances. "You're under arrest!" he cried jubilantly. He didn't seem at all shaken by his prisoner's gruesome appearance; maybe he assumed his captive was wearing makeup too. "And you might as well stop struggling; we know how strong you are, and I guarantee that rig'll hold you anyway."

Let me go! David commanded. *This is all a terrible mistake; you've got the wrong man and you'll lose your job if you don't unlock this cuff* immediately!

He wasn't surprised when the policeman didn't obey. He tried to slip the shackle off, but it wasn't going to work, not unless he tore his hand off with it. He frantically ripped at the chain again; it still didn't break free, but this time tortured metal screeched.

"Hey, stop that!" shouted the cop. "I told you, you can't get away!" Another frenzied pull, another

247

squeal. "All right, damn it, I'm authorized to use this and you brought it on yourself!" Throwing open the curtains, he turned and grabbed a broom with a dull black handle.

Warily keeping his distance, he thrust the brushless end at David like a spear. David tried to dodge, but the fetter hampered him too much; it jabbed his shoulder.

A crackling shower of blue-white sparks; he gasped and fell to his knees.

Sobbing, he kept jerking the chain, but the shock had leeched his strength and now the bed frame wouldn't even groan.

The prod plunged in again and again, until he was half-blind and nearly paralyzed, until he huddled, shuddering and whimpering, on the floor. Three more cops dashed in from the hall.

"We got him!" said the cop who'd served as bait.

"Way to go!" one of the newcomers replied. "And I said it'd never work; shows what I know. Read him his rights yet?"

"Are you kidding? I just now got him subdued. He's even tougher than they said he was!"

"Then let's get him gagged and completely restrained and attend to the chickenshit afterward."

At last I've got nothing to lose, David thought. If I'm such a coward that I can't make myself do it even now, then I deserve to be dragged away in chains.

He closed his eyes and concentrated.

Icy slivers stabbed up his legs. For an instant he was back in his grave; he sunk his fangs into his free hand and the pain swept the fancy away. The cold danced up and up, and then he was nothing but shadow; he twitched the vacancy that had been his forearm, and the cuff was hanging empty.

"Jesus, look, you can see *through* him!" screamed one of the cops. Guns roared.

David flinched, and a second later he was on the other side of the bed; shorn of substance, he could move faster than anything alive. Too bad he couldn't use his newfound speed to flee, but his body was already starting to disperse.

He struggled to reclaim his flesh. At first nothing happened, but finally lightning blasted down his nerves and made him real again.

Ignoring the pain of reintegration, he leaped up off the floor at his tormentors. It had seemed to take at least ten seconds to restore his body, but the policemen were still pivoting to face him. He grabbed one and slammed him into the wall, punched a second in the kidney and backhanded him across the jaw as he fell. The third got off a shot, a near miss that whined past David's ear before he dropped him with a kick to the knee and a blow to the back of the head.

That left the bait. Unlike the others, he hadn't drawn his gun; perhaps he'd forgotten he had one. His face ashen, his mouth working soundlessly, he thrust again with the prod.

David parried it with his forearm, seized it, yanked it away. Reversing it, he rammed it into his opponent's stomach. The bait made a choking sound and fell.

David yearned to keep jabbing him, fifty times, a hundred; but he drew a ragged breath, turned, and threw the prod across the room instead.

The alarm was still keening; more sprinting feet

were pounding down the hall. He knew he couldn't spin another veil.

So he melted. Apparently it wasn't too soon to do it again, because he didn't die. He sprang at the window, wincing despite himself in anticipation of an impact that never came.

An instant later the ground was flashing by eight stories below. Light as air and swift as an arrow, he hurtled nearly a block before his limbs began to lose cohesion.

He congealed in an elementary school playground, between a row of teeter-totters and a jungle gym. The thirst boiled up like lava.

Chapter Thirty-six

A fitful wind gusted out of the southeast bearing drumbeats, snatches of song, and a tang of smoke. Occasionally coughing, the rustle of paper, or the whir of an electric motor sounded from the radio in the back of the van. Tattered clouds scudded across the moon, and a gray cat darted back and forth across the grass, toying with a mouse that wasn't there.

Steve lowered his binoculars and took a sip of coffee from the red plastic thermos cup sitting on top of the dashboard. "Don't keep that up too long," he said. "You don't want to burn yourself out."

David released the cat. Baffled, it peered wildly about before bounding away into the darkness. Then David lifted his own binoculars, sighting on the only illuminated first-story window on this side of the hulking concrete dormitory.

"I guess Dumont's pulling an all-nighter," Steve said after a moment, "just like the idiots over at the exorcists' jamboree. Thank God; I like to *hear* him, and since he doesn't snore, our wonderful, state-of-the-art, incredibly expensive bug doesn't pick up a damn thing when he's asleep. I sure wish we were closer; I wish we could sit right on top of him all the time. Maybe in a few minutes you should go invisible and sneak up for a closer look again."

David nodded.

"You know, if Liz or Wally had had two functional brain cells to rub together, they would have gotten the hell out of town instead of organizing a witches' hoedown. Now that the police have found Kaz's body, and Virgie, Joe, and of course dear old Carter have disappeared, they must understand that they're in danger. I guess they think their magic can protect them. Maybe they think only magic can protect them. Or, since the cops don't have any wizards on their payroll, maybe they think it's their duty to stand and fight. Or maybe they stuck around just because their lives are here."

David shrugged.

"God damn it!" Steve exploded. "Will you talk to me? You've hardly said a word the last three nights!"

Dumont coughed; David scanned the sky and grounds. "Sorry," he muttered, "I didn't mean for it to get on your nerves. Okay, I'll talk, I'll give you a piece of news. If I'm still alive when this is over, I'll still keep you posted on where I sleep."

"You mean you *want* me to kill you?"

"No, not exactly. I'm not encouraging you, but I want you to continue to have the option." He chuckled bitterly. "See, I used to think I was this 'nice' monster, but I'm not so sure anymore. Now I wonder if maybe I do deserve to die. But I can't make up my mind; you do it for me."

"If I'm supposed to do that, you'd better tell me what's happened."

"Yeah, all right. You know I got caught at Tampa Bay Regional Medical Center?"

"More or less. I heard about it on the news, and since the guy they trapped didn't kill any cops, I figured he was you. If you remember, I tried to ask you about it, but you just stared at me."

"Well, I only escaped because I finally managed to

252

turn into mist. Like I told you, it would kill me to stay in that form very long, so after I slipped out of the hospital I flew as far away as I could, then landed when I felt myself beginning to disintegrate.

"I reformed my body in an empty school yard, where I thought I could rest undisturbed. I sat down on the ground with my back against a big oak tree that would hide me from people passing on the street and tried to calm down and decide what to do next.

"My luck was still running true to form. Not five minutes after I arrived, a pretty Asian woman, a white guy pushing a pink baby carriage, and their little twin sons came down the sidewalk, the parents strolling but the kids almost prancing with impatience. As soon as they turned into the playground, the boys started running, and a moment later one was sweeping back and forth on a swing while the other stood balanced in the center of one of the teeter-totters shifting his weight to make the ends go up and down. They'd left their parents and their little sister far behind, but they weren't more than fifteen feet from me.

"Since I still hadn't drunk, I was in a bad way, parched and feverish. As I peeked around the oak, my perceptions oscillated. One moment the twins were cute, happy, healthy little boys. But the next their hearts pounded and the swing shrieked and the seesaw thudded against the ground in time. Then they were just strange, squealing animals, just tantalizing, fragrant bags of blood, and I ached to lunge out and bite one open.

"I knew I should try to sneak away, but I couldn't make myself get up and do it. I closed my eyes and dug my fingers into the tree trunk. Part of the time, when I was at my sanest, I tried to mesmerize the

253

father into taking everybody home, but I couldn't focus my will and nothing happened.

"Eventually I forgot why I was holding myself back.

"When I looked around the oak again the boys were climbing on the jungle gym. Midway between us, their parents stood watching, and a pace or two behind them sat the carriage.

"At that point I was only a creature, so of course I decided to take the easiest prey. With luck maybe I could carry the baby off and drain her before the others even realized she was gone.

"Desperate as I was, somehow I still crept up quietly. The mother and father were standing close with their arms around each other, and their bodies hid me from the kids. When I was three feet from the infant, the woman shifted; I was sure she was about to turn, and I almost fell on her snapping and punching before I saw that she wasn't.

"The baby smelled like soap; she was asleep. I clapped my filthy hand over her mouth and her brown, slanted eyes popped open. She squirmed and fought but couldn't make a sound.

"So I don't know why her mother finally spun around. Maybe it was maternal intuition, or maybe she smelled me.

"Her eyes were exactly like her daughter's. For some reason, that meant something to me; I snatched my hand back, then shoved the stroller at her. The ground was uneven and it almost upset, but her husband caught it.

"For a moment they were too scared or stunned to run. I knew I had to get rid of them fast, before the thirst overpowered me again, so I kind of roared, stretched out my arms, and lurched at them. The woman grabbed up her screaming baby and then they

254

wheeled and dashed toward their other kids.

"I chased them. At first it was to keep them moving, but before I'd gone ten feet it was to bring one down and drink. Fortunately, reforming my body from shadow hadn't straightened out my leg and I couldn't catch anyone.

"Once they disappeared I stumbled back to the baby carriage and beat it against the oak tree. After half a dozen blows my head cleared.

"And then I wracked my brain, but I couldn't find a way out of my dilemma. If I went back to Tampa Bay Regional, the police would nail me, but I obviously couldn't control myself long enough to hike the rest of the way back to the Taurus and then drive to another hospital. The only way I could avoid killing someone healthy was to commit suicide.

"Well, at first I thought, All right, then I will die; I'll keep the promise I made after I murdered Ed. At least I'll go out knowing that Carter never managed to pull me down to his level, and what the hell do I really have to live for anyway?

"I closed my eyes and tried to dissolve. My instincts told me I was too weak and it was too soon, that the attempt would probably destroy me on the spot, but if it didn't I'd simply soar toward the stars until I faded into nonexistence. It would be a lonely, spooky death, but a lot less painful than ramming a stake into my own heart or letting a bunch of policemen shoot me to pieces.

"But then I had second thoughts: I'd dragged you into this mess, so how could I abandon you when I knew you didn't stand a chance against Carter by yourself? How could I just roll over and die if it meant that Liz, Wally, and my mom and dad would die too? How could I let Carter survive to revel in murder and torture until the end of time? God damn it, I had to live!

"Anyway, that's what I told myself. Maybe I was only making excuses. Maybe I'm so selfish that I want to live no matter what the cost, or maybe I chickened out.

"At any rate, just as the cold pins and needles started pricking my feet I tore open my eyes, waited a second for my toes to thicken back into complete solidity, then headed for a lighted two-story wooden house on the other side of the street.

"I rang the doorbell; a stocky middle-aged guy with jug-handle ears, receding silvery hair, and bushy black eyebrows answered it. When he saw my face, he tried to yell and slam the door, but I lunged inside and grabbed his throat before he could do either.

"We staggered around banging into the walls for a few seconds, and then I finally got my teeth in him. Apparently his wife heard us struggling, because just as I was sucking my first mouthful she charged down the stairs, screamed once, then started pummeling me.

"Without even raising my head, I hit her back. I wish I could say I didn't mean to do it so hard, that I tried to pull my punch, but the truth is, at that moment I was too far gone to care.

"When I'd drunk myself sane enough to look around, she was lying on the floor and I had chips of bone and scraps of flesh and brain stuck to the back of my hand.

"I turned off the lights and locked the door when I left. Since they haven't made the papers, I guess no one's found them yet."

"David—"

"There's more. Yesterday evening I sneaked into the VA and, even though it was tough, managed to check the records and find my usual kind of victim. But to-night I visited a seedy little nursing home Carter's never even raided, and they'd put in security from hell! Eventually I figured out how to get at a few of the patients but not their charts, so I wound up killing a sleeping woman I didn't know anything about. She was ancient, bedridden, and incontinent, but it's entirely possible that she still had a sharp mind and loved life as much as anybody.

"God knows how much more harm I'll do before this is over. In one way, it doesn't matter. Even if I'm lucky enough to be able to kill the prey I prefer from here on out, I've already become what I've become."

"Look," said Steve, "I'm not making any promises, but right now I really can't see myself killing you. Not if you go away to another city after we destroy Carter, at least until all this Vampire Killer hysteria dies down and they pull the guards and alarm systems back out of the hospitals. Because now that I've been around you for a while, I'm pretty sure you're not truly evil."

"Give me a break."

"You're not. You love people and have a conscience. When you . . . hunt, you're just doing what you have to do to survive, the same as every other man and ani-mal in the world. And you weren't just rationalizing there on the playground. Your friends and family *do* need you. We do have to murder Carter. And, cold-blooded as it sounds, if a few innocent, healthy people have to die to give us our shot at him, in the long run the world will still be better off."

David shook his head. "I don't know if I buy any of that, but thanks for trying. You know, you keep surprising me. When I first asked you to help me, I half-expected you to turn me down. Then later I was afraid that when you saw me asleep and unshrouded you'd destroy me out of sheer revulsion. And—"

"I never looked at you during the day; I could tell you didn't want me to."

"Thanks for that, too. And as I was saying, I was just about sure you'd condemn me when you heard what I just told you. How come you're so generous and understanding all of a sudden?"

"I'm no different than I ever was; you just never got to know me before. I tried to make friends but you wanted to believe I was a prick."

"Yeah. In a way, that's the story of my life. The story of my death, too, come to think of it. I—"

"You cripples keep late hours," said the radio.

"My God," Steve whispered, *"he's inside!"*

Chapter Thirty-seven

Steve frantically started grabbing his weapons; David snatched his Browning off the floor, threw open the door, and sprinted up the sidewalk and across the slippery grass. He'd never hated his limp so much; Carter could bite Dumont at any second! Shielding his face with his forearms, he dove at the window.

He crashed through, landed hard, sprawled breathless on a linoleum floor with shards of tinkling, snapping glass raining down all around him.

It was a typical institutional bedroom with a low, narrow bed and a metal dresser, but photos and posters of outer space scenes, brilliantly colored tropical birds and fish, and scantily clad models with glistening bronze skin brightened the sickly yellow cinder block walls. Atop the long formica desk bolted to the wall opposite the bed were crowded stacks of books, a tape recorder, a portable TV, and a stereo; the speakers sat at the ends of the otherwise empty shelf above.

Dumont slumped slack-jawed and glassy-eyed in his wheelchair, his crotch wet and stinking of piss. Carter stood behind him, one brown, clawlike hand resting on his shoulder.

David lurched to one knee and whipped up his gun. "You'd better step away from him," he said.

Carter jerked Dumont up out of his chair, held him so that his limp, twisted body largely concealed

259

Carter's own. "Just how good a shot do you think you are?"

"Tonight we're going to settle what's between us, no matter what that takes. I'd rather not risk shooting him, but I will if I have to."

"What a ruthless fellow you've become. Alas, Kenneth, my friend's callous disregard for your safety has somewhat hastened your demise. If he cared about your welfare, it might have proved amusing to keep you alive a bit longer, but since he doesn't I might as well drink you now."

Dumont started thrashing; Carter murmured and stroked his hair, and his arms flopped back down at his sides. "Strong will," the elder vampire observed, then bent his crumbling face to his captive's neck. David tried to pull the trigger, and the familiar paralyzing pressure ballooned in his brain. He hammered at it, felt it begin to fade immediately, saw that he was still going to be too late.

Bullets thundered through the shattered window.

The first slammed into Carter's left shoulder, through his torso, and out the other side, nearly severing his right arm. The second crunched into his upper back; chunks of leathery flesh leaped from the point of impact. The third smashed in just below the second. Still clutching Dumont, he fell; the handicapped student wound up on top of him.

Steve ripped open his khaki shoulder bag, grabbed a cross, and threw it into the middle of the floor.

It blazed like a sun come down to earth. His guts churning and his muscles knotting in agony, David collapsed and writhed, broken glass grinding against his skin.

Steve clambered through the window, rifle in hand. "Are you all right?"

260

"What . . . does it look like?" David croaked. "But it's just . . . the cross . . . *he* didn't hurt me."

"I'll get rid of it in a second," Steve replied. His eyes glittered, and he was panting as though he'd just run five miles.

"Not till . . . you make certain . . . Carter's dead."

"I am certain, but don't worry, I remember the drill. Is Dumont all right?"

"Not . . . sure."

Steve knelt beside the two intertwined bodies on the other side of the room, gently turned the handicapped student's head from side to side. "Look, Ma, no tooth marks!" When he tried to pull one of Carter's arms open it wouldn't move, so he set his rifle on the floor and seized it with both hands. "I guess this is what they call a death grip.

"You know, I never killed anything bigger than a bug before. Not ever. Well, I guess in a way I still haven't, but you know what I mean. God damn, do you think I'm going to have to cut his arms off? When I saw him I was really grossed out, even though you warned me what to expect, but I'm glad he wasn't wearing a mask; I don't know if I could have fired if he looked like some ordinary guy I'd never seen before. As it was, I was scared to death I'd hit Dumont, but still, I just . . . I just shot him. Did you ever think we'd nail him so easily?"

Suddenly, despite the excruciating incandescence of the cross, David was afraid they hadn't. Half-blind with glare and pain, he strained to peer closely at the visible portions of Carter's body. "Hurry!"

"I am."

The tugging bounced Dumont up and down. Beneath him something seemed to seethe and ripple, but perhaps it was only shadows shifting. "Stop messing . . .

261

with his arms! Flip them over . . . and destroy his head!"

Steve giggled crazily. "Sure, why not? I've got nine bullets left. Look, we've put Dumont through too much already. I don't want to dump him on his face or get him all splashed with corpse gunk or let him come to still cuddled up with *this*. Hang in there; I'll be finished in a moment."

Abruptly thrusting Dumont aside, the lips of his wounds squirming and puckering, Carter sat up.

Steve wailed and grabbed his rifle, but at the same instant the revenant caught his wrist; bone cracked.

David labored to raise his arm until he noticed the Browning wasn't in his hand anymore. Grunting with effort, he turned his head but couldn't see it anywhere.

Carter tore the rifle away and slid it under the desk, then threw Steve down and pinned him. "No one's hurt me like that since nineteen-eleven," he said. "If only you'd followed up immediately, if only you hadn't assumed I was, if not dead, at least as helpless as my protégé there, you would have ended me. But of course you had no way of knowing that mere proximity to a cross wouldn't inconvenience a vampire as old and powerful as I.

"Now I'm going to hurt you."

He began slowly raking his fingertips down Steve's face, carving bloody furrows. Steve struggled furiously, but couldn't buck him off.

Gasping and shuddering, bits of glass stabbing and gashing him, David wormed his way toward the bed. Intent for the moment on his revenge, Carter didn't seem to notice.

The revenant took Steve's left ear between his wet red thumb and first two fingers, then jerked it. It ripped away showering crimson drops, and the human started shrieking.

David labored to lift his hands, failed, tried again. Finally he gripped the sheet and pulled.

It scarcely moved. Someone had tucked it under the mattress, and he was too feeble to drag it out.

Carter walked his fingers down Steve's torso. Steve kicked and contorted, lashed back and forth, still couldn't break loose.

Whimpering, somehow David sat up, just barely managed to grab the sheet higher up before he toppled back onto the floor. This time his weight drew it free.

Steve clamped his thighs tight together; Carter's ragged brown digits wriggled between them anyway.

David swept the sheet across the floor; Steve screamed.

As soon as the cloth covered the cross, David's strength came flooding back. Almost oblivious to the pain still raging through his nerves, he sprang to his feet and hurled himself at Carter.

The corpse-thing looked up just in time, met him with a glancing backhand blow to the jaw. He shook his head and lunged in again. Carter tried to jerk out of his way, but he wasn't quite quick enough; David slammed him back against the desk, and an instant later they were locked together, biting, pounding, and rending one another on the floor.

The hampering alien presence swelled in David's mind. By the time he shoved it out Carter was straddling him, his fists hurtling down to pulp his skull. He wrenched his head aside and chopped at the elder vampire's throat, but Carter ducked, bit, and tore a mouthful of gray, pussy flesh out of his chest.

Then another debilitating fire flared. More glass shattered and phosphorescent blue-white liquid

263

streamed sizzling over Carter's head and shoulders.

Carter howled, rolled away across the floor clawing at himself. He left scraps of ash and charred tissue on the linoleum and an acrid black vapor hanging in the air.

David's skin burned too, but only a few tiny patches of it and only for a moment; Carter's body had shielded him. As he started to stand up, Steve fumbled another fiery bottle out of his satchel. David averted his eyes; there was a crash and the nauseating radiance flickered and died. "Got you again, you son of a bitch! Left-handed, too!"

Grasping the bed, Carter wrenched himself back onto his feet. Smoke still boiled from his body, particularly his mouth, nose, ears, eye sockets, and the half-healed exit wound in his shoulder; he was trembling, and his shriveled face was bubbling, oozing, and flaking away from his skull. "Still not good enough," he said, and although David couldn't see anything to indicate it, somehow he sensed Carter was beginning to dissolve.

No! he roared. *FREEZE!*

Carter kept moving, but his flesh congealed; he snarled, whirled, and unlocked the dead bolt on the door.

David rushed him, sidestepped a kick, grabbed his right arm and swung him into the dresser.

The arm ripped away in his hands.

Carter screamed and clutched his shoulder. Transported with a savage elation, David cast the limb aside and pounced.

At last *he* was on the offensive, he was the one hammering and rending an opponent too slow and clumsy to evade him. He kicked Carter's legs out from under him, then hurled himself down on top of him.

264

Their faces only inches apart, a reek of ancient corruption filling his nostrils, David wrapped his hands around the elder vampire's neck and began tearing Carter's head off. Carter heaved and battered him, but couldn't break his grip.

Across the room, something gurgled.

Without releasing Carter, David jerked around. Dumont still lay where the revenant had tossed him, but now he was wriggling, choking, and dragging feebly at the jointed brown and gray stick that had attached itself to his throat. For a moment David imagined it was some kind of snake; then he recognized Carter's severed arm and hand, the fingers dug in deep and drawing blood. His face grooved and shiny red, his rifle clasped awkwardly in his left hand, Steve stood paralyzed not three feet away.

"Your choice," Carter gasped.

David slammed the other vampire's head down once; it crunched, but he hadn't pulverized it. Then he scrambled away across the floor.

Carter laughed.

Dumont's face was purple, his tongue protruding. When David tried to seize the arm, it beat madly back and forth.

The door thumped shut.

By the time he managed to grab the arm, Dumont had passed out. He strained to twist it and break its hold, couldn't; he gouged his fingers in around the thumb, pried it up, and snapped it.

He fought again to wrench the arm away; the fingers released suddenly and then, the limb contorting like the serpent he'd fancied it was, slashed at his face.

He whipped his head back just in time. Before the arm could attack again, he flailed it against the wall. When all its bones had shattered, it stopped moving.

265

He wasted a precious instant making sure Dumont was still breathing, then leaped up and threw open the door. But on the other side were only an empty corridor and, beyond the door at the end of it, the night.

Chapter Thirty-eight

By the time David hobbled back to Dumont's room, the bite wound in his chest was throbbing fiercely. The handicapped student was still unconscious; Steve was sitting hunched forward in the wheelchair, his face in his hands.

"It's my fault," he said brokenly. "You did your job, you kept him distracted so I could sneak up with the bag and the heavy gun, and if I hadn't lost my shit we would have had him! I—"

David yanked him to his feet and slapped him.

"You're still losing it, and this isn't over! Pull yourself together!"

Steve blinked, shook his head. "I . . . okay."

"Are you all right?"

"I still have one working arm, one ear, and both balls, if that's what you mean. Jesus, that's right, he tore my damn ear—"

David shook him. "Can you drive?"

"I'll do it somehow if I have to."

"You have to; you have to get out of here *now*, before somebody comes to find out what all the noise was about." He knelt, peered about, finally found his Browning under the bed. "Take Carter's arm to Fedora's Pub on Fletcher and wait for me in the parking lot. It's just possible that he can home in on it, so stay on guard. And watch the arm itself; if it starts moving, pour more holy water on it and then beat the crap out of it."

"You're going after him! How do you know where he's headed?"

"Because I know how he thinks. Now let's move!"

Chapter Thirty-nine

The road dead-ended in a faculty parking lot. David wrenched the steering wheel, sideswiped and knocked over a motor scooter, then sped back out onto the street.

Seething with frustration, he slammed his fist down on his thigh. Why did the campus have to be such a damn maze? And why had he wasted time locating his pistol and lifting Dumont onto his bed?

The Taurus rocketed past a stop sign. Tires squealing and horn blaring, a pickup swerved and missed it by a hair.

David turned once more and was finally hurtling south on a straight four-lane road. After a few seconds the cubical concrete classroom buildings gave way to open fields.

The mass exorcism appeared suddenly; it had convened just beyond a thick stand of trees. Several hundred cars parked in a semicircle; inside their arc a black mass of humanity surged and shifted, its contours fitfully illuminated by the flickering golden glow of several bonfires and the sickening incandescence of three huge crosses.

A white Seville had just parked; its taillights winked off and Carter climbed out. His face was still a patchwork of burnt rot and bare bone, but he was moving nimbly again.

David pressed the accelerator even harder; he shouted *Freeze!* The elder vampire raised his remaining hand in a mocking salute and flitted behind a school bus.

By the time David jolted up onto the curb, careened, fishtailing, across the grass, and lurched to a stop behind the Cadillac, he was long gone.

David took a deep breath and refocused his shroud, then stepped out into the smoky air. The field thrummed with a thousand intermingled noises, the voices of a gospel choir knifing through the drone.

Since no one was watching, he decided to render the Seville undrivable, so Carter couldn't use it to flee again. He hurriedly punched out one of its windows, unlocked the door, climbed inside, and ground his knuckle against the ignition until it crumpled. Then, the radiant crosses already leeching his strength and intensifying his countless aches and pains, he limped toward the crowd.

Slipping past what looked like a conga line of swaying, chanting bald people in orange togas, he found himself before an elevated platform. The conservatively dressed young man on the stage opened, reversed, and shook a scarf to demonstrate there was nothing inside it, then lashed it through the air. Little molded plastic cameos of Jesus showered out onto the ground; the audience moaned and scrambled to snatch them up.

Swept this way and that, jostled, at times nearly crushed, David buffeted his way through the milling press. Carter seemed to have vanished off the face of the earth. And where in God's name were Liz and Wally?

Just ahead was a black plastic cauldron full of steaming dry ice; three pudgy belly dancers in G-string bikinis were oozing around it, and a thin, hatchet-faced woman in a long cape and a horned Viking helmet was squatting beside it, gazing raptly into an upraised quartz crystal. Several onlookers were staring just as intently at her, no doubt waiting to hear her reveal whatever secret she was in the process of divining.

David didn't recognize her, but she looked like someone who might know Wally. He tapped her on the shoulder.

She struck his hand away. "Odin's blood!" she growled in an unnaturally guttural voice. "Can't you see I'm scrying?"

"Sorry. Tell me where Wally Fulton is and I'll get out of your hair."

"I don't know him."

"You must; he organized all this. A chubby guy with a round pink face."

"Perhaps the woman knows him; Sigurd does not." She lifted her crystal again.

"Then why don't you put 'the woman' back in the driver's seat for—" Thirty feet ahead, Carter strode between a candle-covered ground cloth and a dozen guys performing slow-motion tai chi exercises.

Shoving and elbowing people aside, David plunged forward; he made it to the candles just in time to glimpse his quarry disappearing behind a freestanding black velvet portrait of Bela Lugosi. Fists clenched and breath rasping, he pursued.

Carter led him directly toward one of the crosses; his eyes blurred and the world began revolving. As he stumbled by the gospelers and a makeshift booth in which a Gypsy was giving Tarot readings, the old woman from the laundromat clutched his arm. He wailed and flung her off, knocking her down and scattering her pamphlets, then saw that she was really someone else.

271

A few moments later he reached the foot of the cross, its searing glare so dazzling that it largely concealed what lay behind it. His eyes squinched shut, he blundered on.

Once the light was at his back, his head cleared. To his left, men, women, and even children were lifting sluggishly writhing rattlesnakes, water moccasins, and copperheads out of wooden boxes. They draped them about their bodies, stroked them, passed them around; one tiny girl with long brown pigtails had one in each hand and another two coiled around her neck. Off to his right, on a bare patch of earth inscribed with a pentagram, gaunt, shaven-headed Frank, now clad in a high-collared scarlet robe, was brandishing a sword and gibbering Latin. And straight ahead, in front of one of the leaping, crackling bonfires, stood Carter, Liz, and his father.

Stan was staring blank-faced at the ground, but, judging from the way she was waving her hands, Liz was arguing vehemently. Carter squeezed her arm as he replied; she slumped, then straightened and started jabbering again.

David pulled his Browning out and charged.

When he was twenty feet away, Carter turned, froze for an instant, then pointed and shouted, "It's him!"

Liz looked and turned white; someone screamed.

Then everyone was shrieking. The crowd exploded into pandemonium, most people stampeding but many fighting their way forward against the tide and a few ministers and occultists like Frank struggling to stand their ground and continue their rituals. The towering cross was flashing, flaming brighter with each pulse. David could feel that his mask was still in place; he squandered an irreplaceable moment staring about in bewilderment, then raised the Browning. Something smashed his legs out from under him and as he fell the gun tumbled out of his hand.

He hit the ground, rolled; a muddy boot stamped down beside his head. He tried to scramble back up, but now other people were kicking him, the bursts of pain a counterpoint to the hellish agony the cross was hammering through his body.

Beyond a forest of darting, dancing legs, Carter led Liz and Stan, both now empty-eyed and quiescent, away from the fire. The revenant was staggering again.

David tried to melt, found he couldn't. Kicking, punching, clawing, snapping bones, and tearing away gobs of cloth and bloody meat, he finally drove his tormentors back and sprang to his feet.

He was surrounded. For a heartbeat the mob hung back, and he imagined his ferocity had cowed them. But then, single-minded and implacable as a horde of army ants, trampling their fallen fellows in their eagerness, they roared and lunged at him.

Whirling, trying not to look directly at the cross, lashing out again and again with all that remained of his inhuman strength, David dodged and battered his way after Carter. He shattered a jaw, flattened a nose, backhanded a fat old man and sent him reeling. Just as he reached the fire they closed in again, hands snatching, grasping, dragging him down.

He ripped free and dove at the flames.

Someone clubbed him as he jumped, slamming him down in a heap at the heart of the blaze. Howling, his thrashing limbs scattering glowing chunks of wood and bits of ember, he somersaulted out the other side.

Clear again, he started sprinting; a dozen skinheads clutching knives, bottles, and lengths of pipe loped out of the darkness ahead.

He spun and raced for the snake handlers' abandoned boxes.

A brown pint bottle whizzed past his ear; another missile jabbed him in the thigh. The pack bayed, thundered at his heels. He vaulted over the little girl with the pigtails, her mashed, trodden face further defiled with double punctures, threw himself to one knee, and yanked open one of the lidded crates.

It was empty. A bludgeon crashed down on top of his skull.

Time skipped, and he was lying facedown in the grass. He twisted and drove his heel into his attacker's shin; the skinhead yelped and fell back against the deputy sheriff charging up behind him.

David scrambled to the next box, plunged his hands into a mass of squirming rope. Hissing and clattering, it stabbed twinned needles at his fingers.

Then Frank was rearing over him, sword held high. "I banish thee!" he cried, then whipped it down.

David jerked aside; the blade crunched deep into the side of the box. He hurled a pair of flailing three-foot diamondbacks into the diabolist's face.

Frank lurched backward, tripped, and fell. David threw handful after handful of maddened snakes, and the shrieking throng recoiled. Clutching a fresh box under one arm and scattering cottonmouths behind him, he dashed after Carter again.

As the cross receded, his strength began to return. Feet still pounded at his back; ahead, beyond the swarm of people still scurrying to their cars, engines roared and horns blared. A woman in a gray felt hat looked over her shoulder. He stuck his hand into the crate, then saw that she wasn't going to scream; apparently his mask was working again.

Dodging and pushing, he zigzagged through the

274

crowd. In the parking lot cars banged and ground together; drivers bellowed, sobbed, and shook their fists. Its front doors hanging open, the Seville sat empty.

David peered frantically about, finally spotted them. Liz's ancient Mazda had crept to the very edge of the jam, but it wasn't moving now; the starter whined and whined but wouldn't catch.

He lunged forward—

—and Wally yelled, "It's him!"

David whirled. Six feet away, circles of sweat under his arms and the border of a tattoo protruding from under his cuff, his friend stood pointing a snub-nosed revolver at him.

David said "You're making a mista—"

"It's you," Wally panted. "I never had my eyes off you, so I'm sure. I'm sorry, David."

David tried to dissolve, but even this far away the cross still hindered him. He shouted, *Freeze!* But Wally fired anyway.

Three shots missed, one burned through his forearm, and two blasted into his stomach and knocked him sprawling on top of the snake box. It only took him a second to shrug off the shock, but when his head cleared Copper was crouching over him aiming an assault rifle at his face.

David rolled; the gun chattered and nearly cut the crate in half. He tackled Copper, brought him down, started him yowling by grabbing and crushing his testicles, then silenced him by bashing a dent in his brow.

Wally was trying to reload, but he'd started shaking so badly the bullets kept slipping out of his fingers; everyone else was running away. David sprang to his feet, wheeled—

And saw that he was too late; the Mazda was moving again. Apparently unwilling to risk being delayed

275

on the congested road, Carter had fled across the fields and was already hundreds of feet away; a second later, the car vanished over a rise.

David slapped Wally's gun out of his hand, then seized him by the collar and jerked him close. "I *saved* you," he said. "I saved your stupid face and you helped *him*."

"Please," Wally whimpered, "try to remember what you were. Try to feel my aura—"

"You know what I'm going to do about your face now? I'm going to stick it in that box over there. Maybe the fucking snakes will like your aura."

Wally started kicking and punching; David half-paralyzed him with a blow to the solar plexus, manhandled him forward and onto his knees. When he flipped up the riddled lid the two surviving water moccasins flattened their heads and opened their creamy-edged mouths. He slowly pushed the writhing human down—

—then yanked him back and released him. "Jesus Christ," he whispered, "get away from me."

Wally clambered to his feet and bolted.

Chapter Forty

Steve scratched at his bloodstained bandages, then gasped and flinched.

"Leave your face alone," David said.

"I can't; it itches." He picked up his steaming mug, sipped, then set it back down on the coffee table beside the Browning and the telephone; his rifle, his satchel, Copper's AK-47, and the aluminum suitcase in which he'd locked Carter's arm lay at his feet. "So what happened then?"

"Basically I just got in the Taurus, waited until I could pull out, and drove away; it was no problem once I looked like a mortal again and no one was actually chasing me." The Pentecostal girl's mangled body floated before his eyes. "God, I still can't believe nine people died."

"With a panicked crowd of that size? We're lucky it wasn't more."

"I never dreamed he could erase my shroud without taking control of my mind or hurting me so badly my concentration slipped. I still don't understand how he did it."

"Oh, really? I figured that out as soon as you told me about it. He weaves more powerful illusions than you do, doesn't he?"

"Sure. He can make people hallucinate a completely

different world. About all I can do is change my appearance."

"Then I imagine he superimposed the image of a shambling corpse over your mask of normalcy, and for at least a moment or two everyone perceived his illusion instead of yours."

"You're probably right. Shit, just when—"

The phone rang.

David jackknifed, almost tumbled off the couch, snatching up the receiver. "Hello!"

"Good evening again," Carter said. "My heartiest felicitations on your escape."

"We still have your arm; it's still okay."

"I know, I can feel it. My captives are intact as well. I propose a truce and an exchange."

"I agree."

"Then ascend the Sulphur Springs tower alone and unarmed. If you give me any reason to suspect you of hostile intent I'll kill them instantly."

"All right, but I want to talk—"

The line went dead. David grimaced and hung up.

"Well?" Steve asked.

"Just what we expected."

"I'll drive so you can rest." When he stood up, he swayed.

"I don't think—"

"I can drive, and I want to be there—or at least as close as I can get."

"Okay, if you can drive fast. I'm supposed to meet him on Bird Street, so Ybor City's not exactly on our way."

Chapter Forty-one

The tower gleamed in the moonlight like an ivory chess king resting on a grassy, irregular square, a square bounded by three roads and the river.

Steve pulled into a deserted package-store parking lot across the street.

"You've got to admit, he picked a good spot," David said. "Nobody could cross that field and climb ten flights of stairs without him spotting them."

Steve snorted. "I know, and I really won't follow you. I'll wait here and open the trunk like we planned. But I still wish you'd take the Browning."

"He might search me, find it, and go crazy. Besides, I can never hold on to the damn things anyway. Uh, you might want to look away and hold your nose."

Steve tried not to flinch and nearly succeeded. "Jesus, even when you were fighting in Dumont's room you didn't let your mask slip."

"Yeah, well, when I get up there I'm liable to need every spark of psychic energy I've got."

"It makes me think you don't expect—"

"He was much stronger than I am before you splashed the holy water on him, and I imagine he's recovered a lot of strength by now. On the other hand, I've learned a couple of tricks he doesn't know I know. So we'll just have to see what happens. . . . You know, I really am sorry—"

"Don't start that again. If we can solve our immediate problem I'll get the rest of my life straightened out somehow, and if we can't it won't matter anyway. Now go take care of business." He extended his hand.

David hesitated, finally shook it. Then he got out, carried the suitcase across the street, tossed it over the chain link fence on the other side, hooked his fingers in the mesh and climbed over.

As he trudged across the grass, a bird chirped; a moment later a warm breeze fanned his face. When he raised his eyes the eastern sky was gray.

Up close, the tower didn't seem to shine; its skin of dingy, graffiti-scarred paint was flaking away, like his own. The door gaped on darkness. His inhuman senses probing ahead, he started up the rusty stairs that spiraled around the hollow interior; his footsteps clacked and echoed up the shaft.

He climbed slowly, conserving his strength. Whenever he passed one of the grimy windows he paused to look down at the Taurus. Steve was still behind the wheel and, as far as he could tell from such a distance, still okay.

Eight stories up, two below the doorway to the balcony, the stairs had buckled; sections of the railing fallen away, they hung from the wall at nearly a forty-five-degree angle. David scaled them like a ladder and they bounced, groaned, and showered chunks of corrosion into the black well below.

The mingled scents of sweat, cologne, and corruption wafted through the opening; hearts pounded.

280

David started concentrating, then stepped out under the stars.

Liz moaned. "Please don't come any closer," Carter said.

They were about ten feet away. Her face streaked with tears and his dad's ashen, they stood on the parapet. Carter sat beside them, a cellular phone by his feet. He'd taken the time to change his torn, blood- and slime-encrusted clothes, and his empty sleeve fluttered in the wind.

Stan said, "Son, I love you and I'm sorry."

"After we arrived I unmasked and explained everything," Carter said. "It helped to pass the time."

"I'm sorry too," David said. "Are you guys okay?"

"He hasn't hurt us," Liz quavered, "but we can't come down. He said we'll step *backward* if he wants us to."

"Stay calm; now that I'm here everything will be fine. Isn't that right, Carter?"

"Presumably," the elder vampire said. "Slide the valise over here."

"Nice tie. Is it a clip-on?"

"No, Liz was kind enough to knot it for me." He cocked his head, listening, glanced over his shoulder at the ground. "The bag?"

"I think you'd have to admit you've deceived me a time or two, so maybe you can understand why I'm a little reluctant to hand over my hostage first." Temples throbbing, David groped; it was impossible to tell if anything was happening.

"Quite. But unfortunately I don't trust you either, so you'll have to do this my way or not at all. I can survive with a single arm if necessary; can you

281

endure abandoning these charming mortals to a grisly demise?"

David felt him prying at his mind. He blanked his face and mimed a stagger, then set the suitcase down.

Stan said "Don't!"

"I have to." He pushed it across the concrete floor, and Carter stopped it with his foot. "The combination's six sixty-six, Steve's idea of a joke."

"I must remember to thank him for the compliment." A muffled thumping sounded, the arm fumbling around, making sure the bag wasn't booby-trapped. Liz shuddered.

Satisfied, the master vampire stripped off his tie, jacket, and shirt. His shoulder terminated in black spongy tatters and splintered bone; his bullet wounds hadn't fully closed. He looked over the parapet again, then squatted and opened the suitcase.

David's head was pounding; he wondered how much longer he could focus his will and attend to the conversation at the same time. "Okay, now you've got it. Let them go."

"Not quite yet. I'm still as weak as a kitten, and I'd be at your mercy without my shield. You'll have to wait until I'm reattached."

He picked up his arm and pressed it back in place. Leathery rot began to liquefy and seep across the division. Liz retched and swayed; for a second David was afraid she'd lose her balance, but Stan grabbed her elbow and steadied her.

As his dead flesh knitted Carter prowled along the balcony peering down. Hoping to distract him, David said, "I'm glad you decided to do this tonight. I was afraid you'd wait until tomorrow."

"Because it's nearly sunup? My new home isn't terribly far and *I* can fly. I see your confederate waiting faithfully by your car, so I trust you won't be inconvenienced either."

"You can cut the shit. I understand you well enough to know you won't let me leave here alive, not after I came so close to destroying you."

"Indeed. You don't appear discomfited at the prospect."

"I'm not. No matter how hard I tried to avoid hurting anyone, I spread misery wherever I went. Of course, I have you to thank for part of that, but I did enough damage all by myself to convince me that dead people shouldn't walk around. Just let Liz and Dad go and I'll die happy."

Carter flexed his arm, curled his fingers into a fist, chuckled. "My poor dunce. If you truly fathomed me you'd realize that I couldn't possibly permit you to 'die happy'—and you wouldn't expect me to cleave to my word in *any* particular."

"What do you mean?"

"I mean that unless you'd care to watch *both* these mortals plummet to their deaths, you'll have to choose one and drink him. When you've bitten the one you condemned I'll release the survivor."

"God damn it, you can't—We had a *deal!*"

"I'm afraid I've changed the terms. Do you accept them?"

Liz said, "Don't do it! He'll only break this promise too!"

"She's right," Stan said. "Save yourself and kill him when you can."

Carter slipped on his shirt. "They have a point: I *might* cheat. But if you want to try to save one,

283

what other option do you have?"

"All right!" David snarled. "Just . . . just give me a minute to select."

"Come now, there are only two of them, and as you pointed out, the dawn creeps on apace. I have a quarter if you'd like to flip it."

"No. . . . I pick Dad."

Liz sobbed.

"Now that wasn't so difficult, was it?" Carter tied his tie. "Just remain where you are, and I'll send him to you. Step down, Mr. Brent. You'll find you can walk to your son, though you still can't struggle."

Wide-eyed and trembling, Stan shuffled forward. When David touched his arm, he cringed. "Dad, I—"

"If . . . if you think you should do this at all," Stan said, "then you made the right choice. Liz has her whole life ahead of her. Just do it fast and *kill* me; don't make me come back."

The hot air was clotting around him, numbing his mind. He strained and strained and still nothing happened. "Carter, you always hinted that you've learned everything there is to know about vampirism. Before I . . . do what you want, will you tell me one thing?"

The corpse-thing quickly surveyed the ground. "What would you like to know?"

"Have I lost my soul? Are we damned no matter what we do?"

"Of course; you can take comfort in the knowledge that when you perish you'll tumble into perdition whether you've committed patricide or not. And if you don't want to see *Liz* tumble, I suggest you honor your father's wishes and commit it with dispatch."

Making his hands shake, feigning clumsiness, David fumbled Stan's collar away from his throat. His skull ringing with agony and the tower revolving like a carousel, he called into the incalescent night. And finally, his dry eyes pulsing, he kissed his father's neck.

Something hummed.

Still nearly invisible against the darkness, the cloud of wasps he'd collected at the house in Ybor City rose above the parapet and swarmed on Carter. Stinging furiously, crawling under his clothes and into the ragged cavities in his head, they coated his upper body in an instant.

David bellowed, *FREEZE!*

The elder vampire tried to dissolve, but couldn't. Reeling and flailing, he staggered into Liz. She screamed and stumbled; her heels slipped over the edge. Arms windmilling madly, she toppled farther and farther into space.

David lunged forward, slammed Carter aside, caught hold of her belt just before she fell.

His arm around her waist, he dragged her to where his father stood gaping and unconsciously fingering his unbitten throat. "You can move normally now; get down the stairs!"

Stan said, "I'll help—"

"You can't! Run!" *Go!* He shoved them toward the doorway. Their first steps were stiff, their second quicker.

Pain blasted through his skull, and David collapsed.

His head and shoulders still a mass of hornets,

his nose hole and eye sockets seething with them, Carter loomed above him. He started to jump up, and the corpse-thing's toe crunched against his temple. He rolled, tried again, nearly made it; another kick shattered his jaw and hurled him back against the parapet.

Snatching frantically, his whole torso dangling, he barely stopped himself from tumbling over.

Carter crouched to spring. Then he grunted and doubled over. His moldering frame wracked with spasms, he managed to flicker into mist for a moment, and when he solidified some of the insects were gone.

Again David shouted, *Freeze!* Then he wrenched himself up and attacked.

He cracked a tibia with a kick of his own, smashed in ribs; Carter clutched at his mind but to no avail. He lashed out again and the elder vampire blocked the blow and jabbed his fingers at David's eyes.

The world burst, vanished; he convulsed.

A blow to the side of the head knocked him sprawling, and stomp kicks pulverized his knee caps. He swiped at the drone of the wasps but couldn't connect.

Something click-scraped, click-scraped: Carter was limping away. A missile boomed inside the tower.

The darkness diminished and swirled into shapes.

One leg still crooked, Carter squatted in front of the door; he gripped the grillwork landing and began to straighten. The damaged stairs shrieked as they ripped away from their moorings; down in the shaft, Liz wailed.

His patellae still grinding through the throes of

286

regeneration, David desperately looked about. Apparently Carter had thrown the suitcase, but the cellular phone was less than a yard away. He grabbed it, sat up, and flung it as hard as he could.

It bashed Carter's head to the side; the grill slipped from his grasp as he lurched to his knees. His flayed fingers clawing and his useless legs thrashing, David scrambled across the concrete and grabbed for his throat.

Rasping and squealing, shaking and swaying, the staircase slowly tore itself out of the wall. Clambering on all fours, Liz in the lead, the humans had descended almost two stories when the weakened section screeched and began to drop.

Liz leaped. Vibration nearly bucked her off, but she made it to the stable stairs. Gripping the rail, she whirled and stretched out her hand, hauled Stan to safety just as the steps under his feet plunged crashing and clanging into the pit below.

Carter struck David's hands aside, pulped his nose with a sweeping backhand blow. David grappled again, but a cancer swelled in his mind; his suddenly wooden fingers missed their hold. The master vampire reared, then slammed both fists down.

David's spine snapped.

He tried to punch, tried to kick, failed; he knew he could recover but not in time. Reeking of decay, most of the wasps finally dead or fled, Carter straddled his waist and started ripping.

"You lose," the corpse-thing said. "Everyone is still going to die."

You don't know it, but you're lying again, you son of a bitch.

David clenched his will and smashed the alien intrusion out of his head; cold jabbed up his legs and made him shadow.

Shorn of substance, he didn't need a spine. He stabbed his hand into Carter's heart and congealed, blending their flesh and fusing their bodies together.

Waves of distortion lashed down his arm; he screamed and blacked out. When he came to, Carter was tugging feebly at the new appendage rooted in his breast. "At last," the revenant croaked, then slumped on top of him.

When he could manage it David dragged himself around to face the east. Soon a red light bloomed and he started burning. Much to his surprise, it didn't hurt; just before the end he thought he felt a tear slide down his cheek.